An Angel Came for You

By David J Howell

I would like to dedicate my book to two great men:

Firstly to my dad, Maurice Howell, who bravely fought multiple sclerosis for twenty years and who is sadly missed by Emma, Jackie, Michelle and I.

Secondly to Michael Goddard who very recently lost his brave fight against cancer and who will be forever missed by his family.

My story is written in memory of these two great men: may they rest in peace.

Chapter 1

The early morning sun slowly breathes a refreshing new light throughout my bedroom signalling the start of the seventh day of a life I no longer understand or even care for. Just like the six mornings that have passed before, I am once again awoken with a jolt to the sound of my alarm clock ringing in my ears. Instinctively, I look over to the other side of the bed just hoping, beyond hope, that the past week was just a really bad dream.

Just for a second, in my sleepy state, I am sure that I catch a glimpse of my little boy laying next to me with his cheeky little grin but it's just my memory playing a cruel trick on me and in a heartbeat reality kicks back in.

As my eyes begin to focus on the cold empty sheets that are still neatly folded on the other side of the bed, I start to feel that same sinking feeling all over again.

Another day without Tommy; another day where I will once again spend my every waking minute contemplating just how little meaning my life has without him.

I really can't see how my life will ever move forward. Why has this happened to me? I'm struggling to understand how it is even humanly possible for me to find myself five years back in my past.

After finally escaping the worst four and a half years of my life living with Charlie and knowing that part of my life is finally over, I should be starting my new life with my little boy, but without him I can no longer function.

For the past year I have religiously prayed every night to my dad for a way out of my abusive life with Charlie. I would remember back to the hopes and dreams Dad had for me. He wanted me to live a happy and fulfilled life. Through my prayers, how I begged him for forgiveness for not living up to his expectations.

For years I have desperately prayed to my angel to take me back to a happier time; a time before I met Charlie. I now know you should be very careful what you wish for because I have to spend the rest of my life bitterly regretting that wish.

I haven't ventured out of my bedroom since the day I lost Tommy. Day after day I just lay on my bed, the very place that Tommy spent his last night with me before vanishing from my life.

All I have left now are my personal memories of his three short years imprinted deep in my mind. I am not ready to face the world without him. Mum knows I need time alone but doesn't know why. It hurts that she doesn't even know her grandson existed; the little boy that she adored has been erased from her mind forever. She has no idea what I am going through. She checks on me now and again and I know she is really worried about me. I know I am going to need her more than ever now but I can't face anyone just yet.

I think of Dad and all the happy times we had together and it makes me smile. I just know if dad was here now my life would have been so different. He would never have let Charlie treat me the way he did. Dad knew me inside out and I couldn't hide anything from him. He would have stepped in; Charlie wouldn't have stood a chance. Dad was always protective of me; I was his little girl. Not a day goes by when he's not in my thoughts.

All I do now is lay here day after day, lost in my thoughts, thinking back to how good my life used to be. Before I met Charlie I had such a happy life.

I couldn't have asked for a better childhood; I loved my parents dearly. Bringing me into this world wasn't easy for them; they had been trying for a baby for three years. Sadly during that time they suffered two miscarriages. I know it hit them hard and they almost gave up hope on me but third time lucky. I was born Sarah Louise Connell in the summer of 1992.

Mum and Dad decided not to have any more children after me, maybe they didn't want to go through that pain again or maybe they thought their family unit was complete. I will always remember Dad sitting me on his knee, I must have been about five, and saying "Before you were born mummy and daddy wanted to meet you so much but the angels decided that the time wasn't quite right so you went back to them for a while and they looked after you for a bit longer." Dad had a beautiful way of looking at life.

When I was about ten, Dad would say to me the day we are born is the day we are sent down to earth as a gift from the angels. We should try to live our lives the best way we can until the time comes to go back to them. He wasn't a deeply religious man but he was a great believer in karma - what goes around comes around. He would say to me treat people as you would like others to treat you.

I look back at my childhood with great affection. I loved the village I was born in; it's about ten miles outside of Cambridge. It was a great place to grow up. It was very quiet but, like most villages, it had a real community feel about it.

My dad worked as an HGV driver for a local haulage firm. He occasionally worked nights but was mostly at home with us in the evenings. He was very much a family man and loved spending his spare time with mum and me; I felt loved.

In the warm summer months Dad and I would often walk a little way up the bank of the river Bedford that winds its way through the village. Dad liked to fish and Mum used to make up a packed lunch for us and we would take the short walk up there together. I loved to sit and watch him fish in those warm summer evenings; sometimes in the school holidays I would stop with him until the sun set.

I enjoyed our annual holidays; the lazy days on the beach and the summer days out. Life seemed so carefree back then. I was a daddy's girl. Mum was the responsible one, Dad just wanted to play games with me. I remember Mum would smile and say "Sometimes it's like having two kids in the house."

As I grew up Dad would always remind me how important good manners were as well as respecting others feelings and always to try to see the best in people.

I remember when I was eleven and I started secondary school. My new school was in a small market town twelve miles from our village which meant getting a school bus for the trip. The school seemed so big and intimidating and for the first time in my life I felt so lost and alone. Being so far from home I just wanted the day to end. That night, after that long first day, Dad soon noticed how quiet I was. He had a knack of knowing when I was upset. He would give me a reassuring smile and say "It's in a dad's job description to know when his little girl needs his help." He put his arm around me and in a soft voice asked me what was wrong. I told him about my day and he gave me one of his special dad hugs and, in his usual reassuring voice, said "If you are ever feeling alone and need me I will move heaven and earth to help you, but if for whatever reason I'm not around at the time, your guardian angel will always be there waiting to help you."

He would say to me "I believe when we are born we all have a guardian angel assigned to us to help us all through our lives. They will never be far away from us and if we ever find ourselves in need of help, we can talk to our angel and they will always listen and find solutions for us."

Dad always had a knack of making me feel much better about myself. I remember Mum would give Dad such a disapproving look and tell him to stop feeding me "all those fairy-tales."

As I reached my teenage years I retreated into myself a little. I was shy but I did have a small circle of friends. I was doing ok at school and at fourteen I moved to the upper school which was full of history; the main building was once an Abbey and home to the Benedictine monks. I found maths my best subject and my maths teacher encouraged me.

Like many teenagers in my year I spent most of my time in my room. As well as studying, I enjoyed reading romantic fiction, listening to music and watching the latest US television programmes of the day.

At sixteen I left school and went to Cambridge College where I studied business studies. Mum and Dad were really happy that I decided to go on to further education. Dad said it was always good to have a good career to fall back on.

College was very different from school and I really enjoyed it and made a new circle of friends.

Kate, Mum's friend, offered me a Saturday job at the cafe she owned. It was ten miles away; Mum would drop me off and I would get the bus back. I loved earning my own money.

Over the next year I studied hard and was doing better than I could ever have expected. Kate would give me extra days at the cafe during my holidays and she became a really good friend to me.

Up until this point, my life had been kind to me.

Chapter 2

It was about this time that I noticed my parents seemed distant, they didn't seem their usual selves, it was the little things I noticed, like they would stop talking when I came into the room. I couldn't really put my finger on it, they just didn't seem happy anymore and I really didn't want to admit it but I thought they were going to split up. I threw myself into my studying and tried to put it to the back of my mind.

A few weeks later when I was sitting in my room, Mum came in.

'Sarah, could you come downstairs, your Dad and I need to have a word with you.'

Well, I thought, this is it, they are splitting up but what they were about to tell me was a million times worse and will stay with me for the rest of my life.

As I entered the room Mum was holding Dad's hand and he looked up at me. 'Sarah come and sit down love; I need to speak to you.' He spoke softly and there was sadness in his voice, the type that I had never heard before. He took my hand gently and looked into my eyes. 'I need you to be brave,' he said. 'You know I love you more than anything.' he paused for a moment and then squeezed my hand tighter. I noticed tears in his eyes and his hand started to tremble so I held it firmly to stop it shaking.

'What's wrong Dad?'

He started crying, something I had never seen him do before, and it started me off too.

'Tell me what's wrong?'

Mum put her arm around him and he looked at her then back at me before taking a deep breath.

'There is no easy way for me to say this to you... I have got cancer.'

My whole body went cold; I couldn't take it in. He sat there and looked so lost and vulnerable. I hugged him for what seemed an age, never wanting the moment to end. I started to babble.

'We can fight it! You will get better won't you? Please tell me you will.'

Dad looked at me with such a sorrowful look. 'No Sarah, I have had all of the tests and its terminal. There isn't anything they can do for me.'

I hesitated for a moment. 'How long?' I asked knowing that I really didn't want to hear the answer.

He held my hand tightly. 'Three to six months if I'm lucky.'

The next hour didn't feel real; I just snuggled up to him. Neither of us spoke, we were just lost in our own thoughts. Dad was the only thing that mattered. I wanted to spend every waking minute with him. I couldn't imagine my life without him.

Over the next few months my college work suffered. I just couldn't face it and I hardly went in. They were very understanding but Dad was my only thought.

It was so painful for me to see him deteriorate so quickly. I had to stay strong for him but I cried every night when I was alone. I was no longer Daddies little girl. Our roles had changed; Dad relied on Mum and me now. The nurses' that came round were a godsend but it was still hard. Every night I would pray for him and I asked his angel to look after him.

Over the next four months I had to grow up quickly. I couldn't imagine my life without Dad as I always thought he would be with me forever. He had always been my teacher, my hero, my best friend and most of all, my Dad.

Towards the end he became mostly bedridden. It was really hard to watch my Dad go from the strong man he was to the weak, frail man I saw in front of me. He was adamant that he wanted to be at home and Mum and I didn't want it any other way.

One night, just before bed, I went into his room to wish him a good night just like I had done every night in those last few months. He was asleep so I tenderly kissed him on the forehead and silently crept out. As I got to the door I heard a frail voice call out my name. His voice was hardly recognisable; weakened by the cancer. I looked around and he gestured me over. I sat on the bed and leaned over to him. He smiled and I sat patiently as he struggled to get his words out.

'Sarah' he said 'I know I don't say this enough but you have turned into a beautiful young woman. I know I am biased but the man that you eventually choose to be with will be the luckiest man on earth. I am so proud of you.'

'Come on Dad' I butted in 'you need to rest now, tell me in the morning. We can sit in the garden and have a good chat. It talks of being a good day.'

Dad started to get agitated.

'No, please let me finish.' He paused for a minute to catch his breath. 'It has always been my dream for you to find a decent man to take good care of you and one day for you to get married. I regret I won't see that day and I won't be able to walk you down the aisle or take my grandchildren to the park but I will always be with you in spirit. Remember, no matter what, I will always be proud of you. All I want is for you to live a happy life like your mum and I have.'

It really upset me to see Dad struggling to breathe. I sat with him for a while until his breathing returned to normal. He smiled at me just before he drifted to sleep and I gave him a hug then quietly left the room.

I was woken early the next morning by a gentle knock on my bedroom door. Mum walked in and I instantly saw the pain etched on her face. I knew straight away.

'Its Dad isn't it, he's gone hasn't he?'

She nodded. I leapt out of bed, my only thought was to comfort her and the moment I hugged her she burst into tears which set me off. Both of us chose to stay in that moment for a few minutes.

It suddenly dawned on me that Dad was saying goodbye to me last night: he knew. I looked at her.

'Mum, I need to see Dad.'

She gently took my hand and led me to their bedroom. She pulled back the sheet. He looked so peaceful, just as if he was sleeping; we sat by the bed for a while. Mum and I held hands and talked about all the good times we had had together.

Whether it is just my imagination, I don't know, but I felt that he was still there listening to us. I knew this would be the last time I would see him and I wanted to remember him as he was.

After a while our conversation dried up and I sensed Mum needed to be with Dad for a bit longer before we reported his passing. I got up and gently squeezed Mums shoulder, looking up at me she smiled.

I don't know how I got through the next fortnight, everyday just blurred into the next. The day of the funeral arrived and Mum and I took our seats at the front of the Crematorium. I gripped her hand tightly, desperately trying to keep it together for her.

My eyes became transfixed on the photo of my Dad, Jack Connell, which sat proudly on top of his coffin. It was a picture of him taken before he became ill; the way I will always remember him. It hit me really hard, it made me realise just how fragile life is and how quickly things can change. A feeling of sadness washed over me at the thought of Dad lying in the coffin and I remember thinking, he is all alone in there and how much he hated being alone. Then I thought, Dad's not laying there, he is everywhere and anywhere he wants to be. That made me smile.

It was a really beautiful service and it was so nice to hear all the lovely things spoken about Dad. The vicar talking about his life made me realise how much I missed him. I remember thinking, I hope all the beliefs he held so dear about the afterlife have come true and he is with the angels now, looking down on us.

Mum said Dad's wish was for us to play "I Have a Dream" at the funeral and when the song started Mum looked at me and held my hand. The words were so fitting for Dad and I cried all the way through, Mum was a bit more in control but had a few tears. She gently pulled me closer to her and I realised just how much I needed her in that moment.

The house was so empty without Dad around. Mum was putting a brave face on for me but I knew she was hurting inside as I often heard her crying late into the night. Life would never be the same for us again. I knew Dad would have wanted me to be strong for her and I tried my hardest.

Over the next six months we grew closer. Although it was hard at first with a lot of awkward silences and not really knowing what to say to each other, Mum and I needed each other and I think we needed that time together.

I don't think either of us could have got through those six months alone.

Chapter 3

As time went on, Mum and I got into a rut and closed the rest of the world out of our lives. We never admitted it to each other but we felt safe in our little bubble. I was actually relieved when, one evening, Mum said we should talk.

'We can't go on like this,' she said 'we need to restart our lives.'

Mum was ok for money as dad had life insurance. My college were very understanding but I felt I had missed so much and I made the decision to quit. I had to find a job so Mum said she would have a word with Kate to see if she could get me some more part time work. I hadn't been in since Dad died but Kate was very understanding and when Mum rang her and explained that I had left college, she said she would like me to come and work for her full time.

Kate suggested I work a couple of day's a week at first and slowly work up to a full week. She was a really good friend to us both over those six month's. It was really nice getting back to work although it was hard leaving Mum at first. Kate was really good, she didn't push me too hard and because she knew Dad, she was a sympathetic ear for me. I repaid her kindness by working hard.

I found it a trek to work on the bus so I decided to learn to drive. I picked it up quite quickly and, to my amazement, eight months later I passed first time. Mum was thrilled for me.

'Dad would have been so proud of you.' She said smiling and reaching into her bag. 'This is from me and Dad,' she handed me two thousand pounds, 'it's out of the insurance money; he would want you to have it.'

I bought myself a little red Ford Fiesta and it really helped me to have my freedom. The first time I went out, I thought of Dad. I looked up and whispered, "thank you Dad."

I was getting on well at the cafe and, with Kate being such a good friend as well as a boss, working there was really enjoyable.

I started to have evenings out with a few of my good friends but Mum wasn't going out and I still felt that emotional pull to be with her. I also felt closer to Dad when I was with Mum.

Life carried on very much like that for the next two years. I was still working at the café when I reached my twenty-first birthday. That was when I met John for the first time. At twenty-five he was slightly older than me. He would come into the café a few times a week and I was instantly attracted to him. He told me he was a car mechanic and lived on his own. I was drawn to his kindness and how genuine he was. I would flirt with him and drop a few subtle hints that I liked him, but, like me, he was a little shy. I was really flattered when he finally asked me out as I think he had been building up to it for about a month.

After a few weeks I took John to meet Mum and she really liked him. I knew Dad would have really liked him too. John was a breath of fresh air; he made me feel alive again. I felt really comfortable around him and he liked to spend time at mine. I think Mum enjoyed the company too and she always made him feel at home. Life felt really good with John. I found myself spending more and more of my spare time with him. He was the type of man I could see myself settling down and spending the rest of my life with. I could even see us having a family in the future.

Over the next few months life was perfect and I couldn't imagine my life without John. However, a cloud of doubt had started to brew up deep inside of me. I felt I was somehow letting Mum down. I felt she still needed me and I was not spending enough time with her.

So, after about six months, I made one of my first bad life decisions. I stupidly ended it with John. He was really upset and stopped coming into the café but I just knew Mum was still grieving for dad and I had to put her first. I needed to be there for her.

Mum was really upset when she realised she was the reason for us splitting up. 'I really love you' she said 'but it is really unhealthy for us to spend so much time together. You should go and try to get him back. You are an adult, you need to live your life and not worry about me.'

I really regretted finishing with John and really missed him. I so wanted to go and see him and beg him for another chance but, like the coward I am, I couldn't bring myself to go and see him.

For the next six months I often thought about him and the future I had thrown away. If only I had swallowed my pride and asked him for another chance. I tried to put the past behind me. I didn't see him again after we split but I still had feelings for him and cherished my memories of our time together. He was my first love.

A few weeks later, on an ordinary Thursday afternoon, my friend Julie phoned me out of the blue, suggesting we go to a club on Saturday night. I wasn't really into clubs but I agreed for her sake.

I would describe Julie as my part time friend. I had known her since school and she popped in and out of my life when it suited her, usually when she was between boyfriends. It was always her that would ring me. I gave up ringing her a long time ago as she would always be too busy. Don't get me wrong, it suited me that way. Julie was fun to be with and we always had a good time but she could be a bit bossy and overpowering but never in a nasty way.

Julie and I met up on Saturday morning to go clothes shopping as I didn't have anything for that night.

As we looked through the racks of clothes, Julie picked out a dress for me. 'Try this on' she said.

As I put it on I caught a glimpse of myself in the booth mirror, the dress was really short, tight fitting and not really me at all. I stepped out of the booth to show her.

'I'm not sure this is really me.' I said pulling the hem down as far as I could.

'It's perfect!' she said grinning. 'You will get used to it. It's about time you had a bit of fun in your life.' She ushered me back into the booth to get changed.

I reluctantly bought the dress and we headed home to get ready for our big night out.

Julie had ordered a taxi and later on that evening, after picking me up, the taxi driver made his way to Julie's house. As we arrived the driver gave two short blasts of his horn. I tried not to laugh when Julie walked towards the taxi. She was all over the place; desperately trying to walk in a straight line in her high heel shoes. I still wasn't sure about the dress but Julie was wearing a similar one and it put my mind at ease.

The club was brimming that night. We bought a drink and found ourselves a seat. I decided I was going to let my hair down and enjoy the night so after a few more drinks we headed to the dance floor.

'We'll have to do this again,' I shouted to Julie over the music.

'Definitely' she replied.

We danced for what seemed like hours and my feet began to ache so I waved my hand at Julie. 'I'm going to sit down now' I shouted whilst pointing over at our table. 'I'm feeling a bit light headed.'

We collapsed into our seats and Julie smiled at me.

'I don't know if you have noticed but that guy over there hasn't been able to take his eyes off of you all night.'

I looked over and he caught my glance and smiled. I quickly turned back to Julie as I could see he was getting out of his chair.

'Oh God!' I said. 'He's coming over.'

As if on cue he strolled up to our table. 'Hi ladies, having a good night? I'm Charlie.'

'Hi Charlie, I'm Julie and this is my mate Sarah.'

Charlie nodded at Julie but quickly turned his attention to me. 'You work at the cafe in Huntingdon high street don't you?' he smiled as he spoke.

'Yes that's right' I replied.

'I normally go in there once or twice a week. I should think you probably recognise me!'

'No, sorry, I don't but we do get hundreds of people in a day.'

'Can I have your number? Maybe we can go for a drink sometime?' He handed me his phone expectantly. I typed my number into his contacts and handed it back to him. Giving me a lingering look, he smiled. 'I'll leave you ladies in peace now, oh, and Sarah I will ring you tomorrow I promise.'

Charlie headed back to his friend.

'I think you're in luck there,' Julie grinned 'he seems very keen.'

'I don't know if he's my type. He seems over confident' I hesitated, 'but he's seems quite nice though.'

'Well if you don't want to go out with him, I will' Julie laughed.

As he promised, Charlie rung the next day and we made a date to go to the pub. I said I would meet him at The Three Crowns at three in the afternoon. I didn't want him to know where I lived so soon, at least not until I knew him better. I didn't tell Mum I was meeting Charlie as it was early days.

I deliberately got there a few minutes late as I was hoping I wouldn't be the first to arrive. I opened the pub door and had a quick scan around. I spotted Charlie sitting at the table near the back window and as I walked over he got up.

'You're looking really nice today.' He smiled and leaned in to kiss me on the cheek.

'Thank you,' I replied.

Charlie went to the bar and ordered me a glass of coke as I had to drive home.

I really enjoyed the date and he seemed genuinely interested in me. He explained that he worked in marketing and lived on his own. I don't know why but I poured my heart out about my Dad and how much I missed him and Charlie was really sympathetic. I asked him about his parents but I could see he looked a bit uncomfortable talking about them. He told me he didn't get on with them anymore and didn't really want to talk about it.

'Can I ask you another question?' I said.

'Go on then' he replied looking a bit edgy.

'I was wondering why you asked me out yesterday and not Julie.'

Charlie smiled and laughed. 'Your friend seemed the bossy, overpowering type and you came across as the shy, sensitive type. I prefer shy women plus you're also very attractive.'

We talked into the evening and I told him I really liked him and would really like to see him again.

Over the next few weeks we went out a few times and I told Mum about him.

'Bring him round' she said, 'I'd love to meet him.'

I asked Charlie if he would like to meet my Mum and he said he'd love to. A few days later I picked him up and drove him the ten miles to my house. He was really charming and he and Mum seemed to hit it off right from the start.

Chapter 4

So that was the start of my life with Charlie.

My dream in life was to fall in love with a man with my Dads qualities, get married and have children, show them the way in life with fun and laughter, giving them lots of good memories to cherish which they could take into their adult life. The only trouble with a life dream is sometimes the person you choose to share it with may not have the same agenda.

For the first couple of months life felt really good with Charlie. We really hit it off and it wasn't long before I was spending most evenings with him and I would often stay the night. It was also handy for work as it was only a five minute drive from Charlie's house.

After a couple more months I was virtually living with Charlie. He was very protective towards me and preferred us to stay in. He would say he liked it when it was just us two and to have me all to himself. He had his little routines and would ring me at work at 11 a.m. and 3 p.m. every day. I thought that it was sweet that he was thinking about me.

By this time Charlie and I had been going out for about four months and he suggested that I should move in with him. At first I thought maybe it was a bit too soon but Charlie convinced me it was just a natural progression. He would try to reason it out by saying I was spending most of my time with him anyway.

Mum was a bit unsure at first. She thought it was a bit too early to make such a life changing decision and that there was no rush. I must admit I still had a few niggling doubts but Charlie soon put my mind at ease. I told him that Mum was a bit unsure about me rushing in and that annoyed him.

'You are an adult now,' he said 'and it is your choice and she should butt out. It's none of your Mums business! She's probably jealous of our relationship because she hasn't got a man in her life.'

That really upset me and I jumped to her defence. 'Mum's not like that. She is only looking out for me. I don't like you talking about her like that.'

He apologised and two weeks later I moved in with him. Mum didn't stand in my way but reassured me that my room would always be there if things don't work out. I think Mum still had her doubts about Charlie.

It wasn't long after moving in together that Charlie started to drop hints that he would like us to start a family. Maybe it was because of his own bad childhood that he felt he wanted children so soon in our relationship. To be honest I hadn't given much thought about having children at that point. I always thought it would happen when I was in my mid twenties and after I had been in a relationship for a few years.

Charlie was very persistent and he reminded me of the time when I told him about what my Dad had said, about finding a decent man and starting a family. He would often say "if your dad was here now he would tell you the time is right to have a baby with Charlie." I told him I wasn't ready and we should wait a while. It was nice to think that Charlie wanted children but at the same I didn't want to rush into it and thought we should get to know each other better first.

Charlie wouldn't let it drop. He reassured me that he had a good job and he could easily provide for me and a baby. I kept reminding him that I would feel better if we could just wait a while as I didn't feel ready but gradually he started to get funny with me. He would say things like "it must be because you don't love me enough" and "you don't believe we have a future together." He made me feel so guilty. I did believe in our future together but something in the back of my mind was telling me we shouldn't rush the decision. I felt the time wasn't quite right but I sensed Charlie was upset with me.

Over the next few days he went quiet on me and I really didn't like the bad atmosphere between us. I hated seeing him so upset.

I gave it a lot of thought over the next week. I really wanted us to work out and I did want to make him happy. Maybe having a baby with Charlie wasn't such a bad thing and having a family was something that I really wanted in the future. The more I thought about it, the more I warmed to the idea. Mum and Dad were about my age when they had me and it would probably take me six months to a year to fall pregnant anyway. So, after a lot of soul searching, I decided to go along with his wishes.

That night I made him a coffee and settled down beside him. I took his hand and looked him in the eye. 'Charlie,' I said nervously, 'over the past few weeks I've been giving it some thought and maybe it's not such a bad idea having a baby. We could try for a baby now, that's if you still want to?'

His mood instantly lightened. 'Of course I do. We can start trying straight away; you won't regret it.'

I thought it was best not to tell Mum immediately as she had only just got used to the idea of us living together. I decided I would start dropping hints about us trying a few months down the line.

Chapter 5

Over the next few weeks Charlie's calls to me at work became more frequent. He was ringing me at least six times a day and always seemed to want to know what I was doing and who was in the café at the time. Kate noticed and she didn't mind me taking a call from time to time but she asked me to try and take them during my break as it was affecting my work.

Charlie wasn't happy when I told him.

'So, I can't ring you to see how you are anymore?' his tone was huffy. 'It's not like your job is so important that you can't answer a phone. Why don't you just give it up? It's not like it's a very good job and I can easily provide for us.'

I really didn't like him organising my life and belittling my job.

Next day, during my morning shift, I couldn't believe it when Charlie rang me again; especially when he knew Kate wasn't happy with him keep ringing. No, I won't answer it, I thought and decided it would be best to ignore the calls and put my phone on silent.

During my break I checked my phone and couldn't believe it when I saw I had thirty-six missed calls from Charlie. I suddenly panicked and started to think the worst. Perhaps it was urgent. I knew I had to ring him straight away but it went straight to voicemail. I rang again but again I got his voicemail which was very odd. All afternoon I worried about him and just hoped he hadn't had an accident.

Later, at home, Charlie came in at the usual time. 'Had a good day?' I asked. 'I was really worried about you today.'

I had the tea on the table and as we sat down to eat he gave me an icy stare. He didn't say much and I sensed he was off with me. I didn't push it as I knew from past experience that it wouldn't end well. I became really good at reading his moods and found it easier to try to keep the peace. I knew his job could get a bit stressful and I felt it best to leave him to unwind in his own time.

For the next few hours Charlie was really snappy with me and I could see he was annoyed about something. I plucked up the courage to ask him. 'Are you ok?'

He gave me such a hard look and snapped back.

'Just leave it will you.'

Against my better judgement and feeling a bit nervous, I decided to push it further. 'Is it something I've done wrong?'

'Ok then' he snapped again, 'if you must know, I think Kate is well out of order. If I want to ring you at your stupid little job I don't expect you to ignore my calls. Kate is just a jumped up little waitress and I won't have her telling me what I can and can't do. Okay!'

'If you ring me on my break it's not a problem,' I tried desperately to explain 'but I can't answer when I'm working.'

His following silence spoke volumes. He stayed annoyed with me for the rest of the evening and the tension was too much.

The following day I was so relieved that Charlie didn't ring me at work but I sensed that he still hadn't forgiven me as he didn't ring me on my break either.

Over the next few months I tried to stay on Charlie's good side and that calmed things down a little. I thought that Charlie's work must still have been getting on top of him as he flew into a rage for the smallest of reasons. I wished that he would open up to me.

One evening, as I was clearing up after dinner I started to feel on edge again. Charlie started to lose it big time. I could hear a lot of banging in the front room and it was obvious that Charlie was in a terrible rage. I really didn't want to go anywhere near him but I felt I should try to calm the situation. He couldn't find the remote control and he was throwing things around the room and blaming me. Cautiously, I made my way into the room but he gave it to me with both barrels, calling me a thick idiot amongst other things. I tried my best to calm him down and help look but he gave me a hard shove from behind. Losing my balance I fell to the floor.

'It's your fault,' he shouted 'you lost the stupid thing.'

'It's not my fault you've had a bad day' I sobbed. 'It's not really about the remote is it? I can't take much more of this. If you can't open up to me maybe you should get help for your anger issues.' I had reached the end of my tether and couldn't help but retaliate.

He stopped in his tracks and looked down at me with his piercing brown eyes. Grabbing both of my arms he pulled me to my feet and started to shake me violently just as if I were a rag doll.

'Are you calling me mental?' he screamed in my ear.

I sobbed and begged him over and over again to stop. He hit me hard in the face with the back of his hand and I fell to the floor in total shock. I kept thinking to myself, why does he keep treating me like this? I looked up at him and could see the shocked look on his face.

'I'm really sorry' he said, 'I didn't mean to hurt you, its just things have been getting on top of me lately. It's like, just for a few seconds, I have no control of my actions.' He scooped me up from the floor and gave me a hug. 'You really don't understand what my life's been like' he softly whispered in my ear. 'It won't happen again I promise.'

Chapter 6

Two months after we started trying for a baby, my period was a week late. I put it down to all the stress Charlie's mood swings had been putting me under. I'd started having serious doubts about agreeing to have a baby so soon into our relationship. Sometimes when he went off on one he really scared me and for those few moments there was no reasoning with him. He always apologised afterwards but, after a while, it always happened again.

Being a week late had been playing on my mind all that day and I decided to pick up a pregnancy test on the way home from work. I decided to do the test before Charlie got home and I nervously waited for the result. When I looked down at the stick, to my utter surprise, it read "PREGNANT". I really wasn't expecting it to happen so soon.

I really didn't know what to think. I had thought it would be the happiest day of my life and it still was but I was having serious doubts about Charlie. I just needed time to let it sink in. It was such a big responsibility; I now had a little person growing inside of me.

I sat there anxiously waiting for Charlie to come home. I'd decided I would tell him but only if he was in a good mood. He had been alright for the past few days but I never knew from one day to the next how he was going to be.

To my relief he came home in a fairly good mood. I felt really excited about the pregnancy now and had decided I couldn't keep it to myself any longer. He was sitting on the sofa so I bent down and grabbed his hand. 'Charlie, I have some really good news.'

'Go on then' he smiled back at me, 'what is it?'

‘I’m pregnant!’ I blurted out. ‘We are going to have a baby.’

He jumped up and hugged me. ‘That’s great news!’

I could see in his eyes how much the news meant to him. I just knew it was going to change him: I knew being a dad would help him to open up to me.

I had decided not to tell anybody, not even Mum, until after the first twelve week scan. It was going to be really hard to keep it from her but I felt I had to try.

I excitedly started reading up on my baby’s weekly development and how it was changing. I couldn’t help feeling nervous in those following weeks and I did worry. I was sure everything would be ok but I couldn’t help but think of Mum and the miscarriages she had before she had me.

Being pregnant made me very much aware how then, more than ever, I needed to keep on Charlie’s good side and try not to upset him.

The morning of the twelve week scan arrived and I was so excited. Charlie took the morning off work and we made our way to the hospital with plenty of time to spare. Seeing my little baby on the screen for the first time was one of the best moments of my life. For the first time it all felt real. Charlie didn’t really show any emotion but I think he was pleased.

We went straight to Mum’s from the hospital. I was bursting with excitement at the thought of telling her. I had been dying to tell her for weeks and it had been so hard keeping it from her. As we walked in I couldn’t keep it in any longer and the moment I saw her I excitedly blurted it out. ‘Mum, I’m pregnant!’

Just for an instant, her eyes widened and she looked shocked, then composing herself, she smiled. 'Congratulations. Come here and give your Mum a hug.'

'Mum I think you need to sit down, I'll go and make us a cup of tea.' She obviously needed a few minutes to take it in so I went off to the kitchen.

As I made my way back into the room carrying the tray of tea and biscuits, I could see Mum and Charlie were deep in conversation. I really did think Charlie and I had turned a corner in our relationship as we seemed to be getting on much better. I had learnt how to deal with his temper and, once the baby had arrived, I knew things would sort themselves out. I was really starting to look forward to the future and I put the past hurt to the back of my mind.

I excitedly passed Mum the scan picture.

'Mum, I'm so sorry I kept this from you. I really wanted to tell you six weeks ago but I felt I had to wait until the scan. I didn't want to tempt fate, especially with what you and Dad went through.'

Mum just smiled. 'If anyone can understand that, it would be me.'

Although, at first, it must have come as a big surprise to her, I started to see how much it meant. It was her first grandchild. I just wished Dad had been there to share our good news. It was days like that, that really brought it home to me just how much I missed Dad. I just knew he would have been the best Granddad in the world.

The next morning I couldn't wait to get to work and tell Kate my good news. The short drive seemed to take forever and as soon as I walked in Kate instantly noticed how happy I looked.

'You look pleased with yourself this morning!' She laughed. 'Have you won the lottery or something?'

'No,' I replied, 'it's better than that. I'm pregnant!'

Kate gave me a massive hug. 'Oh wow, congratulations. I am so happy for you both. I bet your mum is over the moon with the news.'

'Yes but I think she needs a little while to get used to the idea. She is really happy though.' I suddenly remembered Kate was also my boss. 'There's no need to worry' I reassured her. 'I intend to work as long as I can, hopefully until I am six to seven months, if that's ok?'

'Yes, of course and if you ever feel a bit unwell or it is too much, you just let me know. Okay?'

That evening Charlie seemed to be in an unusually good mood and after dinner he ushered me off into the lounge. 'Go and sit down. I'll clear up and then make you a cup of tea.'

A few minutes later, Charlie greeted me with a smile and carefully handed me my tea. He sat beside me and gently put his hand on my stomach. Then, looking a bit more serious he said 'I'm worried about you being on your feet all day at work. It's not good for the baby, all that extra strain, especially in the busy times.' He hesitated slightly, 'I think it may be time to give up the job. We can easily manage on my wage.'

To me, my job meant more than just money. I really enjoyed the people I met and Kate was the best boss I could ever have asked for. The thought of just sitting around for six months didn't appeal to me but I thought maybe he was right. I wondered if it would be too much for me especially as my job involved a lot of standing so I gave it a lot of thought. Charlie said it was silly to put me and the baby at risk when he could easily support us so I agreed to give Kate my notice the following day.

When I got to work the next day I was really in two minds about handing in my notice. Kate and the job had been so important to me since Dad died.

Things quietened down about three o'clock so I asked Kate if we could talk. She ushered me to a table in the corner and, looking concerned, asked if everything was ok.

I took a deep breath before replying. 'I am really sorry. I know it is really short notice but Charlie and I have been talking and we think I should give my job up now.'

Kate took my hand and gave me a sympathetic smile. 'I will miss you and this place won't be the same without you but you must do what you think is right. I will be sad to see you go.'

I felt really guilty about leaving Kate in the lurch as she had been really good to me for so many years but, deep down, I knew Charlie was right and I was doing the right thing.

Chapter 7

After working my weeks notice I found it hard adjusting to being at home all day. I missed being at work and wished I had gone on for a few more months. I wasn't ready to sit around doing nothing; Charlie pushed me into it far too soon.

During that time I thought a lot about Charlie's parents and how they were going to miss out on their grandchild. Charlie never spoke about his parents and every time I mentioned them to him he would clam up and then get annoyed, so I never really pushed it. However, I thought that maybe it was time for us to build bridges.

One Tuesday, I had been thinking about it all day and although I didn't know how he would react, I felt I had to try and convince him to make it up with them. When Charlie arrived home he was in an okay mood so, during dinner, I decided maybe it was a good time to bring the subject up.

'Charlie, I know you haven't told me much about your parents and I don't know exactly why you have fallen out but I was thinking, now we have a baby on the way, maybe it could be the perfect opportunity to start again. Make a fresh start with them. I'm sure they will want to be a part of our baby's life.'

Charlie looked up from his dinner. 'That is never going to happen' he said bluntly.

'If you tell me why you have fallen out then maybe I could understand. I'm sure whatever's happened we can sort it out. I don't want them missing out on their grandchild.' I tried to reason with him but he gave me a hard look and slammed his knife and fork down on the table.

'There you go again,' he shouted, 'interfering in things that you know nothing about. You really just don't know when to shut that big gob of yours do you! Just keep your nose out of my business.'

Feeling a little nervous I tried to calm the situation. 'I am here for you. I just wish you wouldn't shut me out all the time.'

Charlie jumped to his feet and threw his plate against the wall and it shattered into tiny pieces. He gave me one of his hard stares before turning to watch the contents of his dinner slowly drip down the wall. Eventually his eyes found their way back to me. 'Why do you always do this to me? You always have to wind me up don't you.' He slammed his fists on the table and stormed out of the room.

I sat there in stunned silence, too scared to move or cry. After a few minutes I composed myself, wiped the wall down and carefully picked up all the shards of broken plate. Although I didn't want to, I reluctantly made my way into the lounge. Charlie was sat watching television as if nothing had happened. He avoided eye contact with me but I could see by his icy stare fixed on the flickering screen that he was still annoyed. I sat down trying not to antagonise him anymore but the atmosphere was very tense.

Charlie's temper really scared me. I thought it would be for the best if I didn't bring up his parents again, maybe it was his childhood that made him like he was. If only I knew his parents and whether they were to blame for his anger, then maybe I could help him.

That should have been the happiest time of my life but I couldn't enjoy my pregnancy. I was always on edge. I had to be careful what I said and did as I just couldn't risk setting off his short temper. I was so scared that if I upset him, to a degree where he couldn't control his actions, that he would punch me in the stomach again like he had before I fell pregnant. He was always sorry afterwards. He would always say that, just for a few seconds, it was like a grey mist enveloped him and he was no longer in control. He would throw anything within reaching distance. I lost count of how many plates he broke and the amount of TV remotes we got through. There was even a hole in the bedroom door where he punched clean through. He said it was me that made him violent and that he wasn't violent before I moved in.

I learnt to read him and calm the situation well before it turned violent. I had become very good at it. I couldn't have afforded for him to lose his temper while I was pregnant. If he had made me lose my baby I would never have forgiven him.

I worried every day about my baby and for the next few months I walked on eggshells. It seemed to work as he had no excuse to be annoyed with me. I enjoyed the peace when Charlie was at work and started to dread the time just before he came home.

I found it really hard to stay occupied during the day as there was only so much housework I could do. I really missed being at work. Not so much the actual work but more the feeling of being part of a team and the banter with Kate. On the plus side I could go and see Mum more often during the week.

After I left my job I got into the routine of going to see Mum most Tuesdays and Thursdays. Spending time with her was the only thing that kept me sane. I didn't tell Charlie, he may have been ok with it but I didn't want to give him an excuse to get angry with me. When I first moved in with him we would see Mum most weekends but it dwindled and he started finding any excuse not to go. I wasn't sure he really liked her.

When I was with Mum I felt I could be myself for a while but Charlie was always in the back of my mind. I often wished I had never met him and deciding to have a baby with him so soon started to seem like a bad decision. I had to make sure I left plenty of time to get back after seeing Mum so that Charlie's dinner would be on the table when he got home.

On one particular Thursday, on the drive home, there had been a car accident and the traffic was stacking back for miles. I felt my heart racing and I just knew I wouldn't make it home on time. I started to get more agitated as the minutes ticked by. I just prayed that Charlie would be held up too but I couldn't see how he would as he came back on a different route on the A14.

The cars were moving slowly and I could see the police in the distance moving the traffic on. I thought it was going to be touch and go whether I would make it home in time. I spent the next forty minutes moving slowly to the front of the queue. I started to tap the steering wheel in a frustrated rhythm, willing the car in front to go faster. I soon got nearer to the front of the queue and it was just me and the car in front.

Just my luck, the policeman put his hand up to me and waved the oncoming traffic by. If he had known my situation with Charlie he surely would have let me through. As I sat and waited, getting more frustrated, I looked at the mangled wreckage of the two cars and a van. I started to feel guilty for my selfish thoughts when clearly at least three people could have been seriously injured. After a few minutes the policeman waved me through.

I had ten minutes before Charlie would normally have been home and I was still at least twenty minutes away. I started to drive a little faster than I felt comfortable with as thoughts of what I would say to him started to flood my mind. I managed to make up good time and I just hoped Charlie had been held up but my heart sank as I pulled up to the house and parked up behind Charlie's car.

I really didn't know what I was going to say to him. I slowly walked up to the house and opened the door. My mouth was dry and my heart was pounding as I prepared myself for the verbal abuse that I knew was coming.

Charlie met me in the hall and, to my utter relief he didn't seem as annoyed as I thought he was going to be. I explained how I got caught in the accident on the way back from Mum's and he gave me a vague smile. 'Yes, I heard about it on the traffic news on the way home. It sounded quite bad.'

I really hadn't expected him to react like that and it threw me. I headed to the kitchen and rustled up something quick for his dinner. He seemed very quiet and deep in thought but he seemed okay within himself and I wondered if maybe I had misjudged him.

I decided to stay in on Friday, catch up with my housework and make something really nice for our dinner. Charlie came home at the usual time and we settled down to eat but I sensed there was something on Charlie's mind as he was avoiding eye contact.

'I've been giving it some thought today' he said, 'and with you not working anymore and money being tighter now, I think it's time that we go down to just one car. I spoke to my mate today and he said he would give me one thousand pounds for your Fiesta. I said he can come and pick it up tonight.'

I couldn't believe what I was hearing. It was my car and he had no right to presume he could sell it without my permission. I was really hurt. My car didn't cost him anything to run. When I gave up my job Charlie gave me very little money. I had to justify every penny he gave me and I only ever asked for money when I really needed it. He even made me feel guilty for asking for money for maternity clothes. However, I never asked him for petrol money as I had been dipping into my savings. He didn't know it but I had just over fifteen hundred pounds saved up.

I could have cried when Charlie's friend came to take my car. He handed the money to Charlie and, without a thought for me, he put it straight in his back pocket. By rights that was my money.

He had promised me before I got pregnant and gave up my job, that money wouldn't be a problem and that I could keep my car. This was all because I was late home. I knew I was going to be so lost without my car. I would be stuck in the house and I had no way of seeing Mum.

Over those next few days the thought of being tied to the house got me down. The town was only a five minute walk away but without money there was no point going, plus I had to be careful spending my savings as Charlie would start to wonder where the money had come from.

Mum understood when I told her we had to sell the car. She told me nothing had to change and that she would pick me up on Tuesdays and Thursdays. I was very grateful as I really couldn't have coped without her.

Chapter 8

My twenty week scan was booked for the following Monday and I was really looking forward to seeing how much my baby had grown. I had no preference on whether it was a boy or a girl but we decided we wanted to know the sex. Charlie took the day off work and we made our way to the hospital. Everything was fine and to actually see my baby move was the best feeling in the world. The midwife asked if we wanted to know what we were having. I nodded excitedly and she went quiet for a moment as she studied the screen. 'Congratulations! You are having a boy.'

Full of excitement Charlie suggested we go to a cafe for a meal to celebrate. I didn't realise he was taking me to Kate's cafe.

As soon as we walked in Kate spotted us and came straight over. She gave me a hug. 'Look at you' she said 'you are really showing now.'

I was bursting with excitement and couldn't tell her my news fast enough. 'Yes I'm twenty weeks now. We have just come back from the scan and we are having a little boy.'

'Oh that's wonderful news. Congratulations. You must be over the moon. Come and sit down and no arguments but your money is no good in here today. Everything is on me.'

I felt so overwhelmed by her generosity. Seeing Kate again reminded me of my old life and how much I missed it. It reminded me just how much Charlie had taken control of my life.

I felt I had to watch everything I said and did when I was around him and I began to wish I had never gone to that dam club with Julie. I often wished I could go back in time and start my life again, just before I met him.

During our meal we sat in almost total silence. I always felt on edge when we were in public. Charlie would be watching my every move and if I said or did anything that he didn't like, I wouldn't hear the end of it when we got back home.

Soon after we finished I thanked Kate. I really wanted to have a proper catch up with her but I didn't feel comfortable enough to do so with Charlie breathing down my neck. I thought about returning during the day without him.

During the next few months I felt more and more isolated without my car. Mum had been really good to me and picked me up on Tuesdays and Thursdays but I felt really guilty and insisted on giving her petrol money, not that she would take it.

I was on edge most of the time and being so heavily pregnant the baby's welfare was my only concern. I didn't want any extra stress. I got used to all the insults and put downs and after a while I started to think "oh whatever, just leave me alone".

Some days he was like a child and would sulk for days for the smallest of reasons, at other times he would shout but at least he didn't lay a finger on me after I fell pregnant. He had grabbed my arm a few times but he managed to control himself; not even he would harm his unborn baby.

The big day was fast approaching and we had decided on the name Tommy. I felt both excited and nervous bringing him into the world as the situation with Charlie was far from perfect.

Chapter 9

At 3.45 p.m. on Wednesday the 14th of January 2015 I gave birth to a beautiful baby boy. The moment I first held him I knew my life had changed forever. I couldn't take my eyes off this cute little bundle lying in my arms. It scared me to think he depended on me for his every need. My life had taken on a whole new meaning.

Charlie was there when he arrived and he seemed happy to become a dad. I was so hoping fatherhood would change him and we could become the loving family unit I had always dreamed of.

Charlie left the feeding and nappy changing to me, although he did hold him from time to time. Things even improved between Charlie and me but only for a short while. The novelty of being a dad soon wore off and after a few months he didn’t really want to know Tommy anymore and was even jealous of the time I spent with him. My baby boy was the most important thing in my life, he took up a lot of my time and Charlie didn't like that.

I preferred it when Charlie was at work. It was so much better when it was just Tommy and I but I still felt so lonely and isolated and lived for my Tuesday and Thursday catch ups with Mum. I knew soon after Tommy was born that he wasn’t going to have the same happy family upbringing as I did. I realised what a big mistake I had made by moving in with Charlie but by that point he had drained me emotionally and I was totally reliant on him financially. He had also become very jealous. He would check my phone messages every day and if we were out he would accuse me of looking at other men if I happened to glance in their direction.

Over the next three years I tried my hardest to give Tommy the best childhood I could. Without Mum I don't think I would have coped. She would pick me and Tommy up on Tuesdays and Thursdays and we would try to find things to do. In the summer months Mum often wanted to take us to the beach but I couldn't as we wouldn't have got back home in time.

Charlie didn't give me much money towards Tommy and my savings quickly dried up. Mum had to pay for our days out which made me feel very guilty but I knew she got so much pleasure spending quality time with Tommy. Mum knew Charlie wasn't very nice but I never told her just how bad he really was.

It wasn't long after Tommy was born that the beatings gradually started again. By this point I was very unhappy with my life. I had stopped trying to reason with Charlie and I would spend all of my time walking on eggshells. He was in charge and he ruled me with fear. He would erupt very quickly, he would throw things at me, kick me or, more often, he would give me one sharp punch to the stomach. He was always careful not to leave a mark where people could see but sometimes he would forget himself and hit my face, then he would hide me away for a week or two until the bruises faded. My only comfort was the fact he never hurt Tommy.

Charlie never took responsibility for his actions; it was always someone else's fault. He would say I pushed his buttons or his job was stressful or he would blame it on his bad childhood.

The mental torture was just as bad. Almost everyday he would make a point of having a dig at me, to make sure I knew I was worthless, useless and ugly. He liked to remind me how lucky I was that he took me on. If I said the wrong thing he wouldn't talk to me for hours, sometimes even days and when he felt I had suffered enough, he would always twist it to make sure I knew it was my fault.

I learned to read Charlie's moods and calm situations well before they turned nasty but that meant taking the blame for his insecurity and never arguing back and that gave him even more control over me.

The only good thing to come out of our relationship was Tommy and without him I don't think I could have carried on, he was the only reason I got up in the morning. I tried to shield him from all of the abuse and at that point I believed he wasn't in danger but at three years old I knew he would be picking up on what was going on and that worried me.

One evening Charlie came home in a really bad mood. I could tell he was trying to pick a fight with me. He had a go at me about his dinner, then about the cleanliness of the house, then the fact I hadn't ironed his shirt. He went on for about an hour but I didn't respond. I'd seen it all before on so many occasions.

Still in a really foul mood he stormed into the lounge and started screaming at Tommy who was sitting watching the television. For the first time Charlie had crossed the line and my parental instincts kicked in. I stood between him and Tommy and I was so angry I began to shake. 'No!' I snarled at him. 'I won't have you bringing Tommy into this. You leave him alone; he hasn't done anything to you.'

My anger turned to fear as Charlie, in a fit of rage, grabbed my face with one hand and squeezed it tight. I had just given him the excuse he needed and had been pushing for. Through my tears I pleaded for him to stop. 'Please' I begged, 'not in front of Tommy.'

'You are lazy' he bellowed into my face. His eyes widened in anger and droplets of saliva flew from his mouth. 'I put food on the table and a roof over your head. All the things I do for you and your little brat and you talk to me like that.' He shoved my face hard and I lost my balance. As I fell to a heap on the floor he stormed out. I heard the front door bang shut and the screeching of tyres. I was sobbing as I looked over at Tommy. He was frozen to the spot, too scared to move or cry but I could see the fear in his eyes.

'Its ok Tommy, you come to Mummy.' I tried to calm my sobbing.

Tommy got up and ran to me, flung his little arms around me and started to cry. 'Are you okay Mummy?'

That one short sentence broke my heart. Tommy should never ever have witnessed what happened and for the first time I thought he might be in danger. I knew at that point that I had to find a way out, for Tommy's sake.

I thought of Dad almost every day but I was beginning to doubt my beliefs in an after life, otherwise I knew Dad would have found a way to help me.

I cried most nights whilst Charlie slept. I constantly prayed to my angel and begged her to get me and Tommy out of the situation. My life was hopeless and my love for Tommy was the only thing that got me through the day. My faith in my angel was the only hope I had left. I prayed every night hoping that there was a way out. I had to believe. I remembered Dad saying, if you believe and really need genuine help, your angel will always come through for you but it would be a subtle sign and you would have to look for it.

Mum and Charlie didn’t like one another and he tried to stop me seeing her but I stood my ground. Without spending time with Mum and Tommy my life wouldn't have been worth living. I wanted to tell her everything that had happened and I nearly did on a few occasions but I couldn’t bring myself to, I felt such a failure. Mum had been through so much and I didn’t want her to have to deal with Charlie as well. I so wished Dad had been there as he would have known how to deal with everything.

Chapter 10

About a week later Tommy had a horrible rash on his arm so I made him a doctor's appointment. The appointment was for Tuesday so I had to cancel my day with Mum. Walking into the waiting room I couldn't believe my eyes. There was John. He recognised me straight away and, just for a moment, all my troubles seemed to be forgotten. I smiled and headed towards him.

'Hello' I said, 'how are you?'

John seemed a little taken aback. 'I'm fine thank you. It's really nice to see you.'

For a few minutes we talked about old times and it got me thinking about the way we had broken up.

'Look John, I'm really sorry about the way we finished, I really regretted it. I nearly popped round your house on a few occasions to beg for another chance.'

He put his hand on mine. 'Really, you don't have to apologise, that was so long ago.'

He was as kind as I had remembered. I had thought about him so often and I had to know what had been happening in his life. 'Did you find someone else?'

'Yes, I met Kerry and she moved in with me four years ago but we ended it about six months ago. We just wanted different things. Anyway, enough about me, I see you are doing okay. You have a son now, I remember you telling me your dream of kids and a happy ever after.'

It was too much for me. 'No, he beats me' I blurted out, 'I hate him and I'm so scared of him but there's no way out for me.'

John's eyes widened, I could see he looked shocked but before he could answer his appointment was called out. As he stood he took my hand. 'Look I'm not in work today, I have the week off. So, if you can, please come round my house after 1 p.m. so we can talk.'

I was shocked and relieved by his reply.

'I haven't moved. Do you remember the address?'

I nodded and agreed to see him later.

John lived about a mile away from Charlie and me, so later that day I walked there with Tommy. Welcoming me in, I noticed the house was just the same as I had remembered and it brought back some really nice memories. John put the children's channel on for Tommy and made us all a drink. Over the next few hours I told him everything.

He had always been a good listener and when I had finished he lent in to me, took my hand and gently cupped it in his. 'You can't go on like this. You need to leave him as soon as possible, he's a bully and things won't get better. Is there anywhere you can go? What about your mum's?'

'You don't know Charlie and what he is capable of. He won't just let me go. He will find me and make my life hell.'

'Does your Mum know all of this?'

I shook my head.

'Ok. We need to sort this. We're going to your mum's tomorrow. I will pick you up at ten o'clock. Can you get hold of Tommy's car seat?'

'Yes it's in the hall. I use it when Mum picks me up. Can you pick me up outside the post office?'

I looked at the clock and couldn't believe it was nearly four. I had been there three hours. 'I feel so much better sharing this with you John but I better go now.'

'Can I give you my number?'

‘No’ it sounded much more abrupt than I had intended. ‘Sorry, Charlie goes through my phone most days and I can’t risk it but I’ll be at the post office at ten with Tommy’s seat.’

On the walk home I felt so much more positive. For the first time in ages I felt there was hope as John wanted to help me. I couldn’t help but wonder what my life would have been like if I hadn’t finished with John.

The closer I got to home, the more I started to doubt myself again. Maybe I would never be free of Charlie as he wouldn’t just let me go. I doubted I was strong enough. Then I thought of Tommy and I knew I had to put him first. He had already been through so much and he deserved a happy childhood.

The next morning I struggled with the pushchair and the car seat, thinking how much easier it would have been for John to pick me up from home but obviously I couldn’t have risked a neighbour telling Charlie.

I didn’t have to wait long at the post office. John pulled up a couple of minutes later.

‘Are you alright?’ he asked.

I hesitated. ‘Yes I think so.’

We put Tommy in his car seat and as we pulled away I asked him if he remembered the way. As he nodded I realised he still had the same car. ‘You still drive the same car!’

With a smile he patted the dashboard. ‘Yes I’ve had it seven years and it’s served me well.’

It felt strange being with John in the same car we had gone out in when we dated. It was almost as if the last five years hadn’t happened. I couldn’t help thinking that the way John and I had met up yesterday in the surgery was a bit of a coincidence. I wondered if my angel had brought him to me to help me. Dad had always said the way they help you is subtle.

It wasn't long before we arrived at Mum's. I took Tommy out of his seat and we walked up the drive. I was really nervous as I had no idea what I was going to say to her.

Slowly I made my way in, calling out to her. She popped her head out from the kitchen door and greeted me with a smile. 'Hello love' she paused, 'oh, hello John' she looked both surprised and puzzled. Looking back at me she said 'is everything ok, you didn't tell me you where coming round today.'

I started to cry and told her everything about Charlie and how I couldn't take anymore. She started crying too and held me tightly. 'Oh Sarah, why did you keep this to yourself? You poor thing, there's no way you can go back. I had no idea he was physically hurting you. You have to leave him. You and Tommy must move back here today.'

'Thanks Mum but I can't do that to you. You don't understand, Charlie will come here looking for me and I don't know what he is capable of.'

Mum looked really concerned. 'Don't you worry about Charlie, he doesn't frighten me. He's a bully. This ends today. You and Tommy are safe here and once Charlie realises he has no power over you he will stop, plus the law is on your side. I won't take no for an answer. You don't have to do this alone anymore; you let me worry about Charlie.' She briefly took my hand. 'I'll go and make your bed up. I hope you don't mind but you and Tommy will have to share the bed for a while. Then again that might be a good thing as he may feel a bit unsettled.'

Mum had basically kept my room the same as when I moved out. My personal things had gone but it still had all the same furniture. I knew it would feel strange moving back in but for the first time in Tommy's life I would be able to focus my attention on being a good mum to him, instead of just somebody's frightened girlfriend.

'Right' said Mum 'time for a cup of tea and a chat.' She tapped the seat next to her for me to sit down. 'So, what's the story with you two?'

I couldn't help but blush. 'Nothing, we met up by chance at the doctors yesterday. It was John who insisted I told you everything.'

Mum gave John such a warm smile. 'I'm so glad you did John. You have always been sensible. Sarah should never have let you go.'

I could feel my face redden further as I became more embarrassed. 'Mum, we are just friends now.' Feeling a little awkward, I turned to John. 'You'll never know how grateful I am for your help today John. Thank you.' I turned back to Mum. 'Charlie gets home at half past six so I think I'm going to go there and tell him I am leaving him.'

'I really don't like the sound of that Sarah.' She was looking directly at me and I could see the worry in her eyes.

'Listen Mum, I need to do this if I'm ever going to be free of him. I have to show him I'm serious and for the first time in my life I need to stand up to him. I need closure.'

John gave me a reassuring look. 'It might be best if I come in with you.'

'No! I really don't want to rub his nose in it plus he will really kick off if he sees you. This is my problem and I don't want to see you get hurt. I have to do this on my own.'

I could see John wasn't really comfortable with this but he wasn't going to argue. 'Okay,' he replied, 'but I won't let you do this alone. I'll drop you off and wait in the lay-by round the corner. You need to be careful. When you go in keep the front door open and don't go any further than the front door. If you don't come back or call me within ten minutes I will come and get you.'

John still worried about me and I liked that, it made me feel safe.

'You do know I'm going to have to leave everything there, Tommy's stuff and mine.' The realisation of what I was going to do started to dawn on me. 'Maybe I should go back to him tonight and we can get my stuff tomorrow when Charlie's at work.'

Mum looked horrified. 'Absolutely not! Anyway, you told me you have to get his approval on clothes so you are better off without them. I will buy you and Tommy new clothes.'

'Mum, I can't let you do that. I haven't any money to pay you back.'

'Sarah, I love you and Tommy more than life itself. Your dad has seen me alright financially and as far as I'm concerned, and I am sure he would have agreed, the money is as much yours and Tommy's as it is mine.'

The hours passed painfully slowly as we waited for half past six. We sat and talked but at times the conversation would stop and we would all lose ourselves in our own thoughts. I started to go through all the different scenarios as to how Charlie may react. He could beg me to stay, he could get physical or he could let me go, thinking I would come back with my tail between my legs.

It was time and John looked at the clock before turning to me. 'Are you sure you want to do this?'

'Yes,' I nodded, 'one hundred percent sure.'

John gave me a sympathetic smile. 'Okay then, we had better get going.'

Mum lifted Tommy into her arms and followed us to the door. She looked really concerned as she pleaded with me. 'Please, please come back. Don't let him bully you into staying. Be strong; just think of me and Tommy waiting here for you.'

I kissed Tommy on the cheek before turning to walk to the car. Now, looking a little upset, Mum called out to John. 'Look after my little girl.'

John smiled. 'Don't worry Mrs Connell I will get her safely back here, I promise.'

I looked around once more, wanting to get an image of Mum and Tommy in my mind to keep me strong. I called back to her. 'I'll be back within two hours Mum, I promise.'

John and I had a good chat in the car and I asked him if we could stay friends, although secretly I was hoping for more. He said that he would be there for me for as long as I needed him.

It was nearly half past six and Charlie would be home soon. I didn't know how he was going to react when he realised I wasn't there. I felt my nerves building the closer we got. I suddenly thought of Dad and that he might be looking down on me and it gave me the extra strength I needed.

We pulled up near the hospital in the lay-by around the corner; my house was just hidden out of view. I turned to John and gave him a nervous smile. 'Well this is it.' I was terrified and I knew John wasn't really happy that I was doing this but I felt it was something I had to do.

'Don't forget the plan, stay near the door and leave the door open. Say what you need to say then leave. I'll put my number in your contacts.'

I handed John my phone before getting out of the car.

'Be careful Sarah and, remember, if I haven't heard from you within ten minutes, I am coming in to get you.' He got out of the car to give me a hug and I smiled back nervously. 'You know I'm really not happy with this. You don't have to do this, you could just phone him.' He looked worried as he spoke.

I touched his arm. 'Honestly I'll be ok.' My smile didn't hide how I felt and as I nervously turned and slowly walked towards the house, my mouth was dry and my heart was pounding, in perfect rhythm, like a drum.

As I got closer I spotted Charlie's car parked in its usual place just outside the house. I stopped dead with fear and started to doubt myself again. I don't know if I can do this I thought to myself. My phone started ringing, it was Charlie. I panicked and dropped it. I picked it up and in my confusion, accidentally hung up on him. I knew this would anger him and I felt a deep dread in the pit of my stomach. I ran to the house, fumbled for the door handle and somehow managed to open it. Charlie came out of the lounge as I walked in. 'Where have you been?' his voice was only slightly raised.

I started to stutter 'Ssssorry.'

'What do you mean sorry? I want to know where you have been and where's Tommy?' Feeling a bit flustered I blurted out 'At Mum's.'

'What's he doing there,' Charlie retorted.

It wasn't going to plan and I started to panic. 'I'm going to live with Mum' I blurted out.

Charlie's mood lightened and he started to smirk. 'Oh, are you now, so you're leaving me then are you? I don't think your Mum will put up with you for long.'

He was so arrogant and I think he was enjoying the whole situation. He was trying to rattle me like he had done so many times before.

'What are you going to do when your Mum gets fed up with you? It's not like any bloke is going to look at you.' The smirk on his face widened and he started to laugh. 'Look at you, you're a right state.'

With that I snapped. 'And whose fault is that? You've made me like this.'

'Oooh, Sarah the little quiet mouse has finally found her backbone.' He was grinning and laughing even louder.

My anger turned to hurt. He always knew how to upset me but this time was different; I wanted to hurt him as much as he had hurt me. Without thinking I made a fatal mistake. 'I have already found someone else.'

Charlie's mood instantly changed. He pushed past me and slammed the front door shut. He gave me a hard shove, almost knocking me over and pushing me further away from the door. As he passed me, he snatched my phone from my hand, before giving me one of his looks. I had seen that look in his eyes many times before and I knew he was on the verge of exploding. 'Is your boyfriend's name on here?' he growled.

With horror I remembered John had just put his number on it so I lunged forward to try and grab it back. Charlie moved it out of my reach and then proceeded to look through my contacts. I begged him for it back and I tried to grab it again but he hit me square in the face with the back of his hand. He hit me with so much force that he sent me flying and I fell into a heap on the floor. Feeling a bit dazed I looked up at him but he was engrossed in my phone. I thought it was my best chance to get away and I made a dash for the door. Charlie looked up and made a lunge for me, grabbed my arm, spun me around and gripped his hand tightly around my throat. He slammed me to the wall still holding my throat.

I could see the fury in his eyes. 'Who's this John and how long have you been seeing him?'

I struggled to breathe and could only reply in a broken whisper. 'A day, we are only friends.'

I felt a sharp, agonising pain in the pit of my stomach as he punched me hard just below my rib cage. He let go of my throat and I fell to my knees. I gasped for air as he grabbed a fist full of my hair, lifted me up and pulled me close to his face. His voice changed and he whined in self pity. 'Why would you treat me, the person you love, like this?'

I looked him in the eye as I struggled to breathe and with tears rolling down my face I whispered. 'I don't love you; I stay with you through fear.'

Maybe that was the wrong thing to say. He tightened his grip on my hair and, in a fit of rage, smacked my head hard against the wall three or four times. Each sickening thud felt like it was in slow motion. I could hardly speak, my throat was swollen and sore but I begged him to stop. His eyes were full of hatred as he threw me to the floor. It didn't feel real, it was as if it was happening to someone else. I felt another agonising blow to the stomach as he kicked me. I instinctively curled into the foetal position to protect myself but he kicked me again, this time in the head. I felt numb, the pain didn't register anymore.

Through my tears I pleaded for him to stop. I had no more fight left in me. The thought that I was going to die kept running through my head.

He kicked me again. I tried to protect my head with my hands and I closed my eyes tightly praying for it to stop. I felt an agonising pain in my scalp as I was lifted up by just my hair, but he soon let go and I slumped back to the floor. My head was pounding and I laid there totally helpless waiting for the next blow but nothing happened, it all went quiet. I laid there quietly for a few seconds, too scared to move. Then, nervously, I opened one eye and could see daylight. The front door was wide open and to my relief I saw John grappling with Charlie. John briefly looked at me, I could see the shock written all over his face and in that moment Charlie struggled free. He took a swing at John and with a sickening thud he hit him in the face just below his right eye. John lost his balance and fell to the floor. I tried to scream but no sound came out.

John struggled to his feet. Charlie took another swing at him but this time John saw it coming and blocked him. John retaliated punching him hard in the stomach then square on the jaw and Charlie fell into a clumsy heap. John stood over him and waited for him to get back up but he didn't. He looked up at John but realised he was no match for him and shuffled off into the corner like a wounded animal. Seeing he was no longer a threat, John turned his attention back to me.

He crouched down beside me. 'Are you okay to get up?' he asked.

I looked at him and nodded and he gently helped me to my feet. I could only take small steps and I needed to lean on him for support as the pain in my stomach was excruciating. I spotted my phone with a nasty crack across the screen, near the door and John picked it up for me. As I stepped out of the door I turned around and took one last look at Charlie. He was looking directly at me and I could see tears in his eyes, I almost felt sorry for him.

John must have driven from the lay-by as his car was parked outside the house. He gently helped me into the passenger seat and I winced in pain, Charlie really had gone too far this time.

As we drove back to Mum's, my face felt warm and tender. I pulled down the sun visor and took a look in the mirror. My top lip had a nasty cut and was swollen and my left eye was badly swollen too. I felt like I had just gone ten rounds with a professional boxer.

I inwardly sighed. I was hurt but I was really relieved that it was over and I never had to see Charlie again.

Looking slightly on edge, John glanced over at me and started to apologise. 'Whatever was I thinking of! I knew I shouldn't have let you go in there alone.'

'No, really John, this is not your fault, it was my choice I really didn't think he was capable of that.'

John gave me a slight smile. 'Maybe you should give your Mum a call.'

I think Mum must have been waiting for me to call as she answered on the second ring. I told her everything that had just happened and that if it wasn't for John it would have been so much worse. When we arrived, she was anxiously pacing the doorstep with Tommy in her arms. John helped me out of the car and I had to lean on him for support. As I limped up the drive Mum rushed over and we met halfway.

She immediately started to fret. 'Oh Sarah you poor thing,' she touched my face. 'The man's a monster. I can't believe he's done this to you.'

We made our way into the house and John gently helped me to the settee whilst Mum started to make a fuss by propping me up with extra cushions.

Now Mum looked really concerned. 'You've got to press charges this time. You can't let him get away with this.'

'Yes Mum, I will do. I never want to see him again but can we do it tomorrow? I can't face anyone tonight. I just want to spend time with you and Tommy.'

I cuddled Tommy and he held onto me tightly, obviously sensing something was badly wrong.

A huge sense of relief washed over me as I realised it was all over. What Charlie had done to me made it so much easier for me to make a clean break. I had to press charges against him as I could never forgive myself if he did it to some other poor woman.

I turned my attention back to Tommy who was clinging onto me for all he was worth. I could see how confused and upset he was and I tried to comfort him the best I could.

'Mummy is going to be okay.' I hugged him tightly and tried to put his mind at ease. I looked him in the eye. 'How would you like it if you and I come here and live with Nana for a while?'

He smiled and excitedly nodded.

Looking at Tommy, I made a vow to myself that from that point forward I would always put him first.

Mum smiled. 'I think its Tommy's bed time. I'll put him to bed tonight, you need to rest.'

Tommy still looked upset as he gave me a kiss goodnight. 'I love you Mummy.'

I held him a little tighter in my arms. 'I'll come up in a minute.'

They disappeared upstairs and I waved and called after him. 'I love you too Tommy.'

John took my hand and tried to reassure me. 'The worst is over now' he said.

'I really do appreciate everything you have done for me today.' I squeezed his hand. 'I couldn't have done it without you, and if it wasn't for you I would still be with Charlie.'

I was so grateful for the way John had helped me and as we sat and talked I really wanted to tell him about all the nights I had lay awake praying and wishing I could go back in time to just before I had split up with him. It was too soon to tell him of the feelings I had always had for him and I didn't want him to think I was on the rebound from Charlie. I just wished I was confident enough to tell him how I felt but the last thing I wanted to do was scare him away. I decided I would have to take it slowly and hope he would stick around.

A few minutes later Mum came back downstairs. 'Are you alright love?' she asked looking over at me.

'No, I ache all over and my heads pounding.'

'Maybe we should go to the hospital to get you checked out.' She frowned as she started to reply and her voice was full of concern but I really didn't feel up to going.

I let out a sigh. 'If I'm not feeling any better in the morning I'll go then.'

'Ok then' her frown remained but she didn't argue. 'I will get you some paracetamol and make us all a cup of tea.'

'Thanks Mum. I'll go and see Tommy.'

I struggled to get to my feet with John's help. 'Do you want help to get upstairs?' he asked.

I smiled. 'No I'll be ok thanks.' I gripped the banister tightly and slowly made my way upstairs, one step at a time.

Tommy was sitting up in bed waiting for me. I could see he was a little confused by everything that had happened and I felt so guilty that I hadn't really explained to him what was going on. It was going to take him a little time to get used to all the changes but I knew from that point forward life for both of us would improve. I could give him all of my undivided love and attention. Life was going to be a lot better for us.

I sat on the edge of the bed, put my arm around him and gave him a gentle smile. 'When I was a little girl this was my bedroom and I had lots of fun times in this house with my mummy and daddy. Now it's your turn to have lots of fun times with me and Nana.'

Tommy looked at me thoughtfully. 'Is Daddy going to come here and have fun times too?'

'No sweetheart, Daddy won't be coming.'

That made me think: Charlie might try to use Tommy to get back at me, even though he had never shown any interest in him whatsoever I knew he could be vindictive.

I lay with Tommy for a few minutes as he cuddled up to his teddy bear. It was actually the bear I had as a two year old, Mum and Dad bought it for me at Christmas and after Dad died I treasured it even more. When I moved in with Charlie I boxed it up until Tommy was born, then I put it in his cot and it became his comfort toy that he would take everywhere. It was quite worn and had seen better days but he loved it.

Tommy fell asleep quickly but I lay there with him for a few more minutes, contemplating our future. I just knew everything was going to be alright. The following day would be the start of a brand new chapter in our lives. Tommy had always been the most important thing in my life and I thought how lucky I was to have him with me. Having him in my world got me through those difficult few years.

I crept out of the room and struggled downstairs to find Mum and John deep in conversation. Mum looked up at me. 'I was just saying to John, I am so glad he got to you when he did, it doesn't bear thinking about what could have happened.'

John helped me sit down and Mum passed me my cup of tea and paracetamol. She tried to lighten the mood. 'This is nice, just like old times.' She smiled at us each in turn.

I had forgotten how embarrassing Mum could be. I looked at John and he gave me such an awkward smile so I changed the subject. 'I will go to the police tomorrow. I won't let him get away with this. It really worries me that he will want access to Tommy though, to get to me.'

Mum shook her head. 'I don't think that will happen, not when you tell them what he has done to you.'

We fell silent for a few minutes.

John looked over at me. 'I think I should go now, I will call you tomorrow.'

I tried to get up.

'No don't get up I will see myself out.'

I felt I needed a few minutes alone with John so I shot Mum a look. She nodded slightly with a knowing smile before getting to her feet. 'I'll just go and check on Tommy,' she said.

As she left I turned to John. 'I bet you wished you'd never bumped in to me yesterday.'

'No, I'm glad I did. Nobody deserves to go through what you had to go through. You and Tommy deserve to be happy and I am glad I could help you.'

My mind raced and before he could say anymore I foolishly blurted out my feelings. 'When I saw you the other day, I realised how I still have feelings for you. I thought about you a lot when I was with Charlie. I thought about how my life could have turned out if you and I hadn't finished. Maybe it was fate that brought us back together.'

John eased himself closer, took my hand and looked me in the eye. 'You have just left Charlie, you are feeling vulnerable and I get that but the last thing you need is to jump back into a relationship with me. What you need right now is to spend time with your mum and Tommy.' He squeezed my hand. 'I will be here for you as long as you need me. I will go to the police with you tomorrow as they will need my statement as well.' As he stood up he kissed me on the cheek. 'I'll give you a call tomorrow.'

Within seconds of the front door closing Mum made her way back in. She must have been lurking just outside the room. 'Are you ok?'

I looked at her and smiled half heartedly. 'Yes I suppose. I think I have just blown it with John. I was hoping that we could get back together one day but I think he just wants to stay friends now.'

Mum smiled. 'Give it time love. Don't forget you have only just come out of a bad relationship and Tommy needs you more than ever. John is a really nice guy and he is worth waiting for. I think he will stick around.'

'I know Mum. I haven't been feeling myself today, I think I will take another paracetamol and go to bed.'

I tentatively made my way upstairs with Mum's help before carefully washing my face. I glanced in the mirror and what I saw really upset me. My left eye was painfully swollen plus I had a fat top lip and a nasty cut. I made a vow never to let this happen to me again.

As I made my way into the bedroom I noticed that Tommy was sound asleep and looked so sweet cuddling his teddy. All I ever wanted from life was for him to have the best life I could possibly give him. I just hoped he was young enough to forget all of this. One day I wanted him to look back at his childhood and know that I did my very best for him.

As I climbed into bed my thoughts turned to John. I hoped that in time John and I could give it another go. As I laid there I thought back to happier times and prayed to my angel for a happy ending with John.

That night I struggled to sleep. I must have laid there for a good hour before I eventually fell into a deep sleep with Tommy safely in my arms.

Chapter 11

I was woken up early the next morning by Mum gently shaking me. 'Come on Sarah you've overslept, you are going to be late.'

Still half asleep I warily glanced over at my alarm clock. 'Mum' I whispered, 'it's early you'll wake Tommy. It's only five twenty-four.' I closed my eyes to try and get back to sleep.

Mum shook me again. 'Come on Sarah you are going to be late for work.'

I started to get a bit annoyed. 'Mum, I haven't been to work for four years.'

Mum gave me another gentle shake. 'Come on Sarah wake up, you are not making sense.'

'Okay, okay I'm getting up now. Can you take Tommy and make him his breakfast please.'

'Tommy?' Mum sounded confused. 'Who's Tommy?'

I opened one eye and noticed that Tommy wasn't in the bed. I quickly sat up and looked at Mum. 'Where's Tommy Mum?'

'Who's Tommy?' she replied.

My first thought was that Mum and Tommy were playing a game with me so I decided I would play along. Tommy and I played hide and seek all the time. He would run off and I would go and look for him, when I got close he would always give the game away and start to giggle. I got up and went into every room calling out his name and listening for his little giggle.

Soon I had checked everywhere and when I got to the kitchen there was still no sign of him. I sat down for a minute as Mum followed me in. 'Okay' I said, 'I give up. Where is he?'

'Sweetheart, are you ok?' Mum looked puzzled.

'Yes I'm fine, you win. Tell Tommy he can come out now.'

'I really don't know who Tommy is.'

I looked at her a little oddly. 'Mum this has gone just a little bit too far now, can you go and get my son for me please.'

'Sarah is this some sort of joke, you haven't got a son.'

I started to cry. I just couldn't understand why Mum would be so insensitive and cruel, especially after everything that had happened to me yesterday. How could she be so heartless and say I didn't have a son, she knew how much Tommy meant to me.

Mum tried to comfort me but I pushed her away. I was so upset with her. She was the one person I needed the most in the world.

'Mum, I need to see Tommy! If you think anything of me you'll go and get him for me.'

She looked me in the eye and I could see she was really upset as well. 'Sarah I really don't know what to say to you.'

I could hear the honesty in her voice and it scared me. 'Mum, what's going on.'

'You don't seem yourself this morning. Maybe you should have the day off work.'

I explained to her that I hadn't worked for four years, since I first got pregnant with Tommy but Mum looked confused. 'But you were working yesterday.'

'No' I replied. 'Yesterday Tommy and I moved back in with you after Charlie beat me up. Remember?' I pointed to my face. 'Look what he has done to my face.'

Mum started to get agitated. 'I don't know who this Charlie is and your face looks fine to me.'

I got up and slowly moved to the kitchen mirror. There wasn't a mark on me and I noticed my hair looked a bit shorter than it did yesterday. I sat back down not knowing what to say or think. Maybe it was a bad dream.

Mum leaned across the table and gently touched my hand. 'I think I will give Kate a ring.'

She went off into the front room to make the call but I listened in on her conversation. I could hear her telling Kate that I wasn't feeling well and that I needed a few days off.

When she came back she sat down and looked me in the eye. 'What's wrong Sarah?'

'I don't know Mum.' I sighed. 'I'm confused. Do you know who John is?'

She gave me a funny look. 'Of course I do, he's your boyfriend. You two have been an item for five months.'

A horrible thought flashed through my mind. 'Mum, how old am I?'

She looked puzzled. 'What sort of question is that Sarah? You're twenty-one years old.'

My mind raced and I got up and started looking around the kitchen. It didn't look exactly like it did yesterday. There were subtle differences but nothing I could put a finger on from memory. I went into the hall looking for a clue, anything to make sense of it all. I started walking towards the front room and it was then that something caught my eye; two sets of keys hanging up on the key hooks. I recognised one set as mine and I lifted them off the hook and studied them.

My blood ran cold. Surely not! There in my hand was my old Ford Fiesta key. I just stood there staring at it for a few minutes before a thought came to me and I quickly put on my shoes, ran outside and down the drive. I stopped in my tracks as I couldn't believe what I was seeing. There, parked next to Mum's car, was my red Ford Fiesta, the car Charlie had forced me to sell four years ago. I unlocked the door and sat in the driver's seat. I just sat there for a few minutes and happy memories came flooding back. I thought back to the time before I met Charlie.

I had forgotten what it was like to drive a car, it had been so long. I glanced at the milometer and it read 48902. I remembered that when Charlie sold it he told his mate it had done 56000 miles.

I needed time to take everything in. If I was twenty-one, that meant Tommy didn't exist; he hadn't been born yet. I panicked at the thought of never seeing him again. Had I lost him forever? I felt sick to the bottom of my stomach. I just needed to see Tommy and lift him up into my arms. Surely this couldn't be real.

I slowly made my way back to the house. Mum was still sitting at the table but she now had her head in her hands and looked upset. I gave her a hug.

'Sorry Mum. I didn't mean to upset you, I'm not feeling well. I think I need to go and have a lie down.'

As I climbed the stairs it dawned on me that I was no longer in any pain. I warily opened my bedroom door still not wanting to believe that I may have gone back in time. My bedroom was different, I just hadn't noticed it when I got up this morning but then again why should I have done, I wasn't really looking for anything out of the ordinary then.

I looked around the room. On the bedside cabinet was my old mobile phone, the one I traded in four years ago and my 2013 diary. I would write in my diary every day back then. The last entry was 24th May 2013 so I checked the date on my phone and realised that was yesterday. I sat on the bed and my thoughts turned back to Tommy. I couldn't bear the thought I may never see him again and that he didn't exist. He wouldn't be born until 2015 and that would only happen if I met Charlie. The thought of having to relive my life with Charlie filled me with horror but the thought of never seeing Tommy again made me feel numb and empty inside. Yesterday I thought I was finally free of Charlie. I could quite happily live in this time if I had Tommy with me but without him it was my worst nightmare.

As I laid there I looked down at the cuddly toys at the foot of the bed and in amongst them was my old bear. I picked it up and immediately burst into tears. The image of Tommy cuddling up to it last night was still strong in my mind. It really brought it home to me that I had lost my little boy. I tried to convince myself that I was in the middle of some horrible dream and that if I went back to sleep I would wake up with everything back to how it was and Tommy would be back with me.

I laid back and soon fell into a deep sleep. It was probably the best sleep I had had in ages.

I woke up with a jolt a few hours later and I instinctively looked round for Tommy. My heart sank as I realised the room was the same. How could I have gone back in time? Where was Tommy? Every part of my body was aching for him.

In the following days I hardly left my room as I tried to make sense of it all. I found myself working out the hours and minutes since I last saw Tommy. Mum was worried about me so I decided not to talk to her about Tommy anymore or about me falling back five years in time. I told her I was not thinking straight and maybe I had a fever.

Chapter 12

So that was where I found myself on day seven. The seventh day I had woken up in that life. The seventh day without my little boy and the seventh day I found myself five years in my past.

That life was beginning to feel real and my future life was becoming just a memory. I couldn't face the world outside my room as that would be admitting I may never have Tommy with me again and he was in my thoughts every moment of my waking day. I had no photos or any evidence that he existed, apart from my memories. I felt so guilty because, in his three short years, I couldn't give him the best start in life, the life that he deserved.

My days turned into nights and nights back into days and nothing changed.

Each day I only had my thoughts for company. Each day I spent the same way as the day before. I just lay on my bed and somehow tried to make sense of what had happened to Tommy. I slowly came to the same conclusion every time and I knew there was a way to have Tommy back in my life and, however painful it would be, in my heart I knew the only choice I had was to get back with Charlie.

In this time frame I was destined to meet Charlie in six months. The thought of living the rest of my life without Tommy was too much so I had to do whatever it took and getting back with Charlie was the price I would have to pay, to have Tommy back in my life.

I really needed to talk to Mum about this but I knew how crazy it sounded. How could I expect Mum to understand when I didn't really understand it myself?

I thought back to my Dad and his faith and I realised that was all I had left. I had to have faith in my angel but I wasn't sure whether I believed or not anymore.

Another week passed and all I could think about was having Tommy back with me but also having to relive my life with Charlie and how that was going to slowly bring me to my knees. So, three weeks with no change. I felt that I needed Mum so I decided it was time to leave the comfort of my bedroom and spend more time with her.

I felt I had to make sense of this time that I found myself in so, when she asked me if I felt ready to get back to work, I knew I must go. I needed to get out and find answers; I also needed John's support so I decided to give him a ring.

I called Kate first but it felt really strange speaking to her after all this time. She asked me to start back at work again the next day and I agreed. I had mixed feelings about going back to work again, as far as Kate was concerned it had only been three weeks but for me it had been over four years.

Next I rang John. I knew he had been really concerned about me so I arranged to go to his after work the next day. In this timeline I hadn't seen John in three weeks so I told him I had been really ill.

Every night I still prayed to my angel, not for me but for Tommy. I prayed that I would wake up the next morning, back in my own time, with Tommy next to me. I was finding it so hard to get my head around what had happened to Tommy. I knew he didn't exist yet but I couldn't give up on him. I talked to him everyday; the thought that he could hear me gave me the strength to keep going.

Chapter 13

The next morning I was woken by my alarm at 5.30 a.m. and as always, my first thought was Tommy but within seconds I realised that nothing had changed. I slowly opened the curtains and the sun was just rising. I looked out at the blue and orange sky and listened to the early bird song. I had always loved this time of the morning.

I was feeling a bit nervous as this was the first day I had ventured outside in over three weeks. It was also the first day in four and a half years that I had had to think for myself. I made my way down the stairs and into the kitchen. There on the side was my packed lunch and I smiled to myself. I had forgotten that Mum always made my lunch for me the night before. Sitting down to my breakfast I thought about the day ahead. I was looking forward to getting out but I wasn't sure what the day was going to bring.

If I was going to make sense of everything I needed to get out there. I finished my breakfast just as Mum came in. 'Are you sure you're feeling up to work today?'

I gave her a smile and nodded.

After freshening up, I picked up my lunch and headed for the door but before I could get there Mum called out. 'Don't forget these.' She dangled my car keys in front of her.

'Thanks Mum. Don't forget I'm seeing John tonight after work.' I took the keys and headed out.

'Okay love, I'll see you later then.'

I took a long look at my car and slowly climbed into the driver's seat. I realised it had been four years since I last drove so I sat there for a few minutes reminding myself which pedal was the clutch and accelerator before looking at the gear pattern on the gear knob. I turned the key in the ignition, nervously selected first gear and slowly pulled away.

For a few minutes I drove like I had just passed my test but it started to come back pretty quickly. The sense of freedom took over and my nerves faded. I had forgotten how much I missed just getting in my car and driving. I started to enjoy the moment but it was short lived as my thoughts soon returned to Tommy. I felt I was somehow letting him down and I should be with him right now, seeing to his needs. I prayed for Tommy as somehow I felt closer to him by talking to my angel.

As I got close to my old house curiosity got the better of me and I parked up on the other side of the road. Charlie would be going to work in ten minutes; he was a man of routine and always left at the same time. I waited nervously in anticipation. Right on cue Charlie opened the door, a feeling of fear overwhelmed me and I had to remind myself that he didn't know me yet. He got into his car and pulled away, it was a different car, it was the one he had when I first met him.

I drove the five minutes to the cafe and as I walked in it felt very much like my first day in a new job. Kate was busy setting cutlery on tables but when she saw me she came over and gave me a hug. 'It's really nice to have you back. I hope you are feeling much better.'

It didn't take long for me to get back into the routine and it soon felt as if I hadn't been away. It was a great feeling working again and my first day flew by. You don't realise how much you miss something until it is taken away. It was nice to see the regulars again too. They always made the job so much more enjoyable.

As my shift neared its end my thoughts slowly shifted to John. I was really looking forward to seeing him again.

Kate closed up the cafe and walked out to the car park with me. 'I'll see you tomorrow' she said as she walked to her car.

I smiled back. 'Okay have a nice evening.'

I drove the short distance to John's and when I arrived he welcomed me in with a hug. I remembered how good that felt. As I walked into the kitchen a lovely smell filled the air so I took a deep breath in to savour it.

'Mmmm, something smells nice,'

'Good. I've made us a lasagne and a lemon cheesecake for dessert. I know it's one of your favourites.'

I turned and smiled at him. 'I've really missed you.'

John gave me a cheeky grin. 'Now is it me you've missed or my cooking?'

I couldn't help but laugh. 'Ok you've got me, it's your cooking.' I had forgotten how nice it was to just be myself and not have to think before I spoke.

Dinner was lovely and I told John that I would spoil him next time.

After cleaning up we settled down in the front room. I remembered how I loved our cosy nights in watching TV.

My mind was miles away when John spoke. 'Do you fancy going to see that new film, Man of Steel, on Saturday night? It's the latest Superman film and it sounds quite good.'

'Oh yes I loved that film, I saw it on TV not so long ago.'

'What do you mean you saw it on TV? It has only just come out at the cinema.' John was giving me a funny look.

I had to think quickly. 'Oh sorry I must've been thinking of one of the other Superman films. I would love to go.'

As the time crept on I thought I'd better get home. 'I've got to go now but I'm really looking forward to going to the cinema on Saturday.'

John gently wrapped me in his arms and gave me a tender kiss goodbye.

On the drive home it dawned on me that by getting back with John my life was on a completely different path. When I was with Charlie I often thought what my life would have been like if I hadn't finished with John and how perfect my life could have been. Now it looked like I may get my answer but it could never be perfect, not without Tommy to share it with us.

Over the next few days I spent the evenings with Mum and it was just like old times. I realised I had no choice but to just go with the flow and make the most of the hand that fate had dealt me.

I picked up my diary and read it, I realised the last few months were mainly about John. The last three weeks were blank so I decided I was going to write my diary again. I was going to write about my daily feelings to keep Tommy fresh in my thoughts.

The next morning I woke up feeling good about the day. It was Saturday so after work John and I were going to see Man of Steel. I saw the film with him just before we split up in my other timeline but it would still be nice to see it again. Kate was going to let me finish work early so I could meet up with him.

At about one in the afternoon, during the lunchtime rush, the café was busy and I had just finished clearing a table in the corner when I turned and my stomach lurched into my mouth. Charlie and his mate Mark were standing there waiting patiently for me to finish. Charlie smiled at me and thanked me before they sat down. I couldn't even look him in the eye. Visions of the beating he had given me the other week flooded my mind and I felt a panic attack coming on. I turned and ran to the kitchen to take a few short breaths and calm my nerves. I told myself I was in control and he just caught me by surprise that was all. This situation probably happened last time but because I didn't know Charlie then, I didn't take any notice. When I got back I was relieved to see Kate taking their order as I wasn't sure I could have coped with him so soon.

It was a busy afternoon with the Saturday rush and it made the day go quickly. I just wanted to get to John's as I had been thinking about him all afternoon. I tried to remember back to the time John and I went out all those years ago.

Kate looked at her watch. 'It's almost five so you might as well get going.'

She didn't need to tell me twice. 'Thanks. I'll see you on Monday.' I smiled and got my things.

I arrived at John's about ten minutes later. He answered the door giving me a puzzled look. 'Why don't you use your key anymore?'

I looked down at my keys. I had forgotten that he had given me one for his place but before I could reply he started talking again.

'The film starts at eight so we have a few hours. Are you hungry?'

'Not really. We could have a burger after the film.'

Tonight will be the last time I go to the cinema if my life plays out like it did before. John and I used to go regularly but I didn't really go out much after I finished with him. Charlie didn't really take me anywhere.

It felt really good to be back in a normal relationship where I could be myself, without having to worry about what I said.

We made our way to the cinema just after seven as it was about a ten minute drive from John's house. I felt a shiver down my spine as we passed Charlie's house. He must have been in because his car was parked outside. I tried to blank him from my mind as the night was about me and John but I felt guilty that I was putting my own enjoyment before Tommy.

We parked up with plenty of time to spare, picked up our tickets and piled ourselves up with popcorn and drinks. I saw this film about eight months ago on TV but I was really looking forward to seeing it again. Our seats were pre-booked, four rows from the back, exactly the same place we sat last time. I remembered the lady I was sitting next to with the distinctive pink jumper from last time as well. Did this mean for the next five years my life was destined to go almost the same way as before?

When I was last here five years ago I finished with John the next Thursday but I didn't think I could do that this time so, in theory, I would be rewriting my own life but that would mean writing Tommy out of my life and I couldn't do that. So maybe I was destined to live the next five years the same way as last time and repeat all the bad times with Charlie. The worst thing of all was this time I would be going into it with my eyes wide open, fully aware of every painful thing that Charlie put me through. I really needed my guardian angel by my side now more than ever.

The film started so I cuddled up to John and lost myself in the moment, trying to forget everything for at least a few hours. The film was as good as I remembered it to be and John said he really enjoyed it.

Afterwards we made our way across the road to McDonald's for a burger. After ordering I followed John as I was curious to see where he decided to sit and, sure enough, he sat in the same place we sat five years ago.

I quickly grabbed his hand and led him to the other side of the room. 'No let's sit over there.' I was trying to prove to myself that I had freewill in this timeframe and didn't have to relive my life exactly the same as I did last time.

John smiled at me. 'Okay suit yourself.'

As we sat and ate our food I thought to myself that it would be the last time John and I would go out before we split up. Maybe my angel had sent me back to this time to give me another chance with John, maybe he was my destiny. This time around I could change parts of my past but I needed my angel to guide me through and help me to make the right choices. In this timeframe I wouldn't meet Charlie in the club for another six months. I didn't want to finish with John on Thursday so I thought that maybe, I could carry on seeing him for another six months. I needed to put all my faith in my angel.

Everything that happened that night was very much inline with what had happened the first time I was there. I was very aware that I didn't have to follow my past and if I decided not to finish with John on Thursday, I would be following a new path

I stayed around John's that night. I used to stop around his a couple of nights a week. Five years ago this would have been the last time I spoke to him before Thursday, the day that I finished with him. Back then I didn't even have the courage to finish with him face to face. I chose the cowards way out and finished with him with a text. I had always regretted that.

On Sunday morning I woke up to an empty bed. I heard the clatter of plates downstairs and the smell of bacon filled the air. Still half asleep I made my way downstairs to see John in the kitchen cooking a fry up.

Looking at me, he smiled. 'Sit down, it's almost ready.'

John was always good to me. I still couldn't believe my dream had come true and I had the chance to change the past. I couldn't imagine having to give him up in six months and go back to Charlie. I really wanted to stay with John forever but I knew I had to put Tommy first. It brought me comfort to think that Tommy was up there with the angels, waiting to be born. Every morning I told him how much I loved him. Tommy was my life and I would go through any mental or physical pain from Charlie to have him with me again. Without Tommy there was such a large empty void in my life.

Mum had invited us round for dinner and later that morning we made our way to my house separately as John needed to get back that night.

I really enjoyed spending the day with Mum and John. I was a bit distant as my mind was all over the place but I tried not to show it. John stayed all day and left about 11 p.m. I walked with him to the door. 'I'll be round after work on Thursday.'

He nodded as that was the day I usually stayed over at his. We kissed and he left.

I thought I had got away with it but Mum had noticed I was a bit distant and asked if everything was okay. I really wanted to tell her everything. I felt I couldn't bottle it up any longer but if I did tell her everything and, if by some miracle, she believed me she would really make it hard for me to get with Charlie and if I did she would probably disown me.

As the next few days passed I thought a lot about the way I'd finished with John last time. Surely it wouldn't do any harm to stay with him for another six months?

Thursday the 27th of June arrived, a date that was embedded in my mind. Last time around I sent John that awful text at about 8 p.m. and as it reached 7.30 p.m. I decided that, instead of finishing with him by text, this time I would ring him to say how much I loved him.

I waited anxiously for the clock to turn eight and I rang him on the dot.

'Hi John how are you?'

'Oh hi Sarah I'm glad you rang. I wanted to tell you I have booked us a table for Saturday night at that new Indian restaurant, the one you said you wouldn't mind going to.'

'Great, that'll be lovely. I can't wait. I'm looking forward to seeing you tomorrow too. I really miss you when we're apart.'

'And I really miss you too. You do know I am happy for you to stay here as often as you like don't you? You have a key and I want you to treat this house like your second home.'

We chatted for another ten minutes before I wished him goodnight and put the phone down.

It was a good feeling knowing I had changed my past. From that point on most things would be new, at least for six months. I vowed to try and enjoy the extra months I had with John as after that I would have to put my future in the hands of fate.

Every night I prayed to my angel for a sign so I would know what to do. Why was life being so cruel to me? Having to go back into a life with Charlie for a second time, knowing every painful moment before it happened was too much for me to bear but I knew I had to do it for Tommy. Every mother knows they would walk through burning coals to keep their child safe and Tommy was waiting with the angels; waiting for me to bring him back down to me.

I picked up my diary and thumbed through the pages until I got to Thursday November 7th and wrote a note. That was the day Julie was going to ring me at 2.22 p.m. asking me to go to the nightclub on the Saturday night.

The next day I woke up feeling quite optimistic about the day ahead. I had got used to being back in this time. My future life had faded into the background and felt like a distant memory.

Over the next few months' life with John was everything I thought it would be but I found myself holding back. All I could think about was the night Julie and I went to the club and met Charlie. I tried to put that date to the back of my mind. The extra six months I had with John made me realise just how much I loved him and the nearer it got to that night, the harder I was finding the thought of going back to my old life with Charlie.

Chapter 14

On the night of Wednesday 6th November, before climbing into bed, I picked up my diary and turned to the next page and read the note I wrote to myself six months ago. Thursday was the day Julie was going to ring me, out of the blue and ask me to go to the nightclub on Saturday.

I had been waiting for this day for six months but the thought of meeting up with Charlie and getting back with him absolutely sickened me. I couldn't imagine having to relive the worst four and a half years of my life all over again. I really thought that I'd left that part of my life behind. I couldn't face going back into that situation knowing every little detail of what he would do to me. However I had to focus on the one and only positive outcome, my little boy. He would be back with me in exactly one year, two months and seven days from now.

I got very little sleep that night and set off to work earlier than usual. There was only one thing on my mind; the phone call that I was going to get from Julie. I still didn't know what I was going to say to her. All I did know was that John was my life and I loved him more than anything. The thought of not being with him anymore was just too much for me to deal with.

All morning I was in autopilot, thoughts of what I was going to say to Julie kept running through my head. I really didn't want to go on Saturday night but every time I convinced myself I wouldn't go my thoughts kept coming back to Tommy. I thought of him up there with the angels, waiting to come down to me. He was relying on me to do the right thing and I couldn't let him down.

I asked Kate if I could take a late lunch from two until three and she was okay with that. I looked at the clock and it had only just turned eleven. The first few hours had really dragged and it seemed ages until lunch. After a few more endless hours of clock watching eventually two o'clock arrived. I felt I needed some privacy and decided to go outside and sit in my car.

I couldn't help thinking about the last six months of my life with John and how happy he had made me. I couldn't bear the thought of throwing all that away and having to go back to being that lonely, scared person again. I really thought that knowing my fate would tip me over the edge. I begged my angel to help me. I felt I was at such a painful crossroads and really didn't know which way to turn. I was torn between Tommy, John and my sanity.

At 2.15 p.m. I sat transfixed by my phone waiting for the call. Right on cue at 2.22 and 23 seconds my phone rang and Julie's name flashed up. It still surprised me how I could predict my future.

I took a deep breath and answered it with a hint of sarcasm in my voice. 'Oh hi Julie, how are you? Long time no see.'

'Hi Sarah, erm, yeah sorry about that, you know how it is. I've been meaning to ring for a while. I've been seeing this lad but it hasn't been working out so I ditched him. Then I thought it would be nice for a bit of a catch up with my old mate Sarah.'

The conversation was going the same way as I remembered it did last time so I played along.

'Yes that would be great.'

'Brilliant. I'm free this weekend. I really fancy going out to a club for a girlie night out, are you up for it?'

'I don't know if I'm really in the mood for a club.' I followed the script from the past.

'Come on Sarah, life's too short; let your hair down you know we'll have a good time.'

'But I haven't really got anything to wear.'

'Well that's not a problem we can go shopping on Saturday morning.'

Julie always had an answer for everything and just like before I agreed. We arranged for me to pick her up around ten o'clock like before but as soon as I put the phone down I started to doubt my decision. I had to tell John that Julie and I were going to a club and I knew he would be ok with it, as he trusted me but it broke my heart knowing why I was going.

I looked at my watch and it was 2.45 p.m. I quickly ate my lunch and headed back inside to start the afternoon shift.

All afternoon thoughts about Saturday ran through my head. My mind wasn't on the job all day and I was really glad when my shift finished. I was feeling low and just wanted to get back to John. What made it worse was he kept dropping hints for me to stay round his more often. If it wasn't for Tommy I knew our relationship would be moving on to the next level but I found myself backing off. Maybe I made the wrong decision six months ago and I should have followed the same path as before and ended it with John. I loved him so much but staying with him made us more emotionally involved and getting back with Charlie was going to hurt us both a lot more. Maybe I should never have messed about with the past.

It only took me a few minutes to get to John's and I let myself in. He greeted me in the hall with a kiss. 'I've just ordered us a take away. Your favourite, chicken curry with egg fried rice.'

I couldn't help but smile. 'Oh thank you. I am so lucky to have you.'

Shortly after the takeaway arrived we sat at the table to eat.

John asked me how my day had been and I saw it as the perfect opportunity to drop Saturday into the conversation.

'It's been busy but ok.' I hesitated for a few seconds. 'My friend Julie rang. She wants to go out with me to a club this Saturday, for a girlie night out.' Nervously I waited for his reaction.

'That sounds like fun, you should go. It'll be good for you to get out without me; you hardly ever go out with your friends.'

I didn't want John to know that I had already agreed to go out so I lied. 'Oh, ok, if you really are sure I will ring her back tomorrow.'

'If you want I could always drop you and Julie off at the club and pick you up later?'

I felt a knot of guilt in my stomach. I couldn't let him do that, he trusted me and I was going to throw it all back in his face. I forced a smile as I replied. 'No, its ok we'll get a taxi. It's easier that way.'

We finished our food and made our way to the front room. I was very much aware that it could be the last evening I spent with John and I found I was questioning myself. Could I really go back to Charlie? They say hindsight is a wonderful thing. Well I had hindsight in bucket loads but it didn't help. Every part of my mind and body was screaming at me not to do it and to stay with John but then I thought I had no choice. What would become of Tommy if I didn't? I needed to have him back with me. In my minds eye I saw him standing with my angel, holding her hand and patiently waiting to be born to me.

I looked over at John as he watched the television and resigned myself to the fact that on Sunday morning I would be telling him it was over. That night I wanted to savour every last minute I had left with him. I had known for the last six months that it was coming but it didn't make it any easier. Even though the memories of my future self had faded into the background, my love for Tommy would never fade and would always shine like an eternal flame deep in my heart. Even then, when I closed my eyes I could still picture every detail of my baby boy.

Later that night, like every other night that week, I had trouble sleeping. I looked over at John and he was so peaceful. I wished I could sleep like him and I tried but I just couldn't get Saturday out of my thoughts. Eventually total exhaustion won.

The next morning I woke suddenly to my alarm. I looked at the clock, then over to John's side of the bed and it quickly dawned on me that he was due to leave for work in twenty minutes. In a panic I got dressed in super quick time as I needed to see him before he left.

He was in the kitchen when I got downstairs and as I rushed in he looked up and smiled. 'Hi sweetie, I wasn't expecting you up yet.'

'I wanted to see you before you left. I just wanted to make sure you really are okay with me and Julie going to the club tomorrow?'

He gave me a hug. 'Don't be silly, of course I'm okay with it.' He gave me that grin of his. 'Just don't go off and start chatting up all those single men.'

My knot of guilt returned. 'Of course I won't, you are the only one for me.'

His grin widened. 'I think I'm going to book us a table for Sunday at that pub near the river. We can have a carvery and afterwards we can go for a drink.'

Looking at his watch he suddenly panicked. 'Is it really that time already? I better get off.'

As he turned to the door it dawned on me that it could be the last time that I'd ever see him. A huge rush of emotion took over me and I ran at him and wrapped my arms around him tightly, nearly knocking him over in the process.

'Steady on' he laughed, 'you'll break my ribs.'

I felt myself welling up.

John looked a little bemused as gently wiped a single tear from my cheek with his thumb. 'Hey, what's wrong?' he asked inquisitively.

Wiping a few more tears away I looked directly at him. 'Whatever happens between us I need you to know you're the best thing that has ever happened to me and I will always love you.'

Holding me tighter, he kissed me tenderly on the forehead. 'Where's all this come from? Don't ever doubt my love for you. I'm afraid you are stuck with me, I'm not going anywhere.'

My heart was breaking and I really didn't think I could give him up. I held on to him tightly, never wanting to let him go.

'I need to go now,' he whispered in my ear.

Giving him one final kiss I reluctantly let him go. As he opened the front door, I saw the concerned look etched all over his face. 'We are okay aren't we?'

I nodded and forced a smile. 'Of course we are.'

John's face lifted and he smiled back at me. 'Well have a good time tomorrow and I will see you on Sunday. Don't forget how much I love you.'

The door clicked shut behind him, leaving the room deathly silent. I stood there for a minute just staring at it totally lost in my own thoughts. A feeling of emptiness overwhelmed me as I realised the choices I had to make had become so real and urgent. I slowly made my way to the front room but my mind kept bouncing back and fourth from John to Charlie. I looked around the room and remembered back, or in this timeframe forward, to the day John helped me to leave Charlie.

At the start of my life with Charlie I thought it was love I felt for him. I wasn't aware of who he really was and how he was slowly and deliberately manipulating me. I was blind to the subtle tale-tale signs that were always there.

My thoughts turned to my angel and I told her how much I needed her in my life right now. I prayed that if I had to go back to Charlie that she protected me from him and brought Tommy safely back to me. I told her my life was in her hands and that I needed her guidance to make the right choice in the next few days.

I became so engrossed in my thoughts that I lost all track of time and didn't realise I had been sitting there for almost two hours. I should have been at work an hour earlier but I wasn't really in the mood so decided to ring in sick. I felt guilty for letting Kate down but it wasn't like I took a lot of time off.

I returned to my thoughts and mulled things over. I thought about Tommy and how much I missed him. The bond I had with him was so strong, I felt I needed to do whatever it took to have him back with me and if that meant starting my life over with Charlie then that's what I had to do.

The lack of sleep must have caught up with me as I found myself dozing off. When I woke it was three o'clock in the afternoon and I had stayed a lot longer than I had expected to. I needed to get home but I took one last look around before I shut the door behind me. The thought of never seeing John again hurt so much.

On the drive home I passed Charlie's house. The house was full of bad memories for me. I could still picture the very last time I was in there and him beating me to within an inch of my life and John saving me. I would always be so grateful to John for that. I felt that I was the victim of a cruel twist of fate for having to return to the life I hated.

Arriving back home Mum greeted me in the hallway. 'Hello love, you're home early.'

'Yes I had a migraine and spent the day at John's. Oh, by the way, Julie and I are going to a club tomorrow night.'

Mum gave me one of her disapproving looks. 'I really don't know why you bother with her. She only wants to be your friend when she is at a loose end.'

I gave Mum a wry smile. 'I know Mum but it's a night out.'

I decided to go upstairs to escape as I knew what Mum was like when she got a bee in her bonnet, she would just go on and on.

I lay on my bed and tried to remember how Saturday went in my other timeline. I still didn't know how I was going to react to Charlie when he started talking to me at the club or on Sunday when I had to go out on a date with him.

I hated Charlie with a vengeance and I was sure my plan to get back with him for Tommy's sake was doomed to fail.

The thought of being intimate with him to conceive Tommy filled me with horror and disgust. I thought of John and a feeling of sadness overwhelmed me.

I closed my eyes and pictured Tommy with the angels. I imagined them playing hide and seek with him and that made me smile. Once again I asked my angel to keep me strong and to get me through the next few days. I knew what I must do to get Tommy back and I was scared. I prayed for my angel to be with me in the coming years and if I had to get back with Charlie, that my angel help me to be brave enough to change my future and escape from him soon after Tommy was born. I just prayed my angel could help me do this.

About an hour later I heard Mum coming upstairs. She gently knocked before popping her head around the door.

Looking a little sheepish she started to apologise. 'Look Sarah, I hope you don't think I was speaking out of turn about Julie earlier. It isn't really any of my business. You're old enough to make your own decisions so I'm sorry for that.'

'Don't worry about it Mum,' I quickly replied. 'I am aware she uses me and I wouldn't have agreed to meet her if I didn't fancy a night out.'

Mum smiled and I could hear the relief in her voice as she spoke.

'Okay I will keep out of it in future. I'm glad we've got that cleared up. Anyway dinner will be ready in ten minutes.'

'Okay I'll be down soon.'

As she shut the door I smiled to myself, I wasn't really annoyed with her, after all she was only looking out for me and I appreciated that. She was right about Julie but what she didn't realise though, was that in the next four and a half years I wouldn't hear from Julie again.

In my future life I often wondered what happened to her. Maybe her next boyfriend was the one and she got married. It probably was for the best that we parted company as Charlie and Julie wouldn't have got on. She would definitely have antagonised him with her outspoken ways and then no doubt, Charlie would have taken it out on me with his fists.

During dinner Mum asked me if John wanted to come round for Sunday dinner. I told her he was already taking me out for a carvery.

'Okay' she said, 'maybe we can arrange for the following Sunday as it would be nice to see him again. I haven't seen him for a month you know.' She smiled. 'I'm beginning to think he is avoiding me.'

What Mum didn't realise was I had been deliberately keeping John away as I knew it was getting close to when I would be meeting Charlie. I wasn't looking forward to telling Mum in a few days that I had met Charlie and finished with John.

I got very little sleep that night. All sorts of things kept running through my mind. I knew Mum would be disappointed if I went ahead with Charlie's date and finished with John but I hoped she would also understand and respect my decision.

Waking up the next morning, I realised that whatever decision I made today, there was no going back on it. Tommy was very much in my thoughts and prayers the previous night. I prayed harder than I had ever prayed before. I asked my angel to be with me throughout the day as I really needed love and guidance from her more than anything.

I headed off on the seven mile journey to Julie's just after 9.30 a.m. On the way I tried to remember how this day went before as I needed to make sure that it went exactly the same way as last time. I couldn't afford to risk doing anything differently as I knew it may change the outcome. I realised if I got back with Charlie it was going to be a difficult thing not to influence the following six months. I worried if I influenced any part of it, then it could result in Tommy not being conceived.

It wasn't long before I pulled up outside Julie's house. I gave a short pip of the horn and about a minute or two later she emerged. She was wearing the same clothes as before which was a good sign.

She jumped into the car smiling. 'How are you doing?'

'Yes great thanks' I replied, 'and how are you?'

'Well not too bad. I'm a bit down after finishing with my boyfriend but hey there are plenty more fish in the sea.' She giggled. 'Have you been seeing anyone?'

Glancing over in her direction I quickly lied. 'No I'm still single.'

I felt bad about lying but it was important that I kept the conversation flowing the same way as last time. Anyway I knew I wouldn't hear from her again after that day so it didn't really matter what I said to her.

We soon arrived in town and I parked up in the same place as last time.

'Right,' Julie said, 'let's get you a dress sorted for tonight. I know this great little shop where I can find something perfect for you.'

We walked the five minutes through town to the shop. Some days I likened my life to a rerun of a bad movie, knowing exactly what was coming next. I hadn't really had many déjà vu moments in the past six months with John as I changed that part of my life path and everything had been new to me. However, after today, any future I had with Charlie was going to be a horrible rerun of the past.

Julie grabbed my arm and pulled me into a shop. 'Come on then, I'm sure I can find you something nice in here.'

We looked around for a few minutes before Julie picked out my dress. 'Try this on.'

As I tried it on I caught a glimpse in the booth mirror and thought it looked tight and short but I was okay with it this time around.

As I stepped out of the booth I played my part. 'I'm not sure this is really me.'

'It's perfect' she said, 'you'll get used to it. It's about time you had a bit of fun in your life.'

Next stop was the shoe shop where Julie picked out a pair of shoes for me. 'I really like these. They'll go well with your dress.'

I tried them on knowing they would fit as these were the shoes I would have to buy if I was to follow my future timeframe. That night would be the only time I would ever wear them as a few months after moving in with Charlie he chucked them out, along with the dress I bought. He told me they made me look like a cheap tart.

Julie picked up a pair of red high heel stilettos and tried them on. She was a bit unsteady on her feet as she walked up and down the shop but that didn't stop her. 'I really love these,' she said, 'I will have them for tonight.'

I thought maybe I should have told her that by the end of the night she would have regretted buying them, that all night she would be having trouble walking in them and in the taxi home she would be cursing those stupid red shoes but then I thought about Tommy and how the night needed to happen exactly as it did last time so I kept quiet. I couldn't influence the situation in anyway.

As we left the shop, I could see Julie was really chuffed with her purchase. Passing McDonald's she looked at me. 'Right lets go for a burger, my treat.'

At the till, and without even asking me what I wanted, she ordered two Big Mac meals and asked for hers to be plain.

It was funny but by reliving this day for the second time, I could see things more clearly. This time around I noticed how Julie was controlling every situation; she chose my dress for me, chose my shoes and she had just chosen what I was going to eat as well. It was even her choice which club we were going to.

We sat down to eat our lunch and Julie rang the taxi firm to book our taxi for later on. She then turned and looked me straight in the eye. 'So Sarah,' a cheeky smile spread across her face, 'what have you been up to in the past year then? Has there been any romance in you life?'

I hesitated slightly as I didn't want to mentally trip myself up. 'I was seeing a guy called John for about six months but I finished with him six months ago.'

Looking really intrigued Julie leaned closer to me. 'Why did you finish?'

I shrugged my shoulders. 'It just wasn't working out.'

'What are we like?' Julie chuckled to herself. 'You and I are like two peas in a pod.'

No we're not I thought, I'm nothing like you. It didn't feel good lying about John, especially as we were still together. It was hard work trying to make this day run exactly as it did last time but I reminded myself why and that Tommy was relying on me.

Julie had finished eating and looked at the time. 'Did you want to start getting back now?'

I nodded and she started to get up.

'Okay then let's go.'

On the drive back to Julie's I felt pleased with myself as I thought the morning had gone to plan. I couldn't believe it was just eight hours until we would get to the club and my fate would be sealed. I had resigned myself to the fact I had no choice but to get back with Charlie. I just hoped I would have the courage to escape Charlie a lot sooner than the last time. I desperately needed a clear sign from my angel, a sign to show me that everything would be okay and I was doing the right thing.

I dropped Julie off and headed back home. It worried me that in six months I would have to give up my job, car and independence. My plan was to get away from Charlie within eighteen months, soon after Tommy was born. I wouldn't have John's support this time around so I just hoped I could be mentally stronger. Charlie could be very intimidating and I hoped I didn't get trapped and sucked back into a life full of despair and fear.

Soon after I got home I decided to have a quick afternoon nap as I was absolutely shattered from a whole week of sleepless nights. I fell asleep almost straight away and must have been out for about four hours. I woke up in a panic as it was nearly half past six and the taxi was due to pick me up at eight o'clock.

I was running a bit too late for my liking. I had a quick shower and rushed to get myself ready whilst keeping one eye on the clock. I just about managed to get ready when Mum called up to me. 'Sarah your taxi is here.'

I looked at the time and it was 7.53 p.m. exactly the time it arrived in the other timeline. I was relieved that things were still going to plan.

I made my way to the door and called back to Mum. 'I'm off now, don't wait up for me.'

'Okay love, have a good time.'

I climbed into the back of the taxi and we set off towards Julie's house. Glancing at the driver, I couldn't resist but ask him if he was Ron.

He looked back at me through his rear view mirror and I could see he was very puzzled. 'Yes love, that's right, do I know you then?'

'No' I lied to him, 'this morning when we booked the taxi the lady on the switchboard said Ron will be driving us tonight.'

'Well that's odd because up until an hour ago I was due to do an airport run and I wasn't given this job until the very last minute.'

I remembered his name because in the other timeframe Julie and I were in high spirits and she started flirting with him, even though he was old enough to be her dad. I remember her hassling him for his name and asking him whether or not he was married. Ron took it all in good fun and said that if it had been twenty years ago he would probably have come to the club with us.

My thoughts soon turned to John and I wondered what he was doing. I wished I could be with him but instead I had to meet Charlie. I knew he and his mate Mark must be getting ready for their night out and the thought sent a shiver down my spine. I had to keep reminding myself that I was doing this for Tommy.

My life had been building up to this evening ever since I lost Tommy six months ago. Within an hour I would be in the same room as Charlie. I felt the same sickening nerves as I had the day John saved me from the beating, the day I finally left Charlie. Now every time I thought about Charlie all I could see in my minds eye was him beating me to within an inch of my life and it always left me feeling cold. I knew my future was now in the hands of my angel; I closed my eyes and prayed to her. I prayed she would look after me and I asked her to get me through whatever fate had in store for me.

I glanced out of the window and saw we were only about five minutes away from Julie's. I took a few deep breaths, tried to compose myself and get myself into a confident frame of mind as I didn't want Julie to pick up on my nerves. I pointed out Julie's house to Ron and as he pulled up he gave two short blasts of his horn.

Julie soon emerged from her house. I remembered last time how amused I was watching her trying to walk down the path in those high heels and, just like last time, it made me smile but as she neared the taxi my amusement turned to real concern as she fell into a heap on the floor.

Both Ron and I rushed to her side. 'Are you alright?' I called out as we neared her.

'No' she snapped back at me. 'Do I look alright? It's my ankle; I can't move it, its killing me.'

She was holding it with both hands but I could still see it had started to swell up.

'Maybe we should go and get it checked out?' I bent over to help Julie to her feet just as her mum came running down the path. She must have heard all of the commotion.

I carefully took Julie's shoes off and Ron and I helped her into the taxi. I turned to Julie's mum before we headed off. 'You stay here, there's no point all of us going. I will take good care of her.'

I helped her to get comfortable as Ron pulled away. 'So' he asked, 'where am I taking you to then girls, the club or the hospital?'

'I think it better be the hospital' I replied without hesitating.

A few minutes later I got a text message from John:

"Have a good night tonight. I'm missing you and looking forward to seeing you tomorrow xx."

We parked outside A&E and Ron helped me to get Julie inside. I paid him and I got Julie signed in. As I went to sit with her I glanced up at the electronic waiting sign which informed me that the current waiting time was two hours. Julie carefully put her foot up and settled back with a magazine.

As the minutes ticked by I started to feel a little self conscious in my short, tight fitting dress and high heels. I tried not to catch the eye of the teenage boy who kept looking over at me and smiling when he thought his mum wasn't looking.

With all that had been going on in the past half hour I hadn't had a moment to think but as I regained my thoughts, it suddenly hit me that this shouldn't have happened. We should be at the club. Something outside of my control had changed my timeline. I was almost certain it was my angel. She had changed my destiny but why? By not getting to the club I wouldn't be setting up a date to meet Charlie.

Through my thoughts I talked to my angel.

'Okay you have my attention and I trust your motives as I know you have both mine and Tommy's best interests at heart and you must have done this for a reason but please help me to understand why. Please tell me, where does this leave me and Tommy?'

I felt my angel had given me a clear sign. By keeping me away from Charlie I believed my angel was telling me my future was with John. Did that mean that both Tommy and my angel had decided he was not coming back to me? Maybe Tommy and the angels had decided to give me a life without Charlie or maybe Tommy didn't want to be reborn into a life of violence. I felt that my little boy was walking away from me. The last bit of hope that I had been clinging to was vanishing and I felt a knot in my stomach. My little boy was moving further away from me and there was nothing I could do about it. I felt so lost and empty.

I looked over at Julie and she was still engrossed in a magazine. I asked her if she was ok and she put down her magazine and gave me such a sorrowful look.

'Sarah I'm really sorry I've ruined your evening. I will make it up to you in a few weeks I promise. We can go out again and maybe find a couple of single guys.'

After my angels intervention I thought it was time to come clean with Julie.

'Julie, remember when I said I had finished with John six months ago? Well that wasn't strictly true, we are still together.'

Julie looked at me slightly oddly. 'Why would you lie about being single when you are clearly still in a relationship? Do you feel sorry for me or something? Am I some sort of sad charity case? Find a date for the poor single girl?'

She was totally over reacting so I bluffed my way out of it.

'I wanted you to enjoy the night so thought that if I said I was single it would put you at ease.'

I could see that she was miffed and she didn't really say much after that. She just buried herself back in her magazine.

I thought I had better ring John and tell him that we didn't make it to the club but were in hospital having Julie's ankle looked at. He insisted on coming and taking us both home when Julie was discharged.

I sat back down and sensed Julie was still annoyed with me as she didn't speak. We sat in silence for almost an hour and then, to my huge relief, the nurse called her in. I thought it was best she went in alone. It really didn't bother me that we weren't speaking; if she wanted to sulk let her. It was not like she had been a good friend to me over the years. After that night in my other timeline, she wouldn't get in touch with me for at least the next four and a half years and I doubted this timeline would be any different.

As I waited for Julie, John walked in. He gave me a sympathetic smile as he sat down. 'You haven't really had a good night have you?'

'No' I smiled back, 'not really.'

A few minutes later Julie hobbled out on crutches. She explained that she had torn some ligaments and would have to rest for a few weeks. She looked at John and with a little sarcasm in her voice said hello. 'Oh, you must be John. Sarah has told me so much about you; in fact she's hardly stopped talking about you.'

Looking back at me she gave me a quick but over exaggerated smile.

On the drive back to Julie's she hardly said a word to me and I really couldn't be bothered to try to smooth things over. I was almost relieved when we arrived back at hers as you could have cut the atmosphere with a knife. Julie got out of the car and, without a word, hobbled down her path.

John turned to me confused. ‘Is it just me or is your friend always that rude?’

I couldn’t help but smile back at him. ‘Don’t worry about her. I don’t think I will be seeing much of her in the future.’

I asked John if he minded taking me back home and he gave me a cheeky grin. ‘Okay but it will cost you a cup of coffee.’

Mum was already in bed when we got back so John only stayed for about an hour. Soon after he left I decided to go to bed. Like most nights I settled down holding Tommy’s teddy but that night was different, that night I had a terrible sinking feeling deep in my heart. The thought of having to live my life without Tommy made me cry. I held his teddy close to me and soon fell asleep.

Chapter 15

The next morning I woke up just after nine. Tommy was always my first thought in the mornings and my last thought at night. I always routinely started my day by quietly telling him how much I loved him. I just hoped wherever he was he could hear me.

As I lay there, I thought about what had happened the night before. I was still convinced that my angel had helped me to make a life changing decision for my own good. I had to believe the angels were guiding me down this path for a reason and I could only hope they were taking good care of Tommy.

I couldn't see how the aching feeling within me would ever ease, even just a little. My heart was breaking. My angel's decision meant that the last bit of hope that I had been clinging too of being with Tommy again had gone forever. I could never have made the decision without my angel's intervention. I just hoped Tommy was safe. The only crumb of comfort I had left was the thought that Tommy was up there holding Dad's hand and he was playing with him in heaven. If he was with my dad I knew he would be happy. The worst thing of all had to be dealing with my grief of losing Tommy all on my own. If Tommy had physically died I would have had all of my family's support and photos to look back on; I wouldn't have had to do it alone. More than anything I wanted to go downstairs and have a good cry on Mum's shoulder and talk to her about Tommy. I had really happy memories of me, Mum and Tommy. Mum adored him and the days we all spent together were really special. I sometimes got upset with Mum when she was happy while I was grieving. I had to remind myself that she was in a different time and didn't have those memories. It was tearing me apart from the inside. Sooner or later I would have to accept Tommy wasn't coming home and I would have to let him go but I wasn't ready to deal with that just yet.

The fear of Charlie had disappeared overnight and I needed to plan my future with John as I felt I wanted to spend the rest of my life with him. I sometimes thought how complete my life would have been if Tommy could be born to me and John but I knew it didn't work like that. If I had a baby with John I would be bringing a new soul into the world.

With a heavy heart I got myself ready and slowly made my way downstairs. Mum was sitting in the kitchen at the table. She looked up at me. 'Hello love. Did everything go alright last night? I thought I heard you and John come in about half eleven.'

'Yes we did, he picked me up. Julie and I didn't make it to the club, she fell and tore the ligaments in her ankle and we ended up in the hospital instead. We have fallen out big time and I doubt I will see her again.'

Mum gave me a half smile. 'Well I wouldn't worry about her too much. She is not a true friend; true friends wouldn't expect anything from you and only give you love and support.'

I was so relieved that my life had moved on from Charlie and I felt so safe being back home with Mum.

John was taking me out for Sunday lunch and I was really looking forward to seeing him. I gave him a quick call and told him I would be leaving shortly. I gathered up my overnight bag and called out to Mum on my way out of the door. 'See you tomorrow.'

'Bye love, see you tomorrow.'

When I got to John's it felt like things had changed for me and it felt like I didn't need to hold back anymore. There would always be a massive void in my heart for Tommy and I knew life could never be the same again. I really didn't know how I was going to cope without him but Charlie wasn't an option anymore. I was going to need John's love and support more than ever and I couldn't do it without him.

We drove the three miles to the pub. I had always liked it there, it was in the middle of nowhere with a river running by its side. It was beautiful in the summer months but not so scenic on a cold drizzly November afternoon but whatever time of year they always did a good roast. During the meal John and I had a really good talk and I got the impression he wanted to take our relationship to the next level. The meal was its usual high standard and we finished our dessert just after two o'clock.

However, I'd had something else on my mind all day. This day, at 3 p.m., in my other timeline I met Charlie for our first date at The Three Crowns. I suggested to John we should go there now for a drink. John just gave me his usual easygoing smile and agreed.

I really didn't know what I was expecting to find but my curiosity was drawing me there. We arrived at 2.51 p.m. but as John got out of the car I called him back in.

He gave me a puzzled look. 'What's up?'

'Can we wait a few minutes?' I gave him the excuse I had indigestion but really I wanted to go in at exactly the same time as before. When I next checked my watch it was three o'clock. I looked over at John. 'Okay then, let's go.'

As I opened the main door I instinctively looked over to where Charlie would have been sitting last time. I really didn't know what I was expecting to see but obviously

Charlie wasn't there. Even though most of the tables had been taken, strangely the table where Charlie and I had sat was empty. After getting drinks, John coincidently walked right up to that very same table. We sat down but I found it really weird sitting with John at the same table at exactly the same time that I should have been there with Charlie. I looked around and some of the people looked vaguely familiar. Sitting there with John felt like a turning point in my life. Up until yesterday I had kept all of my feelings for him on hold because I thought today I would be sitting here with Charlie, rerunning the next four and a half years the same way. I now found myself back with John about to start a new chapter in my life.

Feeling a bit nervous I took John's hand and leant into him. I looked him in the eye and took a deep breath. 'John, I have really enjoyed our ten months together. You have made me really happy. I hate it when we are apart and I want to spend the rest of my life with you.'

He smiled and squeezed my hand tighter before replying. 'I really miss you when we're apart. I know it is probably too soon and I don't want to get between you and your mum but I'd love, more than anything, for you to move in with me. No pressure, I just wanted to put it out there for you to think about.'

It was like music to my ears. I was so happy that John felt the same way as me. I thought back to all of those lonely nights with Charlie, wishing I had never left John and now I had a chance to live this new life with him. I was overwhelmed with excitement. 'What is there to think about? I would love to move in with you.'

John jumped up and hugged me tightly, lifting me right off my feet.

‘You won’t regret this,’ he said. ‘I love you more than life; I know we’re going to be really happy together.’

I could see how much this meant to him and I too wanted it more than anything. Committing to spend the rest of my life with John felt so right and something I had always dreamed of, even before I was with Charlie. Charlie was the biggest mistake of my life. I now knew that my old life, along with Tommy, could only ever exist in my mind.

The last few days had been quite a roller coaster ride of emotions but in the end I believed my angel had guided me to this outcome. Tommy would never be more than a heartbeat away from my previous thought. I just needed him to know that I would never abandon him and he would always be number one in my heart. I just hoped one day he could forgive me but there wasn’t anything I could have done; the choice was taken away from me. I believed that spiritually, this was the path chosen for me.

John and I spent the next hour excitedly talking about our plans. I could see a lot of my dad’s qualities in him. I knew he was the right man for me and he would treat me right. I told him I needed to square it with Mum before I moved in as I still worried about her but I knew, in my heart, that she would be okay on her own. In my other life, when I lived with Charlie, she was happy.

We set off back to John’s. We passed Charlie's house and his car was parked outside. With him living so close, I would have to be prepared that I may bump into him from time to time. I didn’t know how I would feel about that as he hadn’t been in the café for quite a few months.

As we pulled up onto the drive at John’s, I felt the need to sort things out. I didn’t want to make the same mistakes with him as I had with Charlie.

'When I move in I insist on paying my way with a fifty fifty split on bills.'

He nodded before pulling on the handbrake and turning to smile at me. 'We can work all the fine details out later.'

Once inside John made me a cup of tea and settled down beside me on the settee so I snuggled up to him. I had always felt safe with him. I remembered Dad's dying wish was for me to find a good man to settle down with and my biggest regret was that Dad wasn't there to see John.

Dad passed far too early and I knew Mum would always miss him terribly. I told John that I really wanted to commit to him but I still worried about leaving Mum alone. He looked at me sympathetically. 'I know your mum likes it when I stop over, so there's no reason why we can't stay over and we have a spare bed here so she is always welcome to stay.'

The next day I felt in such a happy place. I was buzzing at the thought of starting a new life with John but still felt bad for leaving Mum. John suggested that after I had moved in I should stay over at Mum's once a week to spend quality time with her. That was one of the reasons I loved John so much, he was always so thoughtful.

My Monday shift at the café finished and I headed home but I felt a bit apprehensive about telling Mum I was moving in with John. It wasn't going to be straight away as we had agreed on two weeks time but it was still going to be difficult to tell her.

As I arrived, Mum was already serving up our dinner. Over the next half hour I nervously picked at it, trying to find a good time to tell her about my move. I couldn't seem to find the words and missed the moment. As I helped her tidy the kitchen, I felt I should just come out with it so I took a deep breath and started. 'Mum, there's something I need to tell you.'

She looked at me curiously and smiled. 'Oh, this sounds intriguing, is everything ok?'

I took hold of her hand and gently led her to the sofa.

'John and I have been talking and we feel it's time for us to move in together.'

'That's great news,' Mum smiled. 'John's a really good lad. I had a feeling it wouldn't be much longer.'

I hesitated for a moment before replying.

'Are you going to be okay on your own?'

Her smile broadened. 'Look, you are twenty-two years old now. You are just starting your adventure. All I want in life is to see my only daughter living a happy fulfilled life. I know John's a really good man and will look after you. Anyway you are only moving ten miles away, not the other side of the world.'

Deep down I knew Mum was going to be okay but I just couldn't help worrying about her. I wished, more than anything, that Mum and Dad could have had another thirty years together. Life can be so cruel sometimes. I remembered how upset Mum was in my other timeframe when I finished with John but how she told me that I had to live my own life.

Giving Mum a hug, I let out a little laugh. 'You're not getting rid of me that easily. I will still come back and bother you every week.'

I knew Mum was trying not to cry as she gave me a half smile. 'Look at my little girl, all grown up.'

Over the next few weeks Mum and I had a lot of mother daughter time. John totally understood that I needed to spend as much quality time as I could with her before moving in with him.

One day I jokingly said to Mum that she wasn't to go renting my room out just yet. She chuckled and promised that it would be my room for as long as I needed it to be but quickly added "well at least until you give me my first grandchild, then he or she will need it."

Within seconds I was reduced to floods of tears. The thought that Mum would never play a part in Tommy's life was too much for me to take. I desperately wanted her to remember Tommy and how much she loved him. I couldn't bear the thought that his memory had been erased from hers and everybody else's mind and I was now the only person that could keep his memory alive.

Mum looked so confused and apologised for saying the wrong thing. I desperately wanted to tell her about Tommy and how much my heart was breaking for him but I had to lie and say that I was just getting emotional about my future.

Saturday arrived and it was finally the day that John and I would move in together. I was going to really miss Mum but I felt the time was right for me and John to be together properly.

I didn't have many belongings to take with me as it was mainly clothes and personal items. Mum and I managed to get everything into both of our cars and I set off for my new home with Mum following closely behind. Looking back in my rear view mirror, a feeling of sadness overwhelmed me. I still worried about Mum being alone but I wasn't really sure why as I knew she was happy on her own in my other timeline, when I lived with Charlie.

John was waiting for us when we arrived and he helped us unload our cars. It didn't take us long to unpack as John had cleared me some wardrobe space for my clothes. He made us a cup of tea and insisted on taking us out for lunch as a thank you to Mum.

He drove us the mile or so to The Mill restaurant. It had a lovely setting on a marina and it was nice to sit by the window with the view out to the houseboats. John and I had always liked it there and had been going regularly over the past six months. They served really good food.

As we ate our main course, Mum and John chatted. It meant so much to me to see them getting on so well. After finishing we went into the bar for a drink and stayed for another half an hour before heading back to my new home.

Mum stayed for a few hours helping me to sort a few things but mainly to chat then, when she left, my move started to feel more real.

John must have been finding it strange having to share his house with me after living alone for two years.

'How does it feel having a woman invading your space?' I jokingly asked.

'It feels great,' he gave me a cheeky smile. 'I never planned to live alone forever. I always wanted someone special to share the rest of my life with and one day a family.' Realising what he had just said, he gave me a look. 'Don't worry I meant in a few years.'

I was really glad that John felt that way about our future. I thought he would make a great dad one day and I could easily picture us with a couple of children. This was the life I had dreamed about before getting mixed up with Charlie.

I suddenly felt guilty for even daring to think happy thoughts about our future. The only way I could ever be truly happy in life would be to have Tommy with us as part of our family.

'Are you okay?' John noticed I had become a bit emotional and looked concerned.

'Yes I'm okay, just happy to be here and a bit sad to have left Mum.'

He pulled me to him for a hug.

Over the next few months life with John was everything I could have expected and more. We spent our first Christmas together; four days at Mum's from Christmas Eve and then seeing in the New Year at home. I hadn't seen Charlie for such a long time as he didn't seem to come into the café anymore and I thought that was a good thing but it was always in the back of my mind that he could walk in at any time.

Chapter 16

When I was about fifteen, I remembered Dad telling me that in his early twenties he once went to see a fortune-teller medium and he said it was a really good experience for him. I remembered at the time he told me not to tell Mum as she didn't know he had been and she thought that sort of thing was just made up nonsense. I had always been curious and I had thought about seeing one too. After moving in with John, I thought about it more as it would be nice to see if we would have a long and happy future together. I thought I would give it a go as I didn't have anything to lose.

I found a medium local to me called Claire and decided to give her a ring. She sounded nice on the phone so I made an appointment for that coming Friday the 17th at 7 p.m. I decided not to tell John about the appointment as I thought he may laugh at my beliefs. I made the excuse that I was going out for a few hours to see my friend Claire. I hated lying to him but it wasn't a complete lie as I was going to see someone called Claire, it's just that she wasn't my friend.

All week I had been quietly looking forward to Friday. I really believed that some people could see into the future and communicate with the afterlife but I also believed there were a lot of fakes out there who conned people. I was hoping that Claire was genuine and she could pick up on my life as I was curious to know what my future held in store.

When Friday eventually arrived I went straight to Claire's from work. I typed her address into my sat nav and it came up as being 6.4 miles away. On the drive there I tried to imagine how the next two hours would go and I did wonder whether she was genuine or not. I deliberately didn't give her my full name over the phone as if she was a fraud she could get information about me from social media.

I found the house quite quickly as I was familiar with the village. I arrived a few minutes early so sat in the car and waited. I really didn't know what to expect but I decided that I would let her do the talking and I'd keep quiet and not give anything away.

At just after seven I walked up her path and apprehensively knocked on the door. I saw a figure approach and the door opened.

'Hello I'm Claire, you must be Sarah, please come in.'

Claire was about my mum's age, she had shoulder length blonde hair and a friendly face. It was funny as I thought she would be older and I half expected her to have a head scarf, big hoop earrings and a crystal ball. She wasn't at all like the typical fortune telling gypsy I had been expecting. She put me at ease almost straight away as she ushered me into a room at the back of the house. It was a bright room full of family photos and other personal items. It was just an ordinary family dining room.

Claire pulled out a chair for me and asked if I had ever done anything like this before. I shook my head as she handed me a pen and paper. She asked me to write down my full name and email address so she could keep me updated with newsletters. She sat down opposite me and I handed back the piece of paper. She glanced at it, folded it neatly in half and then into a quarter before putting it aside.

Giving me a warm smile she briefly looked me in the eye before making small talk about my day. I tried to keep my answers to a minimum as I didn't want to give her any clues about me. She came across as a very genuine person who was interested in people but I was still slightly wary. She then went quiet for a moment and briefly laid her hand on mine. She took a few deep breaths then looked me in the eye again before continuing.

'I feel you have had a tough time recently. I see you in a relationship with a man. Oh,' she shivered, 'this man is not nice. He's a very angry man and I see him shouting at you. He is very handy with his fists.' She paused and her face softened. 'I also see a young boy who is caught in the middle. He can only be about three or four. I feel how much you worry about him.'

Looking directly at her I slowly nodded. I felt myself starting to well up but I tried to hold my tears back.

Claire smiled. 'You should try not to worry too much about him, I sense he is a tough little boy and he knows his mummy loves him and is looking out for him.'

Claire briefly rested her hand on mine again and, looking slightly concerned, asked if I was still in a relationship with the man she had been talking about.

I shook my head.

She paused, glanced at me for the briefest of moments and then closed her eyes. A few minutes later, taking another look at me, she spoke. 'I'm aware of an older man. He has a strong presence about him. He's in spirit.' She paused again for a second. 'Your dad passed over quite young didn't he?'

Feeling sadness overwhelm me, I nodded and whispered. 'Yes he did.'

She smiled sympathetically. 'Yes I thought so and I sense your dad was a mentally strong man with strong morals and a kind heart. It was your dad that influenced your decision to come here today. I feel his love for you is very strong and he is still with you.' Pausing briefly she continued, 'I see a new love coming into your life. It's looking very positive and I think you will be very happy with him; I feel this one is for keeps. I feel a strong bond growing between your son and this man. Your son will very quickly regard him as a father figure. I can feel how content you are in their company.'

Claire smiled at me. 'You are going to feel like the cat that has got the cream. I also see a little girl coming along in the near future, a baby sister for your little boy.' She stopped to think for a moment. 'I feel this man is someone you already know from your past. A rekindled love maybe? Yes your future is looking really bright. I feel your life is going to change for the better in the next few years. Is there anything you would like to ask me before we carry on?'

Wiping away a few tears I told her all about Charlie and how he had beaten me for years. I also told her about Tommy, my beautiful boy, how I had met up with John again and how he helped me get away from Charlie. I burst into tears as my emotions got the better of me.

Claire moved to my side and gently cuddled me. 'Its okay' she said reassuringly, 'take your time.'

I composed myself for a few minutes before continuing.

'Everything you said about Charlie happened. John helped me and Tommy escape from Charlie but in this timeframe it wouldn't have happened for another four years from now. About seven months ago I fell back five years in time. Tommy no longer exists, he should be born a year from now but he won't be born now as my guardian angel changed my timeline to stop me meeting Charlie. Now I am with John and everything you described about Charlie won't happen and Tommy can't be born.' I paused for breath but quickly continued. 'I am now living four years in my past and only have my angel to help me. I don't know how but you are the only other living person in this timeframe that knows about my relationship with Charlie and that Tommy once existed.'

Claire sat in total silence as I don't think she knew what to say. It must have been a good two or three minutes before she looked at me again and finally spoke.

'You've thrown me. I am at a loss to know what to think. I still see your future as how I told it to you, I see your violent past and your son Tommy but I don't feel or see any of what you have just told me about going back in time. Your son feels real to me, I don't feel his presence in the spirit world and you have confirmed to me that he has existed.'

I started to see it from Claire's point of view; she must have thought I was either crazy or a fantasist. I started feeling very flustered and I needed to get away so I told her I had to go. She tried her best to persuade me to stay for at least another ten minutes but I really just wanted to go. I handed her the money and made a quick exit. As I got into the car I looked back and saw Claire at the door looking really concerned. I gave her a little smile and drove off.

On the drive home, I tried to make sense of what had just happened. Somehow Claire had picked up on my life with Charlie and Tommy even though it didn't happen in this timeline. She also said about me and John having a little girl which could happen. She then mixed up my two timelines, suggesting Tommy would possibly have a new sister. Obviously I knew it was impossible for Tommy to be in this timeline with a new baby sister but even Claire found it hard to accept that I had gone back in time.

Chapter 17

Over the next five months John and I settled into home life really well. Moving in with each other brought us much closer together and I was so happy that I had been given a second chance with him. I couldn't help comparing my life with John from this time and my other timeline with Charlie.

In my other timeline I would have moved in with Charlie a couple of months ago and today would be the day I would find out I was six weeks pregnant with Tommy. Being reminded of my pregnancy stirred all sorts of emotions within me. My life felt so incomplete every time I thought of Tommy. Days like this really drove it home to me that he had gone for good. I knew there were going to be some really tough times ahead of me, especially the 14th of January next year. I didn't know how I was going to get through that day, the day Tommy was born, especially as there wouldn't be anybody for me to share my loss with.

I had been back in this time for thirteen months and I thought it was only natural to keep comparing my two timelines and I supposed I would do it until I caught up to the day I fell back in time. Sometimes I thought my life would be a lot easier if I had no memory of my other life but, however painful it was, I never wanted to forget my time with my little boy.

Life felt strange; I was living the life I had always dreamed of and I was really happy with John but at the same time my heart was breaking that I wasn't pregnant with Tommy, I really felt I had betrayed him.

I hadn't mentioned it to John but I had been thinking about how much I wanted a baby. I thought my aching for a baby was coming from the fact I would have been pregnant in my other timeline. I had to fight the urge and, deep down, I knew the time wasn't right and I needed time to grieve. I had to accept this timeline was my life and the life decisions and changes I had made had reshaped my life. All the bad things, like Charlie, had gone and I had to try to get on with my new life and make the best of it. I believed John's love for me would get me through. I often thought about Dad and how much I missed him. I often wondered if he was aware of what had happened to me.

Over the following few months I couldn't help but keep comparing my two timelines. I got quite emotional on the 15th of July as this was the day I would have gone for my twelve week scan; I could remember the total joy I felt back then seeing my baby on the screen. Then the scan on the 16th of September, the day I found out I was going to have a boy. Apart from the important days like that, I tried not to let the other timeline take over my life. I needed to focus all of my attention on John and my new life.

Late September arrived and John and I had been living together for about nine months and it was sixteen months since I fell back in time. It was only another fifteen weeks until Tommy would have been born. I felt so guilty and I often felt I had no right to be happy living this new life with John.

I was living my life as I always should have, as an equal. In my other timeline I quit my job four months ago and was forced to give up driving about the same time. My two timelines couldn't have been more different. First time around I was in total despair, worrying about my pregnancy and trying to stay on Charlie's good side, when he had one and I was just taking one day at a time but in this timeline I woke up every morning to the man I loved, the man who made me happy and I looked forward to our future together.

Chapter 18

I woke up on Monday 29th September thinking it was going to be just another ordinary day. I left home half an hour after John, for the short journey to work. We opened up as usual.

Monday mornings were generally quiet and today was no exception but things started to get busier about twelve thirty. I was busy taking orders and not paying much attention to the customers coming in but one couple suddenly caught my eye. I had to look twice as I couldn't believe what I was seeing. There, standing in front of me, was Charlie, he was with a woman. My heart started to race.

The café was full but I spotted an empty table near the window and I showed them to their seats. As they sat down, I couldn't help but notice his girlfriend was pregnant. She looked naturally slim so I could say with confidence that she was five to six months gone. I didn't know why I was so taken aback by this, but then again, the thought he might have met someone else had never entered my mind.

I left it a few minutes and then went over to take their order. Charlie looked up at me and ordered for both of them. I deliberately caught his girlfriend's eye and gave her a smile; she smiled back but quickly broke off eye contact.

Looking at them together, with a baby on the way, it almost felt like my life with Charlie never happened. I couldn't help but keep glancing over at them. She looked about twenty and quite shy but I knew that was the type of girl that Charlie went for. I often thought that if I met him again I would have a panic attack but I felt calm and in control.

As I glanced over again a thought suddenly came to me and I realised this woman was living my old life. All the emotional and physical pain I had suffered was now hers. I just knew Charlie would be treating her exactly the same way he had treated me and I knew he wouldn't love their baby. Then it occurred to me that this was my fault. By not reliving my life with Charlie I had changed this woman's life path. I had probably denied her a beautiful life with a decent man and now she had made my bad life decision.

On the night that the angels stepped in and changed my destiny, it didn't even occur to me that it could ruin some other poor woman's life. I looked over at her and I don't know how but I knew I just needed to find a way to get to know her. She was going to need a friend and I wanted to help her. This was my fault and I couldn't leave her to go through what I went through all alone.

Just for a moment I snapped back into reality and really hoped that Kate hadn't noticed that I had neglected my other customers and was giving most of my attention to Charlie's table. I just couldn't focus on anything else and felt the need to talk to her alone but time was running out as they had almost finished their dessert. A few minutes later Charlie's girlfriend got up and headed for the ladies. I realised that it was the opportunity I had been waiting for and I grabbed some paper hand tissues and followed her in. I unlocked the dispenser and waited. As she emerged from the cubicle I pretended to fill the already full dispenser. After washing her hands she looked at me so I smiled at her and handed over a few tissues. Looking at her baby bump I asked when the baby was due. She smiled and told me the 24th of February. I did the maths in my head and realised that would be about six weeks after Tommy would have been born. I asked if she knew what she was having and I could hear the excitement in her voice as she replied. 'We have just got back from the twenty week scan and we are going to have a little girl.'

It probably wasn't the right thing to do but I gave her a hug. 'Congratulations, you must both be really excited. I'm Sarah by the way.'

'I'm Kirsty.'

She smiled but I sensed she was getting slightly edgy as she kept looking over at the door so I gave her the excuse she needed to leave.

'Well, I'd better get back to work.'

'It's really nice to have met you.' She turned and made a quick exit. I could see how much she feared Charlie already.

I locked up the towel dispenser and as I went to leave I noticed, in her haste to get back to Charlie, Kirsty had left her phone by the sink so I grabbed it and went to look for her. I could see them both getting ready to leave and I started to walk towards them but then I stopped, I had second thoughts and slipped her phone into my pocket. All afternoon I thought of the best way to play it, I could take it round tomorrow after Charlie had gone to work or I could wait for her to pop back in for it.

As my shift drew to an end and we began to tidy up I heard an unfamiliar tune. I realised it was coming from my pocket and pulled Kirsty's phone out. Charlie's name was flashing up so I quickly answered it. 'Hi this is Sarah from the café. We found this phone in the ladies toilets.'

Sounding really grateful Charlie replied. 'Hi, I'm Charlie. The phone belongs to my girlfriend. I will be straight over to pick it up.'

I had to think on my feet or I would have lost my opportunity to see Kirsty again. 'No' I quickly replied, 'we're just about to close. I could come and drop it off in about half an hour if you like?'

Charlie agreed and started to explain the best way to get to his house from the café, not that I needed that information of course. Kate heard our conversation and waved her hand towards the door. 'Go on' she smiled, 'you get off now, seems you're helping out one of my customers.'

About five minutes later I pulled up outside their house. It felt so strange standing outside my old home and knocking on the door after all this time. All sorts of emotions were running through my mind as the door opened. I was relieved to see Kirsty standing there and I smiled and handed over the phone.

'I really do appreciate you bringing it back for me.' She smiled and took it from me.

We stood looking awkwardly at one another for a few seconds. I was hoping she would invite me in but she didn't so I had to think quickly. 'I don't suppose I can use your toilet can I?'

'Yes of course, it's upstairs on your left.' She opened the door, ushered me in and pointed up the stairs. As I climbed each step I noticed how everything was pretty much as I had remembered it. This place had been my prison but it also held fond memories of Tommy.

After a few minutes I made my way back downstairs to find Charlie standing in the hall. I cringed as he leant over and gave me a hug. 'It's funny,' he paused as though thinking about what he was going to say next, 'but I feel like I know you really well. Strange isn't it, considering we have only ever said a handful of words to each other.' He smiled. 'Do you fancy a cuppa?'

'Yes I'd love one,' I nodded enthusiastically.

He showed me into the living room before going off to make a cup of tea. This was typical of Charlie; to the outside world he always came across as a decent man. It used to upset me how other people thought he was a wonderful man yet I knew what he was like behind closed doors. His image to the outside world meant more to him than anything as he craved everyone's respect.

As I sat down Kirsty came to sit beside me and I immediately sensed her vulnerability. I felt a strong connection with her through my life with Charlie and I so wanted to be there for her. I knew Charlie inside out and I could use this to my advantage. I needed to gain Kirsty's trust as I hoped to become a good friend to her but I knew if I was going to become her friend, then I would have to get Charlie on side.

There was an awkward silence between us and I struggled to find something to say to break the ice.

'Have you got any names in mind yet?'

'Since I was a little girl I have always really liked the name Amelia. Secretly I was hoping for a girl, so I'm really happy.' Her smile was so broad and I could see how much having a baby really meant to her. Her eyes lit up when she spoke about her little girl.

'Have you got any children?' she asked.

I smiled vaguely as Tommy's image entered my mind. I sadly shook my head. 'No but I'm hoping to have them one day.'

Kirsty gave me a knowing look and I really started to warm to her. I could feel she was holding back because of Charlie and I knew it would be a lot easier to talk to her if he wasn't here. I wanted to find out all about her but I couldn't with Charlie about.

Before we could talk much more the door opened and Charlie returned with the teas. As he sat down my thoughts turned to John and I realised he would be wondering where I had got to. I stood to leave the room. 'I hope you don't mind if I just give John, my boyfriend, a quick ring to let him know I'll be late home?'

Charlie shook his head and I stepped into the hall to ring him. 'Hi John I'm going to be a bit late home, I had to drop a phone off that was left in the café. I hope you don't mind.'

'No of course I don't mind. You take as long as you need.'

I made sure I was in earshot of Charlie before slightly raising my voice and replying.

'Charlie and Kirsty have invited me in for a cup of tea. I really like them, they're a nice couple. I won't be that long. See you soon.'

I made my way back into the room and sat back down next to Kirsty.

'Do you live far away?' Charlie asked.

'No, I live in the next village, about a mile past the hospital.'

Looking at Kirsty, I noticed she had changed since Charlie came into the room, she had gone very quiet. She was exactly how I used to be with him. I got the feeling that Kirsty may not be as emotionally strong as I was. I really wanted to give her a hug and tell her everything was going to be okay. I was no longer frightened of Charlie as he couldn't hurt me anymore but I was still very aware that if I wanted to get to know Kirsty I would have to tip toe around him.

I turned my attention back to Charlie. 'Are you looking forward to becoming a dad?'

'Yes' he beamed, 'I couldn't be happier. I have always wanted a little girl.'

'So you didn't want a boy then?'

He smiled again. 'Boys are okay but they tend to become mummy's boys and girls become daddy's girls.'

I knew I shouldn't have let it get to me as Charlie wasn't a part of my life anymore but I couldn't help but wonder if that was part of the reason he gave Tommy so little attention. I knew what made Charlie tick and he liked to be in control at all times so I tried to show him my vulnerable side. I knew Charlie would pick up on shyness and a lack of confidence a mile off and I wanted him to realise that I wasn't a threat to the controlling world he lived in.

We chatted for a bit longer before I changed the subject. I needed to make a plan to see Kirsty again and I knew Charlie would have to be involved. 'You should come over and meet John, I think you two would get on really well.'

Looking quite enthusiastic Charlie was quick to reply. 'Tell you what, why don't you and John come over here on Saturday night for a few drinks.'

'That sounds great. I will have to ask John first but I can't see it being a problem.' I glanced at the clock and noticed the time. 'I'm so sorry I've just realised the time, I think I'd better get off now.'

Charlie gave me both of their mobile numbers and I promised to text my number to them later. Like the gentleman he was, Charlie saw me out. I told him I would let him know the following day about Saturday and hopefully I'd look forward to seeing them both at the weekend.

On the drive back I couldn't help but feel pleased with myself, I couldn't wait to tell John all about Kirsty and Charlie.

When I got home John had already got the dinner on the table. We sat down and he noticed the huge smile on my face. 'You look pleased with yourself.'

'Yes I am.' I couldn't help but laugh and feel a bit smug. 'You know I just told you about Charlie and Kirsty, well Kirsty and I are so alike and I instantly clicked with her. They have invited us over to theirs on Saturday night for a few drinks, I hope you don't mind?'

'No of course I don't mind, that would be great. So what's this Charlie like then?'

'He seems really nice,' I hesitated slightly, 'and friendly. I think you'll like him.'

I tried to remember back to the time when I was six months pregnant with Tommy and what life was like for me. I really did worry about Kirsty and wondered how she was coping.

The next day Kirsty was never far from my thoughts. If I could get Charlie to trust me enough, I thought I may be able to spend time with Kirsty alone.

That night I rang Charlie and told him that John and I would love to see them on Saturday night. He was still full of enthusiasm and told me he would get the beers in. It was going to feel really weird going round my ex boyfriends house with John. I just hoped John wouldn't cotton on to what he was really like as that may spoil things for me and Kirsty. I was hoping it would be okay though as Charlie was an expert at putting on a good front to the outside world.

After an anxious few days Saturday finally arrived and I started feeling a little bit nervous. We had arranged to meet up at 8 p.m. and I rang Charlie to make sure it was still okay.

'Yes still okay with us,' he said, 'we don't have many people round and we're really looking forward to it.'

We left at about half past seven as John and I decided to walk the mile to Charlie's so that we could have a few drinks. I knocked on the door and Charlie greeted us with a smile. 'Come in,' he said opening the door wide and waving us in.

I introduced John to him and they shook hands. We made our way into the kitchen where Kirsty was making a few nibbles. I made a point of going over to her and giving her a hug.

'Hi Kirsty, how are you?'

'I'm fine thank you,' she said smiling back.

'This is John,' I pointed at John and he gave Kirsty a smile and wave before saying hello.

Charlie handed John a beer and we all headed into the front room.

Kirsty seemed a little more confident but I noticed she kept looking at Charlie for his approval. I was pleased to see John and Charlie getting on well as they had found common ground with their love of cars. That gave me the chance to talk to Kirsty but I knew I'd better stick with small talk as, although Charlie was deep in conversation with John, I knew that he would still be listening in on our conversation.

I decided to talk to Kirsty about her baby. 'You must really be getting excited now.'

'Seeing my baby moving at the scan made it more real,' Kirsty smiled, 'I can't wait now.'

'The first time you hold her in you arms will be the most unbelievable moment ever.' Just for a moment I got carried away and forgot myself and, just as I thought, Charlie had been listening. He abruptly broke off his conversation with John and turned to me. 'I think somebody is getting broody,' he laughed. Feeling a bit embarrassed I looked over at John who seemed totally unfazed by it all.

The evening just flew past and I really enjoyed my time with Kirsty and felt that I'd made a good impression on her. We decided to call it a night by eleven and got up to leave.

As we headed to the door I turned to Kirsty. 'If you're not doing anything on Wednesday I could pop over for a cuppa?'

Kirsty looked over at Charlie who smiled and gave her a little nod; she then looked back at me. 'Yes that would be great.'

'Okay, I'll see you on Wednesday then.'

Charlie saw us out but before we left I made sure to thank him. 'It was really nice to see you both tonight and we should definitely to do it again. Maybe you could both come round to ours next time?'

'Yes definitely,' he replied. He leant over to hug me and I reluctantly hugged him back.

On the walk home I steered the conversation towards Charlie and Kirsty. 'They're a really nice couple aren't they?'

John didn't look convinced. 'Yes they seem to be,' he paused and frowned, 'but to be honest I'm not sure.'

'What do you mean?'

'Well, Charlie does come across as a decent guy but I couldn't help notice how Kirsty was reacting towards him. She seems scared of him and when you suggested seeing her on Wednesday I noticed she had to get his approval first.'

I couldn't believe John had sussed Charlie out already. I was hoping I would get to know Kirsty a bit better before he found out what he was really like. I tried to look surprised.

'Really? I can't say I noticed.' I tried to throw him off the scent. 'Maybe it's nothing? Charlie seems like a decent guy to me but if he was to say or do anything to me I would tell you straight away.'

John gave me a thoughtful look. 'I don't think he will. From what I have seen of him, I think he will want to keep his Mr. Nice Guy image up, but if he did lay a finger on you then he would have me to deal with.'

I held John's hand tight. 'I really like Kirsty and want to get to know her. I think she would be a good friend. Could you try to be nice to Charlie for my sake?'

John smiled. 'Maybe it's nothing, but if he is treating her badly then I wouldn't want you to abandon her. Just be careful.'

I decided it was best if I kept Charlie and John away from each other as much as possible and that I should concentrate on getting to know Kirsty.

The next morning, I made a point of texting Charlie almost straight away and saying how much we had enjoyed last night. I also asked him to let Kirsty know that I would text her in the week about meeting up on Wednesday.

For the next few days I couldn't get Kirsty out of my head. I text her on Tuesday but I was very aware that Charlie would read the message so I kept it short. I decided that, to keep Charlie on side, it would be best to stick to texts so he could see what was being said.

“Hi Kirsty hope you and Charlie are well. I’m looking forward to seeing you tomorrow. I will be round at nine if that’s ok xx”

About five minutes later I get a short message back.

“Hi Sarah, yes that’s fine. See you at nine then xx”

I woke up on Wednesday morning and felt good about the day ahead. I left the house at just gone nine as I didn’t want Kirsty to think I was some over keen mad woman. As I arrived I soon found a parking space and walked the short distance to her house. She greeted me with a warm smile and invited me in. She showed me into the front room and, after making a cup of tea, sat down beside me. It felt awkward between us at first but after a bit of small talk we soon started to feel at ease with each other.

I steered the conversation towards Kirsty as I was keen to know more about her life with Charlie. ‘Are you still working?’ I asked.

‘No, not at the moment but before I got pregnant I was in my first year as a student nurse. After I fell pregnant Charlie and I thought it would be for the best if I gave it up for now. My mum said she could look after the baby when she’s born so hopefully I can get back to my training then.’

I gave Kirsty a sympathetic smile as I knew Charlie wouldn’t allow that to happen. ‘That’ll be good. So do you drive then?’

‘No, I was going to learn soon after finishing my course but now with the baby and everything maybe it won’t happen for a while.’

I could see how similar her life was to mine with Charlie. 'Well at least you have the baby to look forward to. You must really be getting excited now.'

Kirsty's eyes lit up. 'Yes, I just want to feel her in my arms now, I just can't wait to see her. Are you and John thinking of having children in the near future?'

I couldn't help but think about Tommy and how far pregnant I would have been and it filled me with sadness. 'My dream is to have a couple of children in the future but I don't think John is quite ready yet. Who knows though, in a year or so maybe your little girl will have a playmate.' I hesitated for a moment. 'You probably find it hard to get out and about without a car. Do your family live nearby?'

'Well Mum lives about five miles from here. I try to get the bus over to see her as much as I can but I don't see her as much as I would like.'

I just knew that Charlie wouldn't be bothering taking her over anymore and I knew how that felt. Then I had a thought. 'Well I have a car, why don't I drive you over there now?'

Kirsty shook her head. 'I can't expect you do that.'

'Really I don't mind.' I gently persuaded her to ring her mum and sensed her mum was really pleased to hear from her and would love to see her.

On the way, Kirsty glanced over at me. 'I'm really grateful for this.'

'Think nothing of it,' I replied smiling back at her, 'that's what friends are for.'

Her mum's village was only six miles away and as we got close Kirsty pointed out her house to me. As Kirsty got out of the car I called to her. 'I'll come and pick you up in about three hours then?'

'Oh,' her voice was filled with disappointment, 'I thought you were coming in.'

'I thought you would want time alone with your mum.' I replied.

Kirsty smiled. 'Don't be daft, come and meet mum.'

Walking into the living room, Kirsty introduced me. 'Mum, this is my friend Sarah.'

She stood up and gave me a warm smile and a hug. 'Hi, I'm Kim. It's always nice to meet Kristy's friends. I keep telling her she needs to get out more, especially now she has a baby on the way. It was really kind of you to bring her round.'

I smiled back. 'Really it was my pleasure and it's nice to meet you.'

Neither Kirsty nor Kim could drive and I just knew Charlie wouldn't be bringing her here. I genuinely believed, for whatever reason, Charlie was so bitter and he was jealous of other people's families.

I turned to Kirsty. 'It can't be much fun stuck in on your own all the time. I can always drop you off here every now and then before I go to work and pick you up later. That way you can spend time with your mum.'

Kirsty looked at her mum and then back at me. 'I really can't expect you to do that; it's far too much to ask.'

'No, not at all, I'd love to help you and honestly it's no trouble.'

'If you really don't mind?' She hesitated slightly. 'I'm so glad we met, I think me leaving my phone in the ladies toilets was the best thing I have ever done.'

'Maybe someone up there wanted us to become friends.' I smiled.

'Well,' Kim interrupted, 'I don't believe in coincidence. Everything happens for a reason. If it was in your life plan for you two to meet and become friends, then it is fate.'

I really liked the way that Kim thought about things as it reminded me of my dad. She had the same values and I felt so comfortable around her. I sensed she had an inkling of what Charlie was like but not what he was really capable of and, if Kirsty was anything like me, she would be hiding it well. I could sense Kim's annoyance that he didn't make the effort to bring Kirsty round to see her.

I really enjoyed spending the day at Kim's, she made me feel so welcome and kindly made us lunch. Kirsty seemed so much more at ease when she was with her mum and I had seen another side to her. Seeing her so relaxed helped me to make up my mind, I wanted to take Kirsty there at least once a week. I couldn't help but feel guilty that Kirsty had ended up with this life so I needed to try and make it better for her. Nobody was there for me. I just wished I had a good friend looking out for me back then so I really wanted to be there for Kirsty, no matter what it took.

At three o'clock on the dot Kirsty got a call and, just like at eleven o'clock this morning, I knew, before she answered it, that it was Charlie. He would always ring me at the same time wanting to know what I was doing. Kirsty didn't mention to him that she was round her mums and she told him I had left at around twelve o'clock. I could see Kim was a little taken aback. She never said anything to Kirsty but I did notice the strange look she gave her when she said I had gone home.

Just before four o'clock, I suggested we had better get back. Kim gave me a hug and thanked me for bringing Kirsty over. 'You have a good heart,' she told me.

I blushed and looked over at Kirsty. 'I could always drop you off here on Tuesday or Thursday if you like and pick you up after work?'

Kirsty looked at her mum then me before answering. 'Are you sure? I really don't want to put you out.'

'No honestly, it's no trouble.'

Kim hugged me even tighter. 'Thank you Sarah that is such a kind gesture.'

We arrived back at Kirsty's just after four thirty and as she got out of the car I called out to her. 'Don't forget I will pick you up next Tuesday.'

She gave me a nod. 'Thanks Sarah. I will see you next week then.'

On the short drive home, I couldn't help smiling to myself. Just knowing I had made a small difference to Kirsty's life gave me a warm fuzzy feeling inside but I felt I owed her so much more. The very least I could do was give her my time. I was really warming to her and even though I had only known her a week I already saw her as a friend.

I saw things much more clearly looking in from the outside. I realised that both Kirsty and I deserved so much more than Charlie and the thought that he would probably be treating her as badly as he treated me really upset me.

I gave it a lot of thought in the time before John came home from work. I decided that it was for the best that I didn't tell him too much about Charlie and Kirsty as the last thing I wanted was for him to get involved. If he did, Charlie would see us as a threat and stop Kirsty from seeing me.

All week Kirsty was never far from my thoughts. I knew exactly what she was going through and it was a really odd feeling, to see somebody else living out my old life. I knew I would have to be really careful when I got in touch with Kirsty as Charlie would read her texts. I was well aware how Charlie operated, she wouldn't even be able to erase them as he also looked at the call logs, I tried that once and he knew I had deleted them. I knew I would have to keep the texts to a minimum.

Chapter 19

The following Tuesday I arrived at Kirsty's slightly early but she was already waiting at the door. I was really glad she hadn't forgotten. I had been in two minds whether to send her a text the night before but had thought better of it.

Climbing into the passenger seat she greeted me with a smile.

'Had a good week?' I asked.

'Yes fine thanks. I really do appreciate you doing this for me.'

Kirsty started rummaging through her handbag and pulled out a small book. She opened it a few pages from the back and pulled out a crisp five pound note and gently pressed it into my hand. 'That's for your petrol.'

It really took me by surprise as it was the last thing I wanted. I tried handing it back but she pushed my hand away and shook her head. 'No please take it.'

I felt really bad as I knew that was probably the last bit of money she had. I couldn't let her pay me every time I picked her up. I really couldn't take her money and I didn't want her to think she owed me anything. This was really going to test our friendship.

After dropping Kirsty off at Kim's, I made my way into work. All day I thought about that awkward feeling with the petrol money. I knew what she was going through and how degrading it was relying on others for money, especially when it wasn't family. I really didn't want to take her money. I remembered how good I got at hiding my money from Charlie and now I realised Kirsty was doing the same.

I thought about my savings just sitting there in the bank. John and I were comfortable as we had two wages coming in so we didn't need it and I knew I would feel so much better if I could give Kirsty the money but I couldn't just hand it to her as that would make her feel even more indebted to me. All through the day I tried to think of a solution but I was just going round in circles.

I finished a little bit earlier and drove back to pick Kirsty up. I still felt bad about what had happened that morning and just wished I could help her in some way. Then the answer just came to me out of the blue. There was a way I could give her my money without her feeling bad and it was so obvious, I didn't know why I hadn't thought of it sooner.

Driving back to Kirsty's, I picked my moment carefully and excitedly I put my plan into action. 'Kirsty, could you spare a pound?'

Rummaging through her purse she pulled out a battered old coin. 'Yes. Here you go.'

I looked at her and gave her my best smile before replying. 'I don't know why but I'm feeling really lucky today. Do you fancy going halves on a two pound scratchcard?'

Kirsty looked a bit uncertain and withdrew the coin she was holding out. 'I'm not really into gambling.'

'Oh go on,' I persisted. 'Just this once, surely you can spare a pound.'

She smiled and held out the coin once more. 'Okay then, just this once.'

I pulled into the petrol station and we both went inside. As we approached the till I noticed at least ten different types of two pound scratchcards lined up in the plastic holder.

'You choose' I said turning to Kirsty.

She picked one out and after paying we made our way back to her house as I was worried time was getting on. When we arrived she invited me in as Charlie wouldn't be back for an hour. I stayed for a cup of tea, biding my time with the scratchcard but I soon made my excuses and headed out of the door.

'Oh the scratchcard.' I turned back towards Kirsty and pulled the card from my bag. Standing in the street I frantically rubbed the squares but it soon became apparent that it was a losing ticket. I knew I had to make it look convincing so I screamed out.

'Oh my god, I don't believe it, we have won.' I thrust the ticket in her face, not giving her time to focus.

'Really? How much?' She looked shocked.

I gave her a hug. 'You won't believe this but we've won five thousand pounds. That's two and a half thousand each.'

'Really?' Kirsty stood in stunned silence.

I knew I had better go before she asked to see the ticket so I made my excuses. 'Look I need to go but I will come and see you tomorrow. Just keep it to yourself, there's no need to tell Charlie.'

As I arrived back home it dawned on me that I only had fifteen hundred pounds in my savings account and that perhaps I had been just a bit over zealous. Settling down on the sofa with my laptop, I took a look at my internet banking. I had just over two hundred pounds in my current account, far short of the extra thousand I would need. Then I remembered I had a thousand pound overdraft limit on the account. I knew it would leave me short for a while but I was due to be paid the following week and Kirsty's welfare was far more important to me. I hated keeping secrets from John but I couldn't tell him what I was up to and with a bit of scrimping and saving I knew it wouldn't be long until I was back in credit.

The next day I got up early, just after John.

'You look happy,' he said.

'Yes I'm spending the day with Kirsty.'

'You two seem to be getting on well. Is Charlie behaving himself?'

'Yes he seems to be'

John smiled. 'Well I hope I'm wrong about Charlie, I can't stand men that abuse their girlfriends but she seems happy that's the main thing.'

After giving me a quick peck on the cheek he made his way to the door. 'Well have a nice day and say hello to Kirsty for me. I'll see you tonight.'

With a gentle click the door closed behind him and my thoughts turned to Kirsty. I was feeling quite excited at the thought of seeing her and being able to help her out financially. I pottered around the house for an hour, willing the time to go faster and at the stroke of nine I was out of the door like a shot. I pulled up at Kirsty's a few minutes later; I was running on pure adrenaline.

Kirsty greeted me with a huge smile and I could see was as excited as I was. 'Is it really true about our win yesterday?' she laughed. 'I didn't just imagine it did I?'

I laughed as well and grabbed her hand. 'You better believe it's true. We have won two and a half thousand pounds each.'

Kirsty started excitedly jumping up and down on the spot before spinning me around.

'Steady on Kirsty, I don't fancy delivering your baby today.'

We both laughed hysterically before stopping to catch our breath. This was the happiest I had ever seen her and just for a moment I forgot all about Charlie and the pain she must be going through. Just knowing I was going to make such a big difference to Kirsty's life was payment enough. Seeing her reaction I knew I had made the right choice. It was the sort of thing my dad would have done.

I thought I knew her well enough to know she would hide the money from Charlie, just as I did, but I had to be sure. Giving her a little grin I asked. 'Will you be keeping your new found wealth a secret from Charlie?' I let out a little laugh. 'He has plenty of money and he is always splashing out on himself, so I won't tell him if you won't.'

Kirsty smiled and squeezed my hand. 'Thanks that means a lot to me.'

I knew I would have to keep this from John as well, as the last thing I wanted was for him to think I had won two and a half thousand pounds, especially as I was eight hundred pounds in my overdraft. My savings had all gone but I hoped within a year I could get my finances back to where they were without John noticing. I trusted Kirsty's situation enough to know that she would keep it to herself.

It was so good to hear her in the kitchen cheerfully humming away to herself as she made us a cup of tea. I really liked this new, happy Kirsty but I knew it would be short lived as, no doubt, Charlie would soon bring her back down again.

I was still struggling to get my head around how strange it felt being back in my old house with Kirsty. She offered to make me a sandwich but it still felt like my kitchen and it should be me making it for her.

The day passed too quickly for my liking. We had so much fun together and I now regarded her as my closest friend. Charlie chose us both and he knew what he was doing so I suppose it was inevitable that Kirsty and I would be so similar in personality.

On Wednesday afternoons I got that sinking feeling at the thought of having to leave her with him for another week but I got a little comfort knowing she could be with her mum once a week. As our friendship grew stronger, I felt so much more protective towards her and the thought of Charlie treating her, like he treated me, filled me with frustration and anger. It upset me so much, knowing that our friendship would always be limited to a few hours, one day a week and because of that we could never have a really deep friendship; the type where I could just phone or message her day or night, or pop over in the evening for an hour or two.

I often thought back to the time I was a part of Charlie's controlling world and wondered if Kirsty's life was playing out exactly the same way mine had. Then I would think of my life with John and how much better it was and that made me feel even guiltier about Kirsty. I almost felt I didn't deserve to be happy with John whilst my friend was in this terrible situation.

Over the next few days I withdrew the two and a half thousand pounds, in small amounts, from my account. Seeing the money in front of me made me feel a little better about myself, knowing that the following morning I would be handing it over to Kirsty and how happy that would make her eased my conscience. I hardly got a wink of sleep that night because I was so excited.

The next morning I left soon after John and pulled up outside Kirsty's house. Out of the corner of my eye I could see the curtain twitch then Kirsty briskly walked down the drive and climbed into the passenger seat. I couldn't help but notice what an excitable mood she was in.

'Hello Sarah, how are you this morning?' She smiled and laughed.

'I'm fine thank you.' I leaned over and opened the glove box. 'I have something for you.' I pointed at the open glove box hardly able to contain myself.

Kirsty pulled out a thick white envelope and quickly opened it. Her face was a picture as she realised it was stuffed full of twenty pound notes. 'Is this all mine?' She could hardly speak through her tears.

'Yes, all two and a half thousand pounds of it.'

In her over emotional state she clumsily lunged towards me for a hug and we banged heads. I cried out in pain but as we looked at each other we couldn't help but burst out into fits of laughter; I hadn't laughed so much in years. We hugged and in that moment I realised I had done the right thing.

After dropping Kirsty off at her mums, I spent the rest of the day thinking about her and what a difference the money would make. I felt quietly chuffed with myself as in that moment we had got one up on Charlie.

I lived for my Wednesday's with Kirsty. I was at my happiest when we got together and I was always worried about her when we were apart. I remembered back to when I was six months pregnant and how Charlie was treating me and I could only guess just how similar my old life was to Kirsty's. He was probably putting her down emotionally on a daily basis now.

Now that Tommy was gone I found my only comfort was living my life through Kirsty. It was such a weird feeling for me, to know Kirsty's baby would be taking Tommy's place but I had no ill feeling towards her. I'll probably never know the reason why my angel gave my old life to Kirsty. Everybody's life is in the hands of fate and it's very humbling to know that fate plays a big part in our lives and that every choice we make can change our life path forever.

Chapter 20

As the months passed I felt so close to Kirsty, she started to feel more like a sister to me and I just wanted to protect her. I hated the thought that I couldn't shield her from Charlie and I got more and more frustrated that I had to tread very carefully around him. If Charlie got an inkling of how close we had become then he would almost certainly have put a stop to our friendship.

With only a few weeks to go until Kirsty was due to give birth, I knew I was going to have to back off. I had to let the birth take its course as Charlie would be taking a few weeks off work.

The memories of Tommy were beginning to haunt me again, making me feel so empty inside. He would have been three weeks old and I desperately wanted him back with me. I knew he wasn't coming back to me and I slowly accepted the fact that he had gone for good.

The next two weeks were hell and I couldn't leave it any longer so I decided to send a text to Charlie.

"Hi Charlie hope everything is ok with you and Kirsty and I hope everything is going to plan with the birth. John and I would love to come and see your new arrival when she finally makes an appearance, thinking of you both, Sarah xx"

I didn't have to wait long for a reply.

"Hi Sarah, thank you for the text. I will call you with news as soon as I can and you will be most welcome to come and see baby Amelia. I will be in touch soon, Charlie xx"

If I didn't know Charlie better I would have thought that he was a decent guy but that was Charlie for you. He gave out this perfect image to the outside world but behind closed doors he was a monster.

Another week passed and Kirsty was on my mind day and night. It had been three weeks since I last heard from her and I just hoped she was coping with her final weeks of pregnancy and Charlie.

Finally, at just gone three o'clock on Thursday afternoon and I got a text from Charlie. My heart started to race and I felt myself shaking with excitement.

"Hi Sarah, Kirsty gave birth to our lovely daughter Amelia this morning at 11.44 a.m. Kirsty has been asking for you and if you would like she would love for you to pop in tonight xx"

The text really made my day and I replied straight away.

"Congratulations to you both. We would love to come and see you both and baby Amelia tonight. Really looking forward to it. See you later xx"

I got straight on the phone to John. 'I just got a text from Charlie. They have had the baby this morning and asked us to visit tonight.'

'Okay that's great. We'll go up there for seven o'clock.'

I was so happy and the following two hours flew by.

After freshening up and having a bite to eat we made the short journey up to the hospital. Kirsty was in the same ward that I was in when I had Tommy. We soon found them and seeing Kirsty holding Amelia in her arms brought it all flooding back to me. It felt like I was watching my old life back with someone else playing my role.

Kirsty looked so happy and as I sat beside her, she carefully handed Amelia to me and I gently cradled her in my arms. I had forgotten just how tiny they were as newborns. The moment felt so surreal and it brought back so many memories of Tommy. Sitting there with that cute little bundle in my arms made me realise that Amelia had taken Tommy's place in the world. She was such a beautiful baby and I could see a bit of Tommy in her. I really didn't know how to feel but it definitely wasn't resentment towards Kirsty.

I took just one look at Amelia and I instantly felt a bond towards her. It was almost as if she had been sent to help me deal with Tommy's loss. I knew she wasn't a part of me but the bond I felt was strangely familiar. Maybe it was because of Charlie and that I was reliving my past through Kirsty. I found it so hard to let go of Tommy's life and I knew I had to accept that he had gone for good but I also knew I mustn't get too attached to Amelia. Holding that beautiful baby brought it all flooding back and instantly filled me with regret. I just hoped Tommy was in a better place.

Charlie smiled at me. 'I've said it before, you are definitely getting broody.'

I looked up at John and smiled, I was feeling broody. All my maternal instincts were coming back to me but to be honest I didn't think they had ever left; I had just hid them well. Everyday I ached inside and missed that feeling I had with Tommy. Sitting there holding Amelia focused my mind on Tommy and his memory felt so strong. My head was saying I didn't deserve to try again but my heart was desperate to have another baby.

Visiting time ended so quickly and I really didn't want to hand Amelia back. I so wanted to be a part of Kirsty and Amelia's life but in the back of my mind I knew my feelings were unhealthy.

I wanted to hold my own baby. I felt I wanted to try for a baby with John but I also felt so guilty for feeling like that. I knew I would never forget Tommy for as long as I had breath in my lungs and in my heart he would always be my baby boy. I so hated not being able to share my thoughts and memories of him with anyone. I felt so close to my dad in that moment and I knew in my heart, that he heard my prayers and that Tommy was with him.

That night I prayed to Dad. I asked him for a sign that Tommy was with him and happy. I felt I needed to move forward and I knew being a mum again would make things right but it was so important to me to have Tommy's blessing. I needed him to know that he would live on in my heart until I took my final breath and that another baby would never replace him. I had so much love to give and just an empty place in my heart. I wasn't sure I would ever understand why my angel took Tommy away from me that night.

Over the next few weeks I really missed my time with Kirsty. I longed to see her again but I knew I would have to bide my time until Charlie went back to work. I nearly text her a few times and had to stop myself.

My life with John was all I could have dreamed of and I was so happy with him. He treated me so well and I really felt ready for us to become a family and have a baby of our own. I knew he would make a wonderful dad but I worried it was too soon for him. I really didn't want to scare him off so I didn't say anything but it was so hard for me to adjust to not being a mum anymore.

Two and a half weeks after Amelia was born, I assumed Charlie had gone back to work so I decided to surprise Kirsty and go and see her. I was so excited at the thought of seeing them both that I got very little sleep the night before. I just knew that Kirsty's life would gradually get worse over the coming months and I had to be there for her more than ever. I also knew I would eventually have to find the right time to convince her to leave Charlie.

On the Wednesday morning I woke up pretty early and decided to pop to hers at about ten o'clock. I really didn't know why but I was feeling nervous. I just hoped she was okay with me dropping in on her out of the blue.

My heart was in my mouth when I knocked on the door but I still didn't understand why I was so nervous. Maybe it was because our friendship was a little unusual, not being able to contact each other between visits felt wrong.

I needn't have worried as Kirsty greeted me with a hug and seemed really pleased to see me. Taking my hand she pulled me into the front room. Amelia was fast asleep in her little Moses basket that seemed to be three times too big for her. She looked so tiny and cosy and I so wanted to pick her up and hold her in my arms but I knew would have to be patient. I stood there staring down at her. 'Kirsty, she's so beautiful, you must be so happy.'

As I turned I could see Kirsty's face light up.

'She's the best thing that has ever happened to me and I wouldn't change her for the world.'

After making a cup of tea, we both settled down next to Amelia and started cooing over her. Kirsty looked more relaxed than usual and I could see being a mum definitely suited her.

'I was thinking about you yesterday,' she said. 'I was wondering if you would come round today but wasn't sure as I hadn't heard from you for a while.'

'I was going to call' I hesitated, 'but thought I would give you and Charlie time alone.'

Kirsty lifted Amelia out of the Moses basket and gently laid her in my arms. I instinctively supported her head and made her comfortable. Instantly, I felt overwhelmed with emotion and couldn't take my eyes off of her. Kirsty spotted my tears and put her arm around me, she couldn't hide her surprise though. 'Hey what's up? It's supposed to be my emotions all over the place not yours.'

I wiped my eyes. 'I'm sorry; it's just that she is so beautiful.'

Kirsty pulled me closer and smiled. 'I don't think it's going to be long before you and John try for a baby judging from that reaction.'

She was right, I really missed being a mum and my emotions were being pulled all over the place. I couldn't get over the fact, that this beautiful little girl in my arms wouldn't have had a chance of life if I had gone to that club and met Charlie. I found myself questioning the motivation of my angel and why she decided to stop me meeting Charlie that night and to bring Amelia into the world instead of Tommy.

I held Amelia for the next few hours and after changing her nappy for the second time I started to feel a little bit guilty. 'Sorry, I'm taking over aren't I?' I laughed.

Kirsty smiled back at me from the comfort of the sofa that she was lounging back on. 'No please carry on. I'm making the most of the break. You're a natural; anyone would think you'd been doing this for years.'

The day passed quickly and my mind was so focused on Amelia, I realised I had hardly given the whole Charlie situation a second thought. I tried to leave it as long as I could before making my excuses to leave. I didn't want to give Charlie an excuse to have a go at Kirsty so I left in plenty of time before he was due home.

With all that had been going on, I realised I hadn't managed to take Kirsty to see her mum for about a month but I promised myself I would get back into the routine next week. I remembered back to the time when Mum would pick me and Tommy up and how I really looked forward to my Tuesdays and Thursdays with her. It made such a difference to my life back then. I also knew Kim would really appreciate the time spent with Kirsty and Amelia.

The weeks passed and I lived for my Wednesday's spent with Kirsty and Amelia. Although it would never be the same, spending time with them made Tommy's loss just that little bit more bearable. When I was with Amelia I still found it hard to get my head around the fact that if I was living my old life with Charlie and Tommy, then Amelia wouldn't be here and I wouldn't have met Kirsty.

Chapter 21

The warm summer days made a welcome return and with them came happy memories of all the places Mum took me and Tommy. The park, the river, the soft play area and the local swimming pool; Tommy enjoyed splashing about in the shallow end so much.

Kirsty was really keen when I suggested going to the swimming pool with Amelia. It was the first time I had been there since I lost Tommy and it instantly brought all the memories flooding back. Amelia was a lot younger than Tommy was when I first took him but at only four months she really enjoyed the water. Seeing her and Kirsty bond made me realise just how ready I was for a baby of my own. I felt I would be doing it for the right reasons and really hoped John would feel the same way.

It hurt that I couldn't talk to Kirsty between our Wednesdays's together. I constantly had to remind myself how bad her life would be and how I mustn't do anything that would jeopardise our friendship or make her life any worse.

Over the next few weeks I yearned for a baby more and more. I couldn't help testing the water with John and dropped subtle hints at every opportunity but he didn't seem to pick up on them so I decided it was time for the more direct approach. I made up my mind that over dinner that evening I would talk to him. All day I felt both excited and nervous at the prospect. I really didn't know how I would feel if John said he would prefer to wait.

By the time I got home from work my nerves were taking over. I busied myself with making dinner but all I could think about was how John was going to react to the whole baby idea. Dinner was almost ready and I looked up at the clock, I had timed it to perfection as John would be home any minute. My heart was in my mouth; I felt nervous and excited in equal measurements.

It was such a relief when I finally heard his key in the lock. He greeted me with his usual smile and warm embrace which helped ease my nerves somewhat but still, all through dinner, we sat in almost complete silence as I tried to build myself up to ask the question. I bottled it as I just couldn't find the words. I really didn't know why I was finding it so hard.

After clearing up, we made our way into the front room and I was determined to bring the subject up. I took a minute or two to compose myself and John must have spotted how nervous I looked as he spoke first. 'Are you okay? You're looking a bit on edge.'

I took that as my cue and, with a deep breath, I felt all my pent up emotion come rushing to the surface. Looking John in the eye, I let it all out in one, long confused babble.

'John, I've been thinking and, you can say no if you want, and I will quite understand as we haven't been going out that long, and maybe it's a bit soon, and I know it is quite a big step for you, and you will probably want to wait a while and I do get that and, I know this may come as a surprise to you, but I really want us to have a baby more than anything. I am really sorry for springing this on you like this and it's totally unfair of me. Sorry.' I stopped to take breath and realised John was looking at me like some sort of mad woman. 'Sorry it was a bad idea, forget I said anything, it's just me being silly and over emotional. The last thing I want to do is spoil what we have, it's not like there's any rush is there?

John was laughing and grinning widely. He put his finger on my lips. 'Shh, shh, take a breath; I can't get a word in edge ways. The answer is yes, I would love for us to try for a baby.'

'Really? Are you sure? I don't want to pressure you into it. You don't think it is too soon do you?'

John let out another laugh. 'Don't spoil it now, you were doing so well. I would love for us to try.'

I flung my arms around his neck and kissed his cheek. 'Thank you. You don't know how nervous I was in asking you. This means so much to me and I'm so glad that you feel the same way.'

For the next few days I was on cloud nine and couldn't think of anything else. I so wanted to tell Kirsty about our plans as I knew she would be so happy for us.

Sometimes I got so wrapped up in my new life with John and my friendship with Kirsty that I forgot how her life with Charlie must be unfolding. Kirsty hid it so well, just like I used to, and I had to really look for the clues. I so wished I could ring her up for a chat as I was bursting to tell her but it would have to wait.

The next morning I was itching to go and see Kirsty. I knew Charlie always left for work at about eight twenty but I left it until eight forty-five just to be on the safe side. I was so excited to tell her my news and I knew she would be happy for us.

As she opened the door, the wide grin on my face instantly gave the game away. Kirsty smiled back. 'Oh hello, you look really pleased with yourself this morning.'

I couldn't contain myself a second longer and let it out for the whole street to hear. 'John and I are going to try for a baby.'

'Oh brilliant, that's great news, I knew it wasn't going to be long, I just had a feeling. I am so happy for you both.'

I really enjoyed the time I spent with Kirsty and Amelia. I really didn't know how I would have got through my life without them. Holding Amelia in my arms forced me to come to the realisation that Tommy's life wasn't lost in vain and that Amelia's life was just as important as his. I needed him to know my new baby wouldn't be replacing him.

I couldn't take my eyes off of Amelia as she slept. Kirsty sat beside me and gently whispered. 'You're going to make a great mum. You are so good with Amelia. I just wish Charlie would give her half as much attention as you do.'

Kirsty had taken me totally by surprise. This was the first time she had ever said anything negative about him and opened up to me. Just for a second I was lost for words. I needed to be careful how I responded. Trying my best to look surprised I replied. 'Oh. Really? Isn't Charlie hands on with Amelia then?'

Kirsty started to look unsure of herself and avoided eye contact with me. She looked down at her hands and sighed. 'He was at first but he doesn't seem to care much anymore. He's not as nice to us as you may think.'

I had to think on my feet as it was important that I didn't mess it up and say the wrong thing. I gently rearranged Amelia in my arms, trying my best not to wake her, so I could hold Kirsty's hand.

She gave me a sad and awkward smile as our eyes met and I took a deep breath. 'Kirsty, you are my best friend, you can tell me anything. I haven't said this before but I have had my doubts about Charlie and I can see a side of him that doesn't look nice. I'm worried about you and if you ever need a shoulder to cry on, or someone to listen to you, then I will always be here for you. I will never tell a soul, you do know that don't you?'

Without a word she gave a little nod. I could see I had made her feel awkward and decided to leave it. I squeezed her hand gently before passing Amelia over to her. 'I'll go and make us a cup of tea.'

As I returned, I sensed she was still a little lost in thought. I hated to see her like that and tried to lighten the mood. Talking about my plans for a baby seemed to do the trick. I knew only too well how vulnerable she would be feeling and I couldn't afford for her to push me away. I knew I must stick to the long game. I felt it best not to mention Charlie anymore that day and to concentrate on Amelia instead. I was only too aware that Kirsty put on a brave front for me.

Back home I thought about what Kirsty had said and felt that I was finally getting through to her. I was still frustrated that our time together was limited as I wanted to talk to her more about her situation with Charlie. I just hoped that in time and with gentle persuasion, she would open up to me more.

All week I thought about Kirsty. I wanted to tell Kim about Charlie but I knew that it wasn't my place and it had to come from Kirsty. All I could do was make sure she got to spend quality time with her mum.

The next morning I felt really upbeat about the day and left at the usual time. When I arrived I sensed Kirsty was pleased to see me. I don't think she realised just how much I depended on her and Amelia. Without them in my life I don't think I could have got through it. Kirsty always seemed happy for me to take over with Amelia for a few hours. She would often tell me it would be good practice for me when mine came along.

After a while my thoughts turned to Kim. 'Have you managed to see much of your mum recently?'

With a sorrowful look, she replied. 'Not as much as I'd like. Mum did manage to get over here a few weeks ago, when Charlie was at work but I find it hard on the bus in the mornings. I do try to get over there and feel guilty that she doesn't see Amelia as much as I would like her to.'

I jumped to my feet. 'Well, there's no time like the present. I'll drive us over there now if you like?'

I could feel her excitement as she replied. 'Oh that would be great. I'll give her a ring. She will be made up to see Amelia.'

I really enjoyed seeing Kim just as much as Kirsty did and it had been a few months since I last took her. Strapping Amelia into the car seat we made the short journey to Kim's.

Giving me her usual warm welcome she embraced me. 'Sarah it's really nice to see you again and thank you for bringing Kirsty and Amelia over.'

'It's my pleasure. I'm just sorry I haven't managed to bring them over much in the past few months.'

'Don't be silly, I really appreciate you bringing them but it shouldn't be necessary for you to do it. It should be down to that no good boyfriend of Kirsty's.'

I looked over at Kirsty. 'I'll start driving you over here again every week if you like?'

Before Kirsty could reply Kim answered. 'That's so kind of you. I've always said you have a kind heart but you'll have to let me give you some money for fuel.'

'No, honestly I won't hear of that, you three are like my second family.'

Without a word, Kirsty walked over to me and gave me a hug. She then looked back at her mum. 'There's a bus that passes here at half past three on weekdays. I could always catch that back so I haven't got to rely too much on Sarah to get back home.'

Giving Kirsty some stability back in her life was the least I could do and I knew it would ease my conscience a little. I knew it would make such a big difference to her life and sanity. So over the next few months I made sure I never missed getting her there. It made me feel better knowing that she could be with her mum at least once a week. I just hoped that spending quality time with her would eventually give her the courage to talk about what was happening and to leave Charlie a lot sooner than I did.

Chapter 22

It had been just over three months since me and John had started trying for a baby and I was a little disappointed that it hadn't happened. I think because I fell so quickly with Tommy, I thought it may happen as quickly this time round. John gave me a lot of emotional support and having Kirsty and Amelia in my life helped. I knew I would have to be patient and that it would happen in time.

The months passed, the winter evenings closed in and the festive season was rapidly approaching. My thoughts turned to the four Christmases I spent with Charlie. He always gave me enough money to make sure Tommy had gifts to open on Christmas morning, not even Charlie was that cold hearted but Christmas was one of the loneliest times for me. It was the only time of year where I had to spend nearly two weeks solid with him. His constant put downs and snipes seemed much worse at that time of year. I always felt much better when it was just me and Tommy. Just knowing Kirsty was almost certainly going through the same emotions brought me down and filled my heart with sadness.

John and I planned to spend that Christmas with Mum as we had spent it with his parents the previous year but I knew it wouldn't feel right, knowing my best friend would be having such a horrible time.

The following Wednesday would be the last time I would be able to see Kirsty for three weeks. I often wondered where she would be spending Christmas if my life had been fated to meet Charlie again at that club. It would be me and Tommy reliving our Christmas with him. Life seemed unfair as neither of us deserved to have to spend our lives with him.

I tried to enjoy the Christmas break the best I could but all I could think about was Kirsty and how bad her Christmas would be. By the day after Boxing Day I was just willing the rest of the holiday away, looking forward to the day I would be able to see Kirsty and Amelia again. I prayed for the day when she would be strong enough to leave him.

John and I saw the New Year in at home in front of the television. I was due to go back to work on the fourth and I had arranged to meet up with Kirsty on the sixth. It seemed such a long time since we last spoke.

By this time it had been five months since John and I started trying for a baby and I felt so disappointed on Saturday morning when I came on. John gave me a hug and tried to reassure me but I found it difficult to hide my disappointment and stay upbeat. Wednesday couldn't come quickly enough and seeing Kirsty and Amelia again was the best feeling.

She asked if I had had a good Christmas but I played it down for her sake. 'Yes it was okay, nothing special but it would be nice if John and I could have a new born in time for next Christmas.'

Kirsty gave me a sympathetic smile. 'Sometimes it takes a while with your first but it will happen soon I'm sure.'

I thought back to Tommy and how quickly I fell pregnant with him. 'You were quite quick with Amelia weren't you?'

‘Yes only three months but I really wasn’t expecting it to be that quick. You and John have all the time in the world so don't beat yourself up over it.’

Kirsty must have had the weight of the world on her shoulders and it amazed me how she still found time to try and make me feel better about myself. I was so glad we had become friends.

Chapter 23

The 14th of January was a bad day for me. It was the first milestone I had to face as it would have been Tommy's first birthday. It hit me a lot harder than I thought it would and I realised grief is a lot harder to deal with when you have no one to share it with. There were plenty of silent tears that day.

Kirsty and Amelia got me through the bad days and just knowing that Amelia had her life because of Tommy's absence helped to get me through it.

As mid February approached and almost three years since I fell back in time, I dared to hope I had fallen pregnant. I was over a week late but I daren't get my hopes up and for the following week I was on tenterhooks, just praying nothing changed.

As the week drew to an end I couldn't wait any longer; I had to do the test. I bought some months ago in anticipation of this day. I couldn't face work as I felt I would need time alone if it turned out to be negative so I phoned in sick. It took me all morning to build up the courage to do the test and I sat nervously waiting for the result, almost too scared to look, just hoping it would change. I took a peek and realised I was spot on. I stared down desperately trying to believe it. I was pregnant.

I could hardly contain my excitement; finally, after months of waiting, it had happened. I wanted to tell John but he wouldn't be home for hours. I thought about ringing him but I really wanted to see his reaction. All afternoon I was like a cat on hot bricks, I couldn't sit still and my mind was all over the place. I tried to busy myself the best I could until finally I heard John's car pull up.

I made a dash for the door when I heard his key turn, much to his surprise. 'Where's the fire?' he laughed.

Flinging my arms around him, I just blurted it out. 'I'm pregnant. You are going to be a dad.'

John's eyes widened as the news started to sink in. Within seconds he lifted me off of my feet and spun me around. 'Wow! That's fantastic news. I'm going to be a dad. I told you it would happen, didn't I.'

All evening we talked about nothing else. We decided it was best to keep it to ourselves until we reached twelve weeks but I knew I would tell Kirsty. She was my best friend and I couldn't have kept it from her even if I had tried.

It was only when I got to bed and my mind calmed that the full impact of my pregnancy hit me. The image of Tommy filled my mind and, like so many times before, I couldn't help but cry. I knew the guilt and pain I was feeling would never leave me. Life without Tommy was unbearable and not knowing what had become of him was slowly killing me inside. Every day I felt I was betraying him in someway. I just wish I knew where he had gone.

All night the same thoughts ran over and over in my head and I got very little sleep. I was so happy that I was finally pregnant but there would always be a huge part of me that would always feel guilty about my little boy.

The next morning I woke up in a sombre mood. I was looking forward to seeing Kirsty but I couldn't shake the thoughts of Tommy.

When I arrived Kirsty could tell I was hiding something from her, she could read me like a book. She looked inquisitively at me. 'Is everything okay?'

'Yes, sorry I'm still trying to take it all in.' I smiled back at her.

Kirsty quickly took both my hands and looked me in the eye. 'You're not…'

'Yes I'm pregnant,' I quickly butted in with the biggest grin ever plastered across my face. 'I did the test yesterday.'

'Oh Sarah, that's brilliant news. Didn't I tell you it was going to happen soon? You and John must be over the moon.'

For the rest of the day we mostly talked about babies.

When I first met Kirsty I promised myself I was going to do all I could to help her, little did I know just how much of an influence she was going to have on my life. Every day I thought what a difference she had made to my life, she really lifted my spirits. I felt much more positive about my life thanks to her but I knew, from bitter experience, that her life with Charlie would be tough now. She was hiding it well, probably a bit too well for my liking and if I hadn't have lived her life, I could never have imagined just how unbearable it must be.

Over the next few weeks things went well and I really began to enjoy my pregnancy. I was constantly looking up my baby's progress on the internet and John took a real interest too. I just knew he was going to make a really good dad. He started talking about shopping for the baby and getting the spare room ready. I couldn't believe I was living the life I had always dreamed of.

Tommy was constantly in my thoughts. I lost count of the number of times I was out, heard a small child calling their mum and, just for a split second, I looked round convinced it was Tommy. The only way I could get through those times was to visualise him with the angels. However unfair I felt life had treated me, I had to believe it was his time to go back. The angels blessed me with three years of his life and I hoped, one day when my time came, I would be with him again and finally understand why he had to go. I vowed to never let Tommy's memory fade; I would keep it alive through my new baby, who would always be Tommy's little brother or sister.

The next day I received the appointment for my twelve week scan which was in three weeks time. It made everything feel more real and I was looking forward to seeing my first scan picture. I couldn't wait to show John the conformation letter. He was so excited about our baby and I just wished I could let go enough to be as excited as him. I thought maybe it was time I gave myself permission to be happy too.

John and I had a good talk that night and I could see how much the baby had changed him. He really didn't mind if we had a boy or girl but secretly I thought I would prefer a girl this time as I was worried that I may unfairly compare a boy too much to Tommy. Whether we had a boy or girl I knew he or she would be loved dearly by us both.

Every day that passed I found it harder keeping my news from Kate, some days I felt I would burst if I didn't tell her and came so close. I just couldn't wait until the scan; we

Chapter 24

The new week started and I was in good spirits. Just before leaving for work I had to answer a call of nature and was slightly concerned to see a small amount of blood. I convinced myself it was okay, as it was brown in colour and only a small amount, so I headed out of the door.

All morning I tried to put it to the back of my mind. The lunchtime rush died down and I decided to take my break but I didn't really have much of an appetite. About half an hour into the afternoon shift I started feeling funny; I was getting cramps in my stomach and I really started to worry. Kate soon realised something was up and helped me to a chair. 'Are you okay?' She asked her face full of concern. 'I'll get you a glass of water.'

I started to fear the worst and almost let my news slip. I needed reassurance, someone to tell me that everything was going to be alright but I promised John I wouldn't tell anyone.

'I'm not feeling too good. Would you mind if I go home?'

'Yes of course, you go.'

Back home I decided to go up to bed for a lie down. The cramps continued but each time they became gradually worse. I so wanted to believe that it was just stomach ache and would pass but deep down I knew it wasn't as the pain was becoming unbearable. I needed John with me so I called him at work. Within seconds he answered.

My voice was shaky and I could hardly get my words out. 'John please come home, I need you.' I dropped the phone as another cramp took over. I could just about hear John calling my name over and over again and I screamed out in pain. I just wanted it to stop.

I was so relieved when I finally heard John running up the stairs. He looked directly at me and I think he knew, as without a word, he lay down beside me and held me. For the next few hours John comforted me the best he could through my pain.

The pain worsened and I felt it was going to happen so I hurried to the bathroom. Within a short time it was over and I slumped to the floor, completely drained both physically and emotionally. I lay there hardly believing how quickly my life had changed. I heard a tap on the door as John had realised what had just happened. He helped me back to bed and we lay silently together, he cradled me in his arms as I quietly cried inside. I had no energy left and soon fell to sleep.

I slept until the next morning when I slowly awoke to the realisation that my baby had gone. I reached out for John but soon realised the other side of the bed was empty. I lay there for a while, still not quite able to take it in, and soon drifted back to sleep.

John gently woke me at about ten. 'I have rung the hospital and explained what has happened' he whispered. 'They can see us today between appointments. We need to be there at two.'

I nodded, in my heart I already knew what they were going to say but I knew we had to go. John was really good, he took complete control. He knew I needed time and left me to my thoughts but I knew he was hurting too and I wanted to comfort him.

I thought back to how Mum and Dad must have felt all those years ago. I got comfort thinking of the time when I was five and the story Dad had told me about me having to go back to the angel's. That's the way Dad coped with his loss and I took comfort from the thought that maybe my baby had gone back and was waiting with the angels but would come back to me soon.

Early afternoon arrived and we made the short drive to the hospital. I was so nervous and I dreaded that my worst fear was just about to become very real to me. I tried to keep it together for John.

Just for a moment, walking into the waiting room brought happier memories of my two scans of Tommy flooding back. As we took our seats John glanced over at me, only too aware of the couple sitting next to us. They were excitedly talking about their upcoming scan and finding out whether they were having a boy or girl. I'm sure if they had known my situation they would have been mortified that I was within earshot of them.

John took my hand and pointed to a quieter spot. 'Do you want to move over there?' He whispered.

I smiled back and wiped a single tear from my left eye. 'No honestly, it's okay.'

The couple soon got called in, leaving John and I in our silent thoughts.

It wasn't long before my name was called. John gently helped me to my feet and the midwife guided us through the corridor to a small room. She quickly tried to put me at ease and I explained to her about the previous night. Trying not to cry, I said the words that earlier I couldn't bring myself to say out loud. 'I think my baby's gone.'

She gave me a reassuring smile but it didn't help.

The room fell deadly quiet as she prepared me for the scan. John and I stared anxiously at the screen and, after what seemed like an eternity, the midwife spoke. 'I am so sorry; it does look like you have miscarried.' I didn't hear what she said after that. The thought that she must have to deliver bad news everyday and I was just another sad statistic to her just kept running through my head. After a few minutes she took us to a much smaller room close by.

'Take as much time as you need,' she said shutting the door behind her.

I looked at John and could see he was fighting his own internal battle trying to keep his emotions in check. Every part of me felt numb and, no matter how much I wanted to, I couldn't cry. My thoughts turned to Mum. She was the only person that could possibly understand what I was going through and I desperately wanted to be with her.

I stood and grabbed John's hand tightly, pulling him towards the door. 'I need to go; I need to be with Mum. Can we go and see her please?'

He looked me in the eye before replying. 'Of course we can, let's go.'

We silently made our way back to the car. I could tell John had been knocked sideways and I wondered if the fact he was keeping his feelings to himself, was his way of coping.

On the drive to Mum's I became lost in my own thoughts. She didn't even know I was pregnant so it was going to be a huge shock to her. Looking back I thought maybe I shouldn't have kept it from her.

We pulled up outside Mums and sat for a moment in total silence, neither of us wanting to face what we were about to do.

'Okay then, shall we go?' I whispered to John

Walking up Mum's drive was one of the hardest things I had ever had to do. Just knowing I had to break this to her made me feel sick. We paused as we got to the door. John looked at me. 'Are you ready?' He asked gently.

I nervously smiled back and slowly nodded. John opened the door and gingerly we made our way in. I held John's hand tightly as we quietly made our way to the front room. I caught sight of Mum sitting on the sofa. She looked surprised to see us but before she had chance to say anything, I burst into tears.

She jumped up out of her seat and hugged me tightly. 'Sarah, whatever's happened?'

'Mum' I sobbed, 'I've lost my baby. I'm so sorry I didn't even tell you I was pregnant. We were going to surprise you in two weeks after the scan.'

Mum gently pulled me closer before helping me to the sofa. I rested my head on her shoulder and we sat in silence for a few minutes. I sensed Mum was trying to find the right words but all I needed from her was to be there for me.

Eventually she broke the silence. 'Sarah, I know more than anyone how you must be feeling. Even after all these years it's never completely gone away.' She paused for a moment. 'It's going to feel raw for quite a while. I know there isn't anything I can say that's going to make you feel better but you must realise that these things happen and it has nothing to do with anything you've done. I remember how I blamed myself when I first miscarried.' She smiled as she thought back. 'Your dad didn't help much by going on about you going back to the angels to play with them and how you'd be back when the time was right but he meant well. That was just his way of coping I suppose, he was just trying to make me feel better, bless him.'

Mum briefly looked at John then back at me. 'You mustn't let this put you off. I'm sure you will want to try again in time. Look at me and your dad, it took us three attempts to have you in our lives.'

Mum was right and I tried to put it into perspective. My miscarriage was not in the same league as losing Tommy and with Mum's support I knew John and I would get through it and would try again in time.

Just knowing what Mum and Dad went through, and having been through it twice, made me think, if they had given up then I wouldn't be here. It gave me real hope. I also knew of other people that had gone through this and come out the other end. Mum had made me see things more clearly.

As we talked I suddenly thought about Kate. 'Mum I haven't told Kate what's going on. She doesn't know I was pregnant, she thinks I had stomach ache and was probably expecting me in today.'

‘Would you like me to tell her for you?’

I nodded. ‘Yes please, I don’t think I could find the words right now.’

Mum went out into the hall to make the call. I couldn’t hear the conversation so could only imagine Kate’s reaction to the news. It wasn’t long before Mum returned and gave me a sympathetic smile. ‘Kate asked me to give you all her love. She is so sorry for your loss and her thoughts are with you both. She told me to tell you to take as much time off as you need.’

We stayed for another hour before heading home. It was the first time John and I had really been alone to talk. There was an air of awkwardness between us at first with neither of us really knowing what to say. Taking the initiative I asked John how he was feeling.

He looked at me and sadly smiled. ‘It hasn’t really sunk in yet. To be honest I just feel empty. I'm more worried about you; you carried our baby for nine weeks. I hated seeing you in pain yesterday. I felt so useless seeing you suffering and I couldn’t do anything for you.’

I pulled John close to me. ‘John, I needed you yesterday and couldn’t have coped without you. You were there for me, you couldn’t have done anymore for me and I love you for that.’

After a while John got up. ‘I’ll phone my boss and tell him I won’t be in tomorrow.’

‘No it’s okay, you go to work. I will be okay. Anyway tomorrow’s Wednesday and that’s the only day I can spend with Kirsty.’

'Okay but only if you are really sure?' He looked a bit uncertain but I nodded and he agreed.

The next morning I sensed John was still reluctant to leave me but I knew it would be better for him to get back to work; it would take his mind off things.

Kirsty was blissfully unaware of my miscarriage but I couldn't think of anywhere I would rather have been than with both her and Amelia. I left just before nine and arrived at Kirsty's a few minutes later. I was feeling a little more upbeat about things but I was also a bit apprehensive about telling her what had happened. I put on my best smile and knocked on the door. I was greeted by Kirsty with Amelia in her arms.

She had got to know me really well and saw through my fake smile immediately. 'What's wrong?' she asked ushering me in.

I wiped a few tears away. 'Nothing I'm fine.' I promised myself I wouldn't cry in front of Kirsty but that was easier said than done. She took my hand and led me into the front room. She gently placed Amelia on the floor, surrounded by her favourite toys, before turning her attention to me. As she sat down beside me she took both of my hands and squeezed them tightly. 'Please tell me, has something happened?'

I could hear the concern in her voice and I paused for a moment, breaking off eye contact. I wiped a few more tears away with the back of my hand. Kirsty placed her index finger under my chin and gently lifted my head. I gave her a sorrowful smile as I reluctantly looked her in the eye.

'Is it the baby?' she asked.

I nodded and instantly burst into tears. Kirsty let go of my hands and wrapped her arms around me tightly. It took me a few minutes after the sobbing subsided before I could speak. 'I have lost it, my baby's gone.'

I could see the tears forming in Kirsty's eyes as she replied. 'Oh no, I am so sorry.'

Amelia must have sensed the atmosphere and started to get restless. I looked at Kirsty and asked if she minded if I picked her up. She looked concerned. 'Is that a good idea? Are you sure?'

I smiled. 'Honestly I'm fine, John and I have had a really long talk and we are already thinking about the future. We are not going to give up, we will get through this.'

I gently lifted Amelia up and held her close. She was twelve months old and I couldn't believe she was already shuffling across the floor on her bottom. Time seemed to be flying by. I had been back in this timeline for three years and Tommy would have been the same age as Amelia. Seeing her growing up reminded me so much of Tommy and how he was at her age.

I started to make funny faces at Amelia and my heart melted as she laughed back at me. I noticed Kirsty out of the corner of my eye and she looked so concerned for me. I looked up at her and smiled. We didn't really mention the miscarriage anymore and for the next few hours I focused all of my attention on Amelia.

Kirsty was so supportive and I was really glad I had her in my life but I just wished we could have had a more normal friendship. Maybe one day we would but she was very secretive about parts of her life and didn't mention much about Charlie.

The hours passed quickly and it was soon time for me to make a move. Although I had been dropping Kirsty off at her mum's every week, I hadn't managed to see Kim myself for a while. Then a thought came to me, I wasn't working the next day, so I suggested to Kirsty that I could spend the day with them.

Kirsty's face lit up. 'Oh that would be great, Mum would love to see you again, she's always asking after you.' Kirsty hesitated for a moment. 'Would you like me to mention about the miscarriage, so it's not awkward for you?'

I nodded. 'Yes okay, it might be better that way.'

Noticing the time, I made my way to the door before turning to Kirsty to give her one last hug. 'Thank you for today, you really are a good friend to me and it means a lot. I'll see you tomorrow.'

John arrived home from work at the usual time and we settled down to dinner. I told him about my day with Kirsty and our plans for the next day and he smiled. 'I'm glad you've got someone to talk to. It will do you good to get out tomorrow.'

I could see John still worried about saying the wrong thing to me and knowing I had Kirsty to talk to put his mind at ease. We both knew it would take time to get back to where we were.

The next morning I was in a more optimistic frame of mind. I had been getting very little sleep and spent most nights just laying awake thinking. I desperately wanted a baby and I didn't want to wait too long before trying again. I had been advised that it was best to wait a few months but I felt ready and I knew it could take me another six months to fall pregnant again. I had been reading up on it and found that after a miscarriage you are more fertile and tend to get pregnant quicker the second time around so I didn't want to wait. I knew my pregnancy was just one of those unfortunate one in five chances that results in a miscarriage but I had carried Tommy full term so I knew everything was physically okay with me.

I wanted to test the water with John so I cautiously asked him if we could try again as I really didn't want us to be put off. I could tell he was reluctant to talk about it but he was being really supportive and although he had never been one to wear his heart on his sleeve, I knew he felt the same way.

John left for work and I waved him goodbye before getting ready to see Kirsty. She was already waiting on the pavement with Amelia as I pulled up. I helped her put Amelia's seat in the car and she looked me in the eye. 'Are you okay? I've been worried about you.'

'Honestly' I smiled, 'I'm okay and you needn't worry. John and I are fine about things and we'll be ready to try again soon.'

'Oh I'm so glad to hear that. Miscarriages are more common than you think but I'm sure everything will be okay for you both next time.'

We made our way to Kim's, it felt like such a long time since I saw her last and I was really looking forward to spending the day with them both. We arrived and as we walked up the drive I felt Kirsty pulling at my arm.

‘I told Mum this morning,’ she whispered, ‘about your miscarriage.’

Kim greeted me with the biggest hug. ‘Sarah I’m so sorry to hear your news.’

I put on a brave face as I replied. ‘It’s okay it’s one of those things. John and I won’t give up; we will try again in time.’

Kirsty went off to make us a cuppa and I couldn’t help but smile as I watched Kim and Amelia play together on the floor. I sat down beside them and Kim gave me a sympathetic look before resting her hand on mine. ‘It will happen. You'll see, this time in a year we will all be sitting here. Amelia will be running around and you will be holding a new born baby in your arms.’

I smiled as I tried to capture that image in my minds eye. I knew Kim meant well and I really hoped she was right. I was lucky to have so much support around me. I tried to imagine how I would have coped if I had miscarried whilst I was with Charlie and it really didn’t bear thinking about. As my thoughts turned to Charlie I worried how Kirsty was coping. I tried to picture me at this stage and how I used to hide my feelings from everyone. I didn’t believe that Charlie would be treating her any differently but all I could do was be a friend to her.

I scooped Amelia up in my arms before turning to Kim and smiling. ‘This little one gives me all the hope I need and Kirsty’s the best friend I could ask for. I’m just glad I have them both and you in my life.’

She smiled back but it quickly turned into a frown. ‘I really worry about Kirsty and if it wasn’t for you I don’t think I would really get the chance to see her as much as I'd like. Charlie isn't the man I would have chosen for my daughter. He is very controlling and I think he deliberately keeps her away from me.'

The door opened and Kirsty came back in with the teas so Kim quickly changed the subject before I could reply. I felt for Kim, I really did. She was as much in the dark as my mum had been with me. I felt maybe it was time to start dropping subtle hints to try to get Kirsty to open up to me.

Before I knew it the day had gone by and it was time to get Kirsty home. I gave Kim a hug and she smiled. 'Don't leave it so long next time. You know you are always welcome here.'

On the drive back we sat in almost total silence both deep in thought. I so wanted Kirsty to open up to me but at the same time I was afraid of her pushing me away.

That night I mentioned to John what Kim had said to me about Charlie never taking Kirsty to see her and how grateful she was that I did.

'Well that doesn't surprise me,' John replied. 'I always thought he was a bit like that. It can't be much of a life for Kirsty.'

'Listen John, I so want to help her but I don't know what I can do. She never talks about Charlie so I can only imagine how he treats her.'

John took my hand. 'She won't thank you for it. I have read about this sort of thing where the abuser cuts the victim off from family and friends. It can go on for years and only ends when the victim can't take anymore or gets so badly beaten that the police get involved.'

I felt a few tears run down my face. I was finding it so hard sitting back and doing nothing. I just wished she would reach out to me.

I tried to put all the negative thoughts out of my head as there really wasn't much I could do for her between our Wednesdays together. The weekend came and went and I was looking forward to Monday and getting back to work and normality.

As I arrived for work on Monday morning, Kate spotted me as soon as I walked through the door and made a beeline for me.

'I'm so sorry,' she said taking both my hands in hers. 'You should have told me about the baby, there's no way I would have let you go home on your own if I had known.'

I thought I was done crying in public but Kate set me off again. I wiped away my tears before replying. 'It's happened and John and I are coming to terms with it. We're going to try again when we feel ready but we need to put this behind us first. I just need to get back to normality.'

Kate gently nodded. 'Okay but if you feel you want to talk or find it too much, you just let me know.'

It didn't take me long to settle back into my old routine and staying busy helped me to get my life back into perspective. After a few weeks I managed to convince John that we should try again. We decided that when I did fall pregnant I would need Mum's support so we would tell her straight away.

Kirsty really came through for me over those few months which only made me feel guiltier that I hadn't done enough to help her. I found it so frustrating trying to get her to open up. I tried bringing Charlie into our conversations but she always clammed up and changed the subject. I knew how much she enjoyed our Wednesday's together and thought that maybe that was all I could do for her at that time. I just needed to be there for her.

Chapter 25

Three months after the miscarriage I realised my period was two weeks late. I had been a bit irregular over the previous few months so didn't think too much of it but in the back of my mind I was praying that I wouldn't come on.

A few more days passed and I couldn't wait any longer so I decided to do a test after work. The day dragged but after I finally arrived home I headed straight to the bathroom. I waited impatiently, almost willing it to show up positive. I became light headed as I looked down and read the stick "PREGNANT". I couldn't contain my joy and punched the air before letting out a long, loud 'yes'. I spent the next half an hour pacing the floor waiting for John to come home. My only thought was telling him and I felt a huge rush of emotion as I finally heard his car pull up outside. I headed straight for the door and John only just made it in before I flung myself at him.

'John it's happened, I'm pregnant again.'

Totally taken by surprise he wrapped his arms tightly around my waist. 'That's brilliant news. See, what did I tell you, I knew it wouldn't take long second time round.' I could hear the excitement in his voice as he continued. 'Come on lets sit you down before you fall down. You need to get your breath back.'

I started to get flustered as I realised I hadn't thought of anything else since taking the test. 'I haven't even thought about dinner yet' I apologised.

John let out a little laugh. 'Its okay I'll order us a takeaway.'

I sat down and started to gather my thoughts. A feeling of vulnerability overwhelmed me and I turned to John. 'What if it happens again? I couldn't bear that.'

He gently wiped a few tears from my cheek with his thumb before taking my hand. 'Hey, now you listen to me, I won't have any of that talk. We are going to have a baby so I want you to focus on that thought.'

'Maybe I'm just being silly,' I gave him a half hearted smile, 'but I can't get the thought of Mum's two miscarriages out of my head. I worry about history repeating itself.'

John looked concerned and squeezed my hand tighter to try and reassure me. 'I really think you should talk to your mum this time. I'm sure she'll put your mind at ease.'

I knew he was right but I worried, I felt I wasn't going to be able to relax and enjoy my pregnancy until I reached twelve weeks. It had happened once and that focused my mind on Mum's two miscarriages and I couldn't get those negative thoughts out of my head.

John ordered the takeaway and I decided to ring Mum straight away. I waited impatiently for her to answer the phone and when she did, she hardly got her first word out when I excitedly blurted out. 'Mum I'm pregnant.'

'Oh Sarah that's wonderful news, I'm so happy for you both.'

I could hear the tone in my voice change as I replied. 'I really wanted to tell you this time but I still worry about miscarrying again, especially after you and Dad lost two.'

The line went quiet for what seemed ages but in reality could only have been a few seconds. 'Look Sarah, you really have to put what happened to me and your dad to the back of your mind. There is absolutely no reason why it should happen to you again and you need to understand that your dad and I were just really unlucky.'

I knew she was right and I felt much better talking to her. I felt a little bit more positively about things and decided I was going to try to enjoy my pregnancy. I thought about Dad and Tommy every day and the thought they were together helped me and kept me positive.

Apart from a few doubts, this time around my pregnancy felt so right. I just knew things were going to work out. I felt I had Tommy's blessing now but I knew I would feel even better in six weeks after my scan.

I managed to get through Tuesday without telling Kate, although she did comment on what a really good mood I was in. I felt guilty not telling her my news but I kept telling myself it was only for another six weeks.

The next morning I woke up bright and early and I was really looking forward to spending the day with my best friend. I arrived as punctually as ever, just before nine, bursting to tell her my news and as the door opened she soon spotted my stupid grin. Without giving it a second thought or caring who was in hearing distance, I announced it at the top of my voice.

'I'm pregnant again.'

Kirsty smiled excitedly and ushered me inside. 'I'm so happy for you both. Didn't I tell you things would work out for you?'

I couldn't help but tell her about my fears of losing it again and, almost word for word, she said exactly what John had said.

'Kirsty' I said hugging her tightly, 'I feel so lucky to have a friend like you.'

We spent a few minutes talking about the baby before I suggested we take Amelia to the soft play area. I felt I wanted to get out and enjoy the day, luckily Kirsty agreed and we headed off.

As we arrived it surprised me just how busy it was even on a school day. We stayed for a few hours of play with Amelia; she soon wore herself out and quickly fell asleep. As Kirsty strapped her into her pushchair and gently lowered the back rest to the sleeping position, she turned to look at me. 'Do you fancy lunch? It's on me.'

'Yes, thank you that would be nice.'

It felt so good knowing I didn't have to worry about her treating me to lunch. She must have stashed the money I gave her away somewhere. I knew she had been careful with it and it was nice to know that she could pay her way without me feeling guilty.

As we sat, I must have looked slightly tense as Kirsty took my hand to comfort me. 'You know its going to be alright this time don't you?'

I squeezed her hand and smiled. 'Yes I know. I just worry a bit that's all.'

After lunch and a bit longer playing with Amelia, we decided to head back to Kirsty's. By the time we got back it was almost four in the afternoon.

'Have you got time for a quick cuppa?' Kirsty asked as we headed in.

I stayed for an hour but was very aware that Charlie would be home soon so I made my excuses.

'I'll see you next week,' she said as I left, 'and remember, try not to worry.'

'Yes I know. I'll try not to.'

For the next few weeks I tried to put any negative thoughts to the back of my mind. At eight weeks John and I booked the twelve week scan and it couldn't come quickly enough. I knew John worried too but he never showed it. I'm sure he was trying to stay positive for me.

Week nine arrived and on the Friday, about half way through my shift, I had to take a call of nature. That's when I noticed a few spots of blood. It wasn't brown blood like last time but more red. I just sat there in a state of shock, unable to move. 'Please no, not again.' I quietly whined.

All afternoon I had this terrible niggling feeling that I just couldn't shake. I found it hard to focus on my job and I just wanted the working day to end. I felt a little apprehensive when I needed to take another call of nature and tried to put it off for as long as I could. When I did go and there was no blood I felt a sense of utter relief.

That evening I couldn't bring myself to mention it to John; after all it was probably nothing. Instead, I looked it up on the internet and I read that a little blood was nothing to be initially alarmed about but if it became regular then I should get it checked out.

The next morning I was relieved that everything seemed fine. I hadn't bled since the day before so I tried to put it to the back of my mind as it was only two weeks on Monday until the scan.

With it being such an unusually warm day for October, John and I decided to go to Cambridge for the afternoon. Later on in the afternoon, at about four I started to feel unwell. I noticed slight cramps but dismissed them at first. The pain persisted and when I answered the call of nature I noticed traces of blood again. I started to worry and all I wanted to do was get home. I didn't want to worry John as I wasn't sure what was happening so I kept it to myself. When we got home the cramps seemed to ease and there was no more blood but to be on the safe side I decided to go to bed early to rest.

At two in the morning I was woken by an agonising cramp. John was sound asleep next to me and I didn't see the point of disturbing him so I went into the spare room. I lay there for about an hour unable to sleep. I felt numb at the thought of it happening again but I resigned myself to the fact that it probably was. The pain was excruciating and I prayed for it to stop. Instinctively I knew I had to get to the bathroom and within twenty minutes it was all over. I lay on the bathroom floor and just cried.

I heard John knocking on the door before he let himself in. I looked up at him and he instantly knew what had happened and gently embraced me. After a few minutes he helped me to my feet and back to the bedroom. There were no need for words; he just held me and through total exhaustion I fell to sleep.

Early the next morning the sun gently woke me. I just lay there staring at the wall, trying to make sense of it all. Why had this happened again? History really was repeating itself. I felt so empty and I couldn't reason it out.

I stayed in bed for most of the day, not really wanting to do anything. I knew John was finding it hard too. I sensed he really didn't know how to deal with it or what to say to me. I could see he was desperately trying his very best not to say the wrong thing.

In the early evening John came to see how I was feeling. 'Should I ring your mum and tell her what's happened?' he asked.

I nodded. 'Okay but I really can't face talking to anyone today, not even Mum.'

'Okay I'll give her a ring and ask her to have a word with Kate for you.'

The next day I convinced John to go to work. He didn't want too and I knew he was worried about leaving me alone but I insisted. I couldn't focus on anything and just wanted to be left alone with my thoughts. I tried to do a few chores to keep my mind busy but I still felt numb.

Early Tuesday morning I thought about Kirsty and Amelia. I didn't feel able to see her Wednesday and I needed to get a message to her to explain why I couldn't make it. I decided it was best to write her a quick note.

"Kirsty. I'm really sorry but I can't come over today. I'm so sorry for letting you down. I am not in a very good place at the moment. I've miscarried again and can't face the world at the moment. I hope you understand. Hopefully I will see you in a week or two. Love Sarah xx"

The next morning I dropped the note off at just after ten and made my way back home. I felt bad letting Kirsty down but I just couldn't face her. I headed back to bed and I must have dozed off as an hour or so later I came too to hear loud knocking at the door. I reluctantly got up to answer it and was surprised to see Kirsty standing on the doorstep. She must have walked the mile with Amelia.

Before I could speak she stepped forward to hug me. 'I had to come and see you. I will go if that's what you want but I just needed to make sure you were okay.'

I was so pleased to see her and hugged her tightly. 'No, please come in. Excuse the mess I haven't had chance to tidy up.'

'Don't worry about that, let me do it for you.'

We made our way to the front room and Kirsty pointed to the sofa. 'Sit down, I'll go and make us a cup of tea.'

I lifted Amelia out of her pushchair and held her close. I had got to know all of her favourite children's programmes and found something she liked. At that point Kirsty returned clutching two cups of tea. Amelia settled herself on the floor and became totally engrossed in the television.

Kirsty placed the tea on the coffee table and sat down beside me. She took my hand and I watched as a sorrowful look formed on her face. 'Sarah, I know there isn't anything that I can say or do that will make you feel better but I was so upset for you when I saw your note that I couldn't let you be alone. I thought you could do with a friend right now. If you don't want to talk that's fine, we can just sit here quietly.'

Secretly I was really glad that she had come round. Spending time with them both helped me and I realised that I needed my friends around me. Just knowing Kirsty and Amelia were there for me made everything so much more bearable.

After staying for most of the afternoon, Kirsty looked up at the clock. 'Is that the time? I'd better get back or I'll have Charlie moaning at me.'

As she headed to the door I gave her another hug. 'I really appreciated you coming over today. I would have driven you back but we don't have Amelia's car seat.'

Kirsty let out a little laugh. 'Its okay I could do with the exercise.'

She pushed her arms into her coat and reached for the door but before she could open it I stopped her. 'Are you free tomorrow? I was thinking of going to see Mum and wondered if you fancied coming with me?'

'Yes I'd really like that. It would be nice to see her again.'

'Okay then I'll pick you up at nine in the morning.'

As she left I smiled to myself. I felt a bit better about things and that was all down to Kirsty, she had managed to lift my spirits.

Later, John walked through the door and he looked surprised to see me up and about.

‘Hello love’ I smiled at him. ‘Have you had a good day at work? Dinner won’t be long’

‘I didn’t expect you to be up making dinner. Are you okay?’

‘Yes, I’m feeling better. Kirsty came around to see me and ended up staying the day. She’s coming to Mum’s with me tomorrow as well.’

‘That’s great. It’ll be good for you and it’ll do you good to get out. I think you two are good for each other.’

After dinner we settled down in front of the television. John made a lot of small talk and I sensed that he was deliberately avoiding talking about the miscarriage.

The next morning I felt more optimistic about the future. I arrived at Kirsty’s at nine as we’d agreed and after strapping Amelia into her seat we set off.

When we arrived Mum greeted me with a hug. I held her tightly trying my best not to cry. ‘It’s going to be okay’ she whispered.

After a few minutes she looked over at Kirsty. ‘Hi Kirsty, how are you and Amelia keeping? I can’t believe how much Amelia has grown; it must’ve been eight months since I last saw her.’

Mum disappeared upstairs with Amelia and soon came back with a box full of my old toys. I remembered how she used to get them out for Tommy to play with. Kirsty sat down beside Amelia, who tipped the entire contents of the box all over the floor. I smiled to myself as I thought how Tommy used to take great pleasure in doing exactly the same thing. I watched as Amelia and Kirsty played pass with my old tennis ball that had started to look a bit threadbare.

Mum sat beside me and smiled at Amelia's clumsy attempts at catching the ball before turning to me. 'Kate sends her love and she said don't worry about work, just take your time.' She paused and looked deep into my eyes. 'How are you feeling?'

I shrugged it off and tried not to cry. 'Yes I'm getting through it, one day at a time.'

'No that's not what I'm asking you. How are you really feeling? Where do you go from here?'

I hesitated. 'It hurts Mum and I feel so empty inside. A few days ago I was an expectant mum, now I'm nothing. From the first day I found out I was pregnant, I worked out how the rest of my life would be; the date he or she would be born, I imagined what my baby would look like and how good John would be with him or her, then all of a sudden, for the second time, it's all been snatched away from me. I'm trying to stay strong for John but I don't think I can go through it all again.'

Mum smiled at me sympathetically before pulling me to her to comfort me. She let go and hesitated before taking my hand and speaking. 'When I had my second miscarriage I just wanted to hide away from the world. I didn't want people's pity; I just wanted my baby back. I would look at other new mums and think how unfair it was and that there must be something wrong with me. A few weeks later I decided that I couldn't put myself through it again. Your dad comforted me and yes, he said all the right things, but I never once asked him how he felt.' She gripped my hand tighter. 'How's John feeling?'

‘He seems to be coping but he’s really worried about me.’

‘But how does he feel about the loss of his baby? Does he want to try again?’

It was my turn to hesitate. ‘I don’t know Mum, he’s never told me.’

‘I know.’ She smiled and sighed. ‘That's because he's worried about upsetting you. All he wants to do is get you through it, your dad was exactly the same.’ She continued as I started to sob. ‘Take it from me, you need to sit him down and ask him how he feels about losing his babies. You’ll have to ask him to be totally honest with you and to say exactly what he feels, whether he thinks it may hurt your feelings or not, otherwise it becomes all about you.’

I tried to smile through my tears. ‘You’re right Mum, it’s not all about me and I need to let John in.’

Just at that moment Amelia walked over and passed Mum the ball.

‘Thank you sweetie.’ Mum smiled at her.

Amelia struggled to negotiate her way up onto the sofa so I gently helped her up and she settled herself between me and Mum. Mum swiftly lifted her onto her knee and, much to Amelia’s delight, started singing pat-a-cake.

I looked from Mum to Kirsty. ‘I’ll go and make us all a cup of tea. I wouldn’t want to break up their little sing-song moment.’

I got to my feet and Mum briefly stopped mid verse. ‘Bring the biscuits back with you love.’

Kirsty stood to give me a hand and we returned a few minutes later to the sound of row the boat. We sat listening to Mum and Amelia singing when Kirsty's phone rang.

Mum was very aware of Kirsty's life with Charlie as, over the months, I had told her all about him. I told her how he phoned at eleven and three everyday to check up on her, so it came as no surprise to either of us that it was eleven o'clock and her phone was ringing. Kirsty left the room to take the call and we deliberately kept our voices down, only too aware that Kirsty wouldn't want him to know that she was with us. A few minutes later Kirsty returned.

'Sorry about that, it was Charlie just seeing how I was.'

Mum made us lunch and we stayed until about half three. As we got ready to leave Mum gave me a hug. 'Don't forget what I said. Talk to John, it's the only way forward.'

Holding her tightly, I nodded. 'Yes Mum, thank you, I will.'

Mum was the only person that could truly understand what I was going through which helped me to see things in a new light.

On the way back to Kirsty's, I looked in the rear view mirror at Amelia sitting contentedly in her seat and then at Kirsty. She looked embarrassed as she noticed me looking at her.

'I didn't mean to listen in on your conversation with your mum earlier. I know how much having a baby means to you and I really do feel for you. I want you to know that I'll always be here for you if you ever want to talk.'

‘Thank you, that really does mean a lot to me.’ I turned to smile at her as we arrived back at her house but I could see she looked anxious. ‘Are you okay?’

‘I hate to ask but are you still okay to take me to Mum’s tomorrow?’

‘Don’t be silly of course I am; I won’t let you down. You may as well leave the car seat in the car.’

‘No!’ her reply was abrupt and caught me by surprise but she didn’t seem aware and continued. ‘I’d better take it with me as Charlie might notice its missing.’

After helping her with the seat I arranged to pick her up at nine the next morning.

When I got home I thought about Mum’s advice and really felt I needed to clear the air with John sooner rather than later. I decided I would talk to him when he got home from work, so after we finished dinner and made our way into the front room, I tried to steer the conversation onto the miscarriages but I found it hard to know where to start.

‘How are you feeling?’ John asked me as we sat down. I routinely responded by saying “yes I’m fine” but I stopped myself and instead, I held his hand and took a deep breath.

‘John I want you to be honest with me, I need you to tell me how you are really feeling and how all this is affecting you. Please don’t worry about upsetting me; I just need you to be honest and open.’

He looked uneasy and paused slightly before replying. ‘When you had your first miscarriage all I could think about was you and how you felt. I looked it up on the internet and found that one in five pregnancy’s fail so I just thought we had been one of the unlucky one's. To be honest I was absolutely devastated when it happened again as I hadn't really got over the first one but I had to stay strong for you. I needed to put you first.'

I held his hand a little tighter before cautiously asking my next question. 'What about the future? Do you want us to try again?'

John's tone softened as he looked into my eyes. 'Nothing's changed, I really want a baby with you but right now I'm more worried about you and can't bear to see you go through all this physical and emotional pain. But surely we couldn't be that unlucky a third time. Look at your mum and dad, if they had given up second time around then you wouldn't be here now.'

'Well I'm not ready to give up. I want, more than anything, for us to be a family. I don't need time; I want us to try again.'

Hearing John say he wanted to try again lifted a huge weight from my shoulders and the next morning I woke feeling much better. John had already left for work and a sense of urgency took over as I realised I was supposed to be picking Kirsty up in just over half an hour. I got myself ready and out of the door in double quick time, aware that if I was late Kirsty would be waiting on the pavement with Amelia.

I pulled up outside Kirsty's house to see her struggling down the steps with the car seat in one hand and Amelia in the other. I jumped out of the car and hurried over to her, lifting Amelia into my arms as I got there.

Kirsty looked flustered. 'Thanks, I thought Amelia was going to get away from me there for a minute.'

We set off on the fifteen minute drive to Kim's and I looked over at Kirsty and tried to lighten the mood. 'You do know this is the third day in a row we have spent together don't you? That must be some sort of record.'

'I know,' she laughed. 'It's nice to have adult company during the day. I really miss that since having to give up on my nursing course.'

I decided it was a good time to test her reaction and brought up Charlie. 'What does Charlie think about you starting the course again one day?'

I immediately sensed sadness in her voice. 'No, Charlie wouldn't be happy with that. He is old fashioned, he prefers me to stay at home and look after Amelia.'

I decided not to push her but realised I hadn't got anywhere with the softly-softly approach. I cared too much for her to do nothing so thought maybe I should start to drop hints that I had sussed Charlie out and hopefully that would encourage her to open up to me.

We arrived at Kim's and Amelia excitedly called out "Nanny's house" which made us both smile. Kim gave me a clumsy hug and looked awkward as she greeted me. 'I really don't know what to say to you, I'm so sorry.'

I held her tightly. 'Honestly it's okay. John and I have been really open with each other and talked for ages, we're not going to give up and we will try again. Emotionally we're in a good place now.'

'Oh Sarah, I'm so glad to hear that. I'm sure everything will be okay next time.'

Kim went off to make us a drink and Amelia settled down at the new little plastic table and chair that Kim had bought her a few weeks ago. Deep in concentration she started to colour in her colouring book.

At eleven o'clock on the dot, Kirsty's phone rang and, like every other time, she went out of the room to answer it. With Amelia so engrossed in her colouring we couldn't help but listen in on her side of the conversation.

'Hello. Yes I'm fine thanks. You?'

'No not much just a bit of housework.'

'Oh really? So what time are you getting home then?'

'No, sorry I didn't mean it like that.'

'I know you don't have to answer to me, I was just wondering what time you were going to be home.'

'Okay I will see you at one then.'

Kirsty walked back into the room looking a bit flustered and Kim's face dropped. 'Is everything okay love?' she asked full of concern.

'No not really. Sorry Mum but I'm going to need to get back soon as Charlie's doing a half day today and will be home from work soon. He's on about going out with a couple of mates to watch the football this evening.'

I could tell Kim was slightly annoyed and wasn't going to let it go without having her say. 'Well you shouldn't go running back to him just because he clicks his fingers. I think he has too much say over you. I'm sorry but it has to be said, you need to stand up to him a bit more and you shouldn't be at his beckon call all the time. Who does he think he is treating you like this? If it wasn't for Sarah I would never see you and Amelia.'

Kirsty went quiet so I quickly stepped in. 'Its fine I can take her home.'

The atmosphere had become very tense and we decided it was time to make a move. Kim obviously felt guilty as she gave Kirsty a hug goodbye. 'I'm sorry, I don't mean to have a go love, it just frustrates me to see him treat you like this.'

Kirsty was very quiet on the journey home. I knew exactly how she was feeling and I knew her mum having a go at her like that wouldn't have helped. After dropping her off I headed for home but I couldn't help feeling that I hadn't done enough and maybe I had missed the perfect moment to say something.

Chapter 26

Christmas came and went but I couldn't really enjoy it knowing what a bad time Kirsty would be having. It had been nearly four years since I slipped back in time and only another year until I would catch up with my present time. I couldn't believe how different my two lives had become, even though they had become interwoven.

January the 14th arrived and Tommy would have been two. It was always a bad day for me in this timeline. I could still picture his second birthday in my mind and, despite Charlie's disapproval I made sure he had a good day.

The weeks passed and in mid February I had mixed emotions when my period was a couple of weeks late. I had been avoiding doing a pregnancy test for a week but felt I couldn't put it off any longer. I had been staring at the stick in total silence for what seemed like hours but which, in reality, was less than a few minutes. When the result showed PREGNANT a rush of excitement took over me but the doubts soon started to creep in. I was very aware that it could happen again and I couldn't bear going through another miscarriage.

I had decided a few months prior that if I fell pregnant again I wouldn't tell anyone, not even John. I had to be sure so I struggled through the next four weeks on my own. I constantly worried and every day I thought this could be the day that it starts to go wrong for me. At ten weeks I felt I had reached a milestone and felt much better within myself. I had passed the point when I had miscarried on the last two occasions and felt it was the right time to tell John.

I waited patiently for him to return from work one evening. I timed the dinner to perfection and had it on the table a few minutes before he walked in.

He couldn't help but notice the huge smile on my face but before he had time to speak I just blurted it out. 'John I have something to tell you. I'm pregnant again and not only that, I'm ten weeks and we have a scan booked for a week Thursday.'

He wrapped his arms around me and I could hear his voice trembling with excitement as he spoke. 'Oh Sarah that's brilliant news. Ten weeks eh? It's going to be ok this time, I just know it.'

After dinner we settled down in the front room. We talked about our future and it seemed the news had given John a second wind. He was impatient and itching to buy things for the baby's room but I was superstitious and gently reminded him that we needed to wait. I promised that we could go and have a look round the big baby superstore in Peterborough, the weekend after the scan but also reminded him that we would have to wait until the twenty week scan, to find out the sex of the baby so we really couldn't go overboard.

The next morning I was up early. I was filled with excitement as all week I had been looking forward to seeing Kirsty so I could tell her our news. I pulled up to her house and I could feel all of my pent up energy reaching boiling point. Kirsty opened the door and greeted me. Without a word I took her hand and led her into the front room.

'Is everything okay?' Kirsty asked looking bemused.

I wasn't able to hold back any longer and excitedly told her my news. 'I'm pregnant again and not only that I'm almost eleven weeks and we have the scan a week tomorrow.'

Just for a moment she looked lost for words but she quickly composed herself and, nearly squeezing the life out of me, she gave me a massive hug. 'Oh Sarah I'm so pleased for you and eleven weeks too, that's great news. I had a feeling it would be third time lucky.'

I had hardly sat down before Amelia pulled me from the sofa and ordered me to sit on the floor beside her to build a tower out of her wooden blocks. As I did, she took great delight in knocking them over when I get to about six high.

Kirsty gave a little laugh. 'I'm glad she asked you to do that as I'm getting a bit fed up with that game.'

I loved playing with Amelia, she reminded me so much of Tommy at that age. I'd noticed their facial expressions were so similar and assumed they must have got that from their dad.

Kirsty and I spent most of the day in baby chat mode and I felt a lot more comfortable talking about my pregnancy as I was nearly twelve weeks gone. Looking at the clock I noticed the time was getting on and reluctantly I got up to leave.

For the next week I was on cloud nine as every day was a day closer to the scan. I remembered back to happier times and the first time I saw Tommy on the monitor.

The day before the scan arrived and I woke up in a really happy mood. I had planned to spend the day with my best friend and her little girl and the following day, John and I would see the first image of our baby. For the first time in a long time, my life felt good and in high spirits, I made the five minute journey to Kirsty's.

When I arrived I knocked on the door but got no reply. After trying a few more times I started to get an uneasy feeling. I sensed something wasn't right and I was getting worried as I could hear Amelia. I called through the letterbox and, after calling a couple more times, I saw movement and the door slowly opened.

Kirsty looked up at me but was trying to avoid eye contact. Her left eye was badly swollen and she had bruising around her neck. She instantly burst into tears so I grabbed hold of her and gently pulled her close to me. I helped her down the hall and, entering the front room, I noticed Amelia sitting on the floor happily playing, totally unfazed by it all.

I gently eased Kirsty down onto the sofa and sat beside her before looking her straight in the eye. 'Charlie did this to you didn't he? I bet this isn't the first time either. He treats you badly doesn't he?'

Kirsty hesitated as if considering whether or not to tell me the truth. 'He hits me all the time and has always put me down. I hate him but I'm so scared of him.' She sobbed as she spoke and I moved closer to comfort her.

'I wish you had told me sooner so I could've helped you. You don't have to put up with this anymore, I'm here for you.'

Kirsty looked vulnerable as she quietly replied. 'I remember the day I met you as if it were yesterday. You were a godsend. I had already realised what a big mistake I had made with Charlie but I was twenty weeks pregnant and felt trapped. I prayed every night for a way out but I don't know what I was expecting as I'd lost all hope. I needed help and didn't know where to turn. Then you come along,' she paused as if trying to find the right words. 'I know this is going to sound strange to you but I feel someone up there has sent you to me, to help me. You gave me hope and I live for my Wednesdays plus you go out of your way taking me to Mum's every week. Also there's the money we won; I don't think we just won that randomly, I believe it was sent to us, to help me get through.'

I nodded and took her hand to encourage her to carry on.

'Sarah, I was so worried that if you found out how badly Charlie treated me then maybe I'd lose you and I couldn't risk that. I couldn't have coped without you in my life. I so wanted to tell you but how could I? You have had enough pain in your life with your two miscarriages. I just wish I could have been a better friend to you and been more supportive.'

'Now listen, you are my best friend, nobody else even comes close. You don't know how much your friendship means to me. Without you I don't think I could have got through the past few years and look at me now, it's our twelve week scan tomorrow. So now it's my turn to help you. You don't have to do this alone anymore, I am here for you. I will help you and Amelia through this.'

Kirsty became agitated and pulled her hand from mine. 'I can't let you do that; you can't imagine what he is capable of. He won't just let me go.'

'I know more than you think,' I tried to reassure her. 'I've seen his type before. I think it's time for us to go to your mum's and it may be best to pack some clothes for both you and Amelia.'

I could tell Kirsty was unsure and scared but deep down I think she knew she had to leave so she agreed and went upstairs to pack. I sat beside Amelia and gave her my full attention as I didn't want her to feel anxious. Kirsty soon emerged with a small suitcase.

'Are you ready?' I looked at her and smiled and she smiled back.

'Yes, I think so.'

We drove to Kim's in almost total silence and it brought back memories of the fear I felt when I finally escaped from Charlie. As we pulled up outside her mum's house I looked Kirsty in the eye. 'Are you ready to do this?'

She squeezed my hand and nodded. We walked into the front room and caught Kim by surprise. 'Oh my goodness, what has happened to your face? Please tell me that's not Charlie's handiwork?'

Kirsty flung her arms around Kim and burst into tears so I took Amelia to one side and tried to distract her the best I could, to give them both time to talk. I couldn't help but overhear as she told Kim everything. Her life with Charlie had been so similar to mine and it could quite easily have been me explaining my life with Charlie to my mum. It also dawned on me that Charlie knew exactly what he was doing. He had been deliberately shaping her into being what he wanted her to be.

Kim looked at me briefly before looking back at Kirsty. 'There's no way you can go back there. Please tell me it's over between you and Charlie.'

Kirsty slowly nodded. 'I want to leave him Mum, I can't take anymore but I m so scared of him. He will come here and I don't know what he is capable of.'

Kim held her tightly before beckoning her to the sofa to soothe her. 'I just wish you could've come to me earlier. I promise I won't let him hurt you anymore, you and Amelia must come back home today.'

'Mum, you don't need this. As soon as he knows where I am he will come here looking for me.'

I desperately wanted to comfort her and I quickly sat beside her and gently put my arm around her. I knew exactly what she was going through and I tried my best to console her. 'You don't have to worry anymore, you are safe now and we will see you through this.' Kirsty gently rested her head on my shoulder and I looked over at Kim. 'It might be best if I ask John to come over here after work, just to be on the safe side.'

I rang John and explained to him what had happened and how worried we all were. Without even hesitating he told me not to worry and that he would be with us at five.

I gave Kirsty a sympathetic smile. 'Everything going to be okay, John's coming here straight from work so you needn't worry, Charlie won't try anything tonight.'

Kirsty looked up at me, her eyes swollen from all her tears. 'I am so sorry.' She gave my hand a gentle squeeze before continuing. 'I never wanted to put you and John in this position. You don't know what Charlie's capable of, I really don't want to see John get hurt because of me; I couldn't bear that.'

I smiled as I thought back to the day John rescued me from my beating and reassured her. 'I don't think you need worry about that, I'm sure John can handle Charlie.'

Kirsty became tenser as the hours passed. I knew just how vulnerable she was in that moment and realised we had to keep Charlie away from her for the next few days at all costs. I looked up at the clock and it was almost five. I anxiously waited for John to arrive as I knew Charlie would get home at five thirty and that's when I was expecting it to kick off. I looked out of the window and was relieved when John's car finally pulled up. A few minutes later the door bell rang and I ran down the hall to let him in.

'Is everything okay?' he asked his face etched with concern.

'Yes, for now but I'm really worried about Kirsty, she is very vulnerable at the moment.'

We made our way back to the front room and Kim got up to greet John with a hug. He responded before turning to Kirsty to reassure her as best he could. 'You have nothing to worry about, you are safe here and you have my word that I won't let any harm come to you.'

I returned to my seat on the sofa and looked up at John. 'Charlie will probably ring soon.'

Before John could answer, Kirsty handed me her phone. 'I turned it off this morning; I couldn't face talking to him.'

John smiled reassuringly. 'We will have to turn it on.' He looked back at Kirsty as he spoke. 'It might be better if I talk to him when he rings.'

I think we were all quietly relieved that John had taken control of the situation. As we sat and waited, all the bad memories of Charlie came flooding to the forefront of my mind. I just prayed Kirsty was strong enough to see it through. For the next half hour the room fell into an almost deadly silence, only broken by Amelia's playful chatter.

Kirsty's phone rang at five forty-two and I instantly went cold. We all nervously looked at each other and John paused for a few seconds, took a deep breath and then leaned over to the coffee table to pick it up.

He looked back at Kirsty. 'It's Charlie, are you ready for this?'

Kirsty nervously cleared her throat and croakily said yes. John answered and immediately put the phone on loud speaker so we could all hear the conversation.

'Hi this is John. Kirsty doesn't want to speak to you.'

The phone went quiet as Charlie had obviously been caught off guard.

'Well errr, I don't know what she has been telling you but I need to speak to her, could you put her on please.'

'No, honestly she needs time away from you and she will be staying with me and Sarah for a while.'

'Look,' Charlie's tone changed and we could hear the rage in his voice. 'Whatever you think has happened, you are wrong. She fell and banged her head and with all due respect, this is really between me and her.'

'Sorry Charlie, as I said she has decided to stay with us for a while and needs time to think. As far as we are concerned she can stay with us as long as she wants, I'm going to hang up now.'

John hung up and slid the phone back onto the coffee table.

'Thanks John you handled that brilliantly.' I couldn't help but hug him, I was so proud of him.

'You should be safe now' he said looking over at Kirsty and smiling. 'He thinks you're round our house so he shouldn't bother you here.'

Out of the corner of my eye I could see Kim's face was full of concern. 'But what about you two?' she asked. 'What if he comes and hassles you?'

John turned to smile at Kim this time. 'I'd like to see him try. I've met his type before, he's not likely to bother me but if he does I can handle him. Anyway I'm at home until Monday as we're going for our twelve week scan tomorrow.'

Kirsty let out a sigh of relief as he talked but took my hand when he mentioned the scan. 'I'm so sorry I've got you involved,' she said turning to me. 'You really don't need this hassle right now, especially with what you have been through over the past few months.'

'I'm just glad we got you away from him' I replied. 'You and Amelia deserve so much more from life. We can all look to the future now; you and Amelia deserve to be happy.'

Kirsty's shoulders dropped and she started to look more at ease. 'I'm really glad it's worked out for you both this time, I can't wait to see your scan picture.'

'We will come round straight after the scan tomorrow so you can see it first.'

John pulled his old mobile phone out of his coat pocket, complete with charger and handed it to Kirsty. 'I've put ten pound credit on it and programmed mine and Sarah's numbers in. It's probably best if you keep your other phone switched off as he will hassle you.'

John and I got up to leave as it was getting late but I stopped to give Kirsty one last hug. 'Remember we're here for you, you don't have to do this alone.'

John briefly hugged Kim and tried to reassure her again. 'Any problems ring me, I can be here within fifteen minutes day or night, I promise.'

She smiled up at him. 'Thank you, that means a lot and I'm looking forward to seeing the scan picture tomorrow.'

On the way home, I couldn't help but worry about Kirsty. I knew how much she was going to need us over the coming weeks and I knew we would have to be strong for her but I was also feeling positive. She would get through it, she was safe and she had John and me as back up. I just knew everything was going to be okay.

As we passed Charlie's house I was relieved to see his car still parked up outside. I didn't think he would try anything immediately but, knowing Charlie, he would probably come round when he thought John was at work. Even so, as long as he thought Kirsty was with us she would be safe.

Chapter 27

The next morning I woke early after a troubled nights sleep. My mind had been filled with a mixture of anxiety about Kirsty and excitement about the scan. Whilst getting ready I found a quiet moment to talk to Tommy. I told him that I would be thinking about him when we saw his brother or sister for the first time.

Just before we left for the hospital I rang Kirsty on her new mobile. She seemed to be quite optimistic about her future and I was relieved to hear that Charlie hadn't been in touch but I knew Charlie wouldn't leave it there. John and I planned to spend the day with Kirsty when we left the hospital. All we could do was take one day at a time until she was strong enough to put all this behind her.

We arrived for the scan with twenty minutes to spare. As we sat down John took my hand and gave me his usual warm smile. I felt a little sad as I thought back to the last two times we had been there. I remembered Dad once telling me that, however hard their two miscarriages' had been, it had made his bond with me even closer.

We didn't have to wait long before we were called in. As I settled on the bed I noticed that it wasn't Carol doing my scan today. I took Johns hand and smiled up at the lady doing the sonograph.

'I'm Jane' she said smiling back warmly. 'Carol has decided to let me loose on you today.'

I felt I needed to explain to her about my last two miscarriages but soon thought better of it. John squeezed my hand as we eagerly looked up at the monitor. A few minutes passed and she eventually located our baby. Without taking her eyes off of the screen she asked how many weeks along I was.

'Nearly thirteen weeks now' I replied before smiling at John.

After a few more minutes she looked back at me and I noticed a glimmer of uncertainty in her eyes. 'I just need to bring in my colleague. I will be back in a minute.'

I looked at John and he tried to give me a reassuring smile but he couldn't hide his concern and I worried that something was wrong. Jane returned with Carol who smiled as she took over the scan. I was apprehensive as I looked at John then back at the screen. I tried to reason with myself that maybe the other midwife was newly qualified and not that confident but a few more minutes passed and I really started to worry. I stared at Carol desperately trying to read her facial expression.

'Sarah' she said her face emotionless, 'I think we need to do an internal scan just to get a better view.'

A wave of fear started to grip me as she spoke as I had to have internal scans after both of my miscarriages. I looked at John, giving him a nervous smile. He squeezed my hand tightly as we both turned to concentrate on the monitor. I could see something but I wasn't sure what. Carol studied it for a moment before trying to get a better position. Shortly after she looked back at us and her face filled with sympathy.

‘I am so sorry’ she said, ‘by the size and with no heartbeat I’m afraid your pregnancy stopped at nine weeks.’

I heard her saying the words but she may as well have been speaking a foreign language. I couldn’t take any of it in; I just felt numb. John pulled me close but I kept thinking that it couldn’t be true, that they must have made a mistake. I looked John in the eye, he was trying to hold it together and do his best to reassure me at the same time but his eyes couldn’t lie. The next ten minutes were a blur and as the numbness subsided panic took over. I needed to get out of there.

‘John please take me home, I just want to go home.’

Carol was saying something to John but I pulled him towards the door and we left.

Back home, I just wanted to go to bed. I didn’t want to talk to anyone. I just wanted to be left alone. I didn’t cry, for if I let myself cry then somehow it must be true but it wasn’t true. I still felt pregnant. I hadn’t bled or had any cramps so they must have got it wrong. Plus I had reached thirteen weeks so I should have been safe. I lay there drifting in and out of sleep until eventually I fell into a deep sleep.

I was awoken the next morning by bright sunshine streaming through the small gap in the curtains. I looked at the clock and saw it was quarter past nine. John’s side of the bed was empty and I wasn’t even sure if he had come up last night. I needed to see him so I wrapped my dressing gown around me and slowly made my way downstairs. John must have heard me as he met me at the bottom of the stairs. I looked him in the eye and with great urgency I told him we needed to go back to the hospital. I could tell he was bewildered so I carried on.

'They have got it wrong, I saw my baby on the monitor and I'm still pregnant.'

John took my hand and led me into the front room and sat me down.

'We need to get back to the hospital' I repeated. 'We need to have another scan. I'm not imagining it. I definitely saw something on the monitor.'

I tried to stand but John didn't let me.

'Sarah please don't do this to yourself. It stopped at nine weeks, I saw it myself. There was no heartbeat.' He hesitated for a few minutes. 'I'm really sorry but we have to face facts, nature may take it's course in the next few days but either way we have an appointment at the hospital next week.'

I still didn't want to believe what he was saying to me but hearing it out loud made me realise that, deep down, I knew I had lost my baby. I just couldn't face up to it as I had been so certain that everything was okay this time around.

For the next few days I was lost in my own grief. I just lay on the sofa not really wanting to talk. I just wanted to be alone with my thoughts. It was early on the Thursday morning when reality caught up with me. I noticed a small amount of blood and knew that it had started but it wasn't until the next morning that I started to feel mild cramps. I knew the feeling only too well and knew exactly what the next few hours would bring. The cramps gradually became more and more painful.

I called out to John. ‘I think this is it, it’s starting again.’ My voice trembled and he took my hand. Without a word he pulled me close and held me.

John didn’t leave my side all afternoon and evening. The pain became unbearable and just before midnight nature took its course. I walked back into the bedroom, totally drained. I just needed to be with John and to sleep.

The next morning I woke to an overwhelming feeling of emptiness. I couldn’t get out of bed and face the world I just wanted to sleep and forget. Questions kept running around in my head: what was wrong with me? Why did this keep happening to me? I remembered Dad once saying it was because the time wasn’t right. Maybe the time would never be right or maybe I was being punished by Tommy’s Angel. In her eyes I had denied him life and so maybe now I had to pay the price.

For the next few days I stayed in my own little bubble. I couldn’t even begin to think of trying again as I couldn’t handle another miscarriage. I told John that I couldn't go through anymore pain and didn’t want to try again. He agreed for my sake but I could see the huge disappointment in his eyes.

A few more days passed before I decided I needed to get out. Then I thought about Kirsty and realised it had been almost a week since she had left Charlie.

‘John,’ I called out, ‘I have to see Kirsty. She must think I have abandoned her. Does she know what happened? I need to tell her why I haven’t been round and about my miscarriage.’

John gently squeezed my arm. 'It's okay I've already told Kim about your miscarriage and she said she would break it to her.'

'I really need to see her today, can we go?'

John hesitated and looked down at the floor. I sensed he was hiding something from me and I started to feel uneasy. 'Is everything okay?'

He slowly looked up at me but paused before speaking. I could see he was desperately trying to work out what he was going to say. 'I've been trying to find the right time to tell you. I'm afraid Charlie has got to her, she must have switched her phone back on.' He avoided eye contact and looked back at the floor before continuing. 'I've been speaking to Kim and she told me that Charlie persuaded her to go back with him two days ago. She has left Amelia with Kim.'

My whole body went cold and I stared at John in stunned silence. It had obviously been too much for her and I wasn't there for her when she was at her most vulnerable. I felt I had totally let her down. I shook my head. 'I have to go and see her. I need to see her now; I need to know she is alright.'

John must have realised that I wasn't going to take no for an answer and nodded. 'Okay we'll both go.'

As we pulled up to the house, I noticed Charlie's car parked outside. I looked over at John. 'I don't care if he's there. I am still going in to talk to her no matter what he says.'

'Are you sure you are up to this?' His voice was full of concern for me.

‘Yes definitely, I’ve let her down and I need to put this right.’

‘Well, I won’t let you go alone; I’m coming in with you’

Giving him a half hearted smile I pulled at the car door handle. ‘Okay that’s fine. I just need to have a few minutes alone with her, without him around.’

We walked up to the house and I nervously knocked on the door. It swung open and Charlie stood in front of us, his face red with anger. He looked from me to John and then back at me. ‘Haven’t you two done enough damage already? Just get lost will you.’ He tried to slam the door shut but John quickly wedged his foot in the opening. That really annoyed Charlie and his face turned a darker shade of red. ‘Move your foot now or I will phone the police.’

‘Oh please do, I am sure that they will be very interested to know how Kirsty got that black eye and the bruises around her neck.’ I looked Charlie right in the eye as I replied; I wanted him to know I wasn’t scared of him.

He looked slightly taken aback. ‘Okay so what do you want?’

‘I want to see Kirsty. I need to make sure she is okay and that she’s not being held against her will. If you don't, I will call the police myself and say she has been beaten and I think she is in danger.’

Charlie's tone changed as he began to realise I wasn’t bluffing. He shrugged his shoulders. ‘Okay I haven’t anything to hide. You have five minutes but just you, not your boyfriend.’

John didn't like the idea of me going in alone but I gave him a quick hug and told him everything would be okay and I wouldn't be long. Charlie moved aside and I made my way past him but before he could shut the door John moved to within a few inches of him. 'You lay one finger on Sarah and I promise you, it will be the last thing you ever do.'

'Hey what sort of man do you think I am? You've got me all wrong.' Charlie grinned nervously before turning and shutting the door behind me. He led me to the front room where I spotted Kirsty sitting on the sofa. My heart sank as she looked so lost and forlorn.

I gave Charlie an icy stare. 'Can I have some time alone with Kirsty please?'

A false smile flickered across his face and he reluctantly turned to leave. 'Okay, that's fine I'll leave you for five minutes.'

He shut the door behind him and I went to sit beside Kirsty. I took her hand and she looked up at me and nervously smiled. 'I am so sorry about your baby,' she whispered. 'I was devastated when I heard the news and I haven't been able to stop thinking about it since.'

I felt myself welling up all over again and struggled to get my words out. 'I'm really sorry I let you down. I should have been there for you but I can make up for it now. John is outside, just say the word and we will get you out of here.'

Kirsty loosened her grip of my hand and avoided eye contact. She hesitated for a moment before answering. 'I need a little time by myself to think this through so it may be for the best if we don't see each other for a while. It will only make things worse. Charlie's taken my phone off me and he says you and John are a bad influence and are trying to turn me against him.'

I gently retook her hand. 'What about Amelia? She needs to be with you.'

Kirsty briefly looked me in the eye. 'Charlie said it's best to leave her with Mum for a couple of weeks until everything settles down. Then we can become a family again.'

'Do you still have the phone John gave you?' I whispered not wanting Charlie to hear.

She nodded and whispered back. 'Yes I've put it somewhere safe.'

Charlie came in before we could talk anymore. His arrogant smile made my blood boil but I held my tongue in check and let him speak.

'Is everything okay then?' he asked.

'Yes everything's fine.' I answered curtly whilst smiling through gritted teeth. I really didn't want to leave her with him but I realised I had no choice. Kirsty looked up at me as I stood to leave and I mouthed the words "ring me" before turning away. Charlie gently took my arm and led me into the kitchen before pausing for a moment. He looked me straight in the eye and I felt he was going to try and reason with me.

'I'm really worried about Kirsty,' he said. 'I think she has some sort of delayed post natal depression and I'm worried she's a danger to herself. Life hasn't been easy for me recently and she lashes out at me all the time. Its like the other week, I tried to reason with her and calm her down but she was mad with rage, it was too much, she fell and banged her face bruising her eye. I know she always feels guilty afterwards but she's like a woman possessed. I'm really worried she might hurt Amelia. I need to get her help as she really scares me at times. I think it would better for her wellbeing if you could stay away for a while, just until she is better.'

I couldn't believe what he had just said to me. I was so angry I felt like screaming at the top of my voice, you liar, but a loud banging on the front door stopped me and instead I made my excuses.

Charlie opened the door and as I squeezed past him he gave me a clumsy hug. 'It's just for now,' he said. 'Things will be better in a month or two you'll see.'

As I walked back to the car with John he gave me a puzzled look. 'What on earth was all that about?'

I told him about the conversation and how I didn't believe a word of it. I also told him how I had tried to convince Kirsty to leave him. After talking, we decided we needed to see Kim. I really didn't know what we were going to say to her as I thought she was relying on us to convince Kirsty to come home.

As we pulled up outside Kim's I looked over at John. He looked as depressed as I felt and we made our way up the drive in silence. Seeing Kim's expectant face at the door was too much and all I could do was apologise. 'I am so sorry; I really tried my best to get her to come home.'

Kim gave me a hug and nodded sadly. 'I know you did, it's alright. We will sort this.'

As I went in I saw Amelia sat on the floor playing with a doll. My heart broke seeing her for the first time without Kirsty. She looked so small and lost on her own.

I told Kim what Charlie had said and she vigorously shook her head. 'That's absurd, I know my daughter, she's the gentlest person I know and to suggest that she could harm Amelia is laughable. It's obvious that he knows we are on to him and he's trying to take back control.'

'I know and I'm going to convince her to come home. Charlie is trying to break her contact with us, that's why he took her phone away but she still has the one John gave her. It's Saturday tomorrow so I won't be able to see her alone until Monday and that's only if Charlie goes to work.'

I tried my best to comfort Kim as she started to cry.

'I can't bear the thought of her being alone with him,' she sobbed. 'Goodness only knows how he is treating her. She should be here, at home, with me and Amelia.'

I hated seeing Kim so upset and I just wanted to make everything better for her. I knew how dangerous Charlie could be when cornered and I just prayed that if he pushed her too far she would ring me. We stayed with Kim for most of the day as I didn't want to leave her like she was but eventually we had to leave. As we got ready to go a thought came to me. 'Why don't I pick you up on Monday and we can take Amelia to Kirsty and convince her to come home with us. We stand a better chance without Charlie around.'

'Oh that's a good idea. I'm sure we can convince her between us.' Kim seemed brighter and I arranged to see her Monday.

On the journey home, I felt more optimistic about Monday. I was sure that, with Kim's help and Charlie at work, I could convince Kirsty to come home. The weekend dragged and I couldn't get Kirsty out of my mind. All I could think about was Monday. I had been hoping she would ring me beforehand and ask us to come and get her but I heard nothing.

I didn't get much sleep Sunday night for thinking about what may happen. I had arranged to pick Kim up around ten thirty so I left just before ten. On my way I drove past Kirsty's and my heart sank as I spotted Charlie's car outside. I pulled over and rang Kim with the bad news. I could hear the disappointment in her voice.

'It's alright,' I reassured her, 'I'm not going back to work until next week and Charlie will have to go back to work at some point, I just hope its tomorrow.'

For the next three days I routinely checked, only to see Charlie's car sitting outside every day. By Thursday I had come to the conclusion that Charlie had taken the whole week off. I really needed to talk to Kirsty as I knew exactly how Charlie operated. He would be doing everything he could to make her feel bad about herself and turn her against us. I remembered how Charlie had a way of getting right into my head and making me feel worthless, he would also use Tommy to keep me in line. He had a way of making me doubt myself and if you are told often enough that you are a bad mum then eventually you start to believe it. For a long time he had me exactly where he wanted me.

I knew he would be doing exactly the same to Kirsty. We had backed Charlie into a corner and I just knew he would be throwing everything at her, both emotionally and physically, to regain total control over her. I had a good idea how she would be feeling and just how vulnerable she was.

It really looked like it was going to be Monday before I would get to see Kirsty and I just hoped Kim and I could reason with her when we did.

Chapter 28

John took Friday off work as we had an appointment at the hospital to check that nature had taken its course and everything was okay with me.

We arrived at the hospital a few minutes late and I really didn't want to be there. It was Carol that saw us. She was very sympathetic and, although she said all the right things, I couldn't help but associate her with all the negative things that had happened. As I had expected the scan showed that the baby had gone and nature had taken its course.

'I'm so sorry to be the bearer of bad news' she smiled compassionately but I really didn't want to stick around to hear her sympathy so we made our way back to the car.

'Shall we go and see your mum for a few hours.' John suggested.

I think he realised how much Mum helped me and I really appreciated his thoughtfulness. As we pulled out of the hospital car park I started to reply but mid sentence I glanced over at Charlie's house. 'Stop!' I shouted grabbing John's arm.

He just about managed to look in his rear view mirror before slamming on the brakes and screeching to a halt. He looked really alarmed and wide eyed. 'What's wrong? What's happened?' I could hear the panic in his voice but I was hardly able to speak so I pointed frantically at Charlie's house.

'Charlie's not there, his cars gone. We need to get to Kim's. I will ring her on the way.'

John pulled away again as I rang Kim. 'Kim, Charlie's not at home. This is our chance. We can be at yours in fifteen minutes.'

'Ok I'll be ready and waiting with Amelia, see you soon.'

John looked over at me. 'What if he's just popped out for a minute?'

'Well that's just a chance we're going to have to take. I just hope we can get her alone and convince her to come back with us. All I know for sure is that I won't leave without her.'

Without a word John gave me a knowing smile and nodded.

To my surprise Kim was already waiting on her doorstep. We quickly got Amelia into her car seat and made our way back. I looked round at Kim and sensed she was nervous so I tried my best to reassure her. 'It's going to be okay. I'm sure as soon as she sees Amelia she'll want to come back with us, you'll see.'

With a vague smile she replied. 'I really do hope so; I can't bear the thought of her spending another day alone with him.'

John pulled up outside Charlie's house and we were all relieved that Charlie s car was nowhere to be seen. Standing at the door I looked nervously at John and then at Kim. I knocked, just hoping that Kirsty would answer. I tried three more times and still there was no answer.

'Try her on the phone I gave her,' John suggested.

I rang the number and there was a dialling tone. I listened intently before realising I could hear the phone ringing inside the house. After a minute it went to voicemail so I tried again but again there was no answer.

As a last ditch attempt and more out of desperation than belief I tried the door handle. I was shocked to find the door open and tentatively we made our way in. I called out for Kirsty as we slowly made our way into the kitchen. To my surprise Kirsty's phone was on the kitchen table but there was no sign of her.

John turned to Kim. 'I'll try upstairs, you two look down here.'

After a few minutes it became apparent that she wasn't at home and I started to feel nauseous. 'This isn't right, I'm worried. There is no way that she would just leave the phone on full view like that.'

'Maybe she just popped into town and forgot the phone.' I'm not sure if John was trying to convince us or himself but he wasn't doing either.

'I think we should take it with us just in case Charlie comes back.' I lifted the phone from the table as John looked at his watch. 'It's nearly two' he said. 'Let's go and have something to eat and come back in an hour or two as she may be back by then.'

I didn't really have much of an appetite but I agreed to John's idea. I was so worried about Kirsty and I just prayed she would be home by the time we got back. After lunch we made our way back to the house and to my relief Charlie's car still wasn't there. Kim decided to stay in the car with Amelia while John and I went in.

We soon realised that Kirsty still wasn't back and I felt frustrated, knowing we would have to wait until Monday to try again. I could see the disappointment on Kim's face as we got back in the car and I felt I needed to say something positive. 'I won't give up on her; we will try again on Monday.'

Back at Kim's, I could see how much everything had affected her. I really didn't want to leave her straight away so we stayed for a few hours and decided to leave at Amelia's bed time. Kim thanked us for our help and drew me in for a hug.

'We will come for you at nine Monday morning' I said, 'but if you hear anything in the meantime then please ring me.'

Kim nodded as she wiped a few tears from her cheek.

On the way back we spotted Charlie's car outside the house and I couldn't help but wonder if they had gone out together for the day. Then I thought about the phone and how it was so unlike Kirsty just to leave it out on the table. Maybe he had found it and he knew it had come from us but what would that mean for Kirsty. Also, I couldn't get over the fact that the door had been left unlocked. That was so unlike Charlie; he would always lock the door whenever he went out, he was a stickler for it. Something wasn't right and I really wanted to stop and sort it out there and then but I worried that by doing that, I would make Kirsty's situation even worse.

All evening I thought about Kirsty and it really frustrated me that I couldn't do anything until Monday.

'Kirsty's been away from Amelia for a week now,' I said to John over dinner. 'I hate not knowing what her state of mind is. I need to know she is okay.'

John reached across the table and took my hand. 'We will sort this out, one way or another, on Monday.'

'I could do with Charlie not being there but if he is we are still going, I will threaten him with the police if he stands in our way.' I just felt it had been going on for far too long and John was right we needed to sort it out and soon.

On Saturday morning we decided to pop out and I noticed Charlie's car was still outside his house. I wanted to go and speak to Kirsty then but I knew I needed to be patient and stick to our plan.

Later that evening, just after our dinner, I got a call from Kim and she was hysterical. I couldn't make out a word she was saying.

'It's Charlie!' she screamed down the phone. 'He's banging on my door and shouting at me to let him in, he's upsetting Amelia, I don't know what to do.'

'Phone the police now, John and I are on our way.' I tried to calm her down as John grabbed his car keys. Within seconds we were out of the door. We arrived at Kim's in half the time it usually took and found Charlie banging on the front window.

John jumped out of the car and grabbed hold of his arm. 'What's your problem?' he shouted at him. I'd never seen him so angry.

Charlie quickly pulled his arm away and shouted back in his face. 'I want to see Kirsty. What have you done with her?'

'What do you mean? Are you saying she's not with you?' I could hear the confusion in John's voice and he turned to look at me.

Just then two police cars screeched to a halt right next to us, sirens blaring and blue lights flashing. Their arrival really set Charlie off and he started shouting at the police officers as they approached him. 'They've kidnapped my girlfriend and daughter and won't let me see them.'

The closest police officer took his arm and tried to calm him down but in a real temper he managed to shake him off and lash out. It took three of them to eventually wrestle him to the ground and it was only when his face was pressed firmly to the floor that he calmed down. They bundled him into one of the cars to keep him calm and talk to him.

Kim let us in and, after a few minutes talking to Charlie, two of the police officers came in to speak to us. I told them everything that had happened over the past week and how we went to Kirsty and Charlie's house yesterday.

The officers looked at each other a little oddly and then back at me. 'Charlie has just told us that he hasn't seen Kirsty since yesterday morning just before going to work. Has she got a mobile number we could try? Charlie was quite evasive when we asked him.'

'That's because he took her phone off of her a week ago to stop her contacting anyone.' I glanced over at John and then back at the officer who had spoken. 'Wait a minute, John gave her his old phone last week but when we went round yesterday she had left it on the table in the kitchen which I found unusual. Charlie didn't know about the phone so we thought it was best that we brought it back with us.'

Taking the phone from his pocket John handed it to one of the officers who promptly scrolled through the contacts. He came across the only number that Kirsty had rung and held the phone in front of us so we could see it. 'Do you recognise this number? She called it yesterday morning at nine thirty-two.'

I shook my head and I could see John was shaking his too. 'No but it's a local number.' I replied.

The officer decided to ring the number and it soon became apparent that it was a local cab firm. The officer looked at Kim as if he wanted to reassure her. 'It looks like Kirsty ordered a cab yesterday morning. Because of her emotional state and the fact nobody has heard from her for over twenty-four hours, we are taking this very seriously. My colleague is going to follow up this lead with the taxi firm but if you can think of anywhere she might have gone then it would be most helpful.'

'This really isn't like Kirsty,' Kim paused and took a deep breath, 'Charlie must have really scared her this time, she wouldn't just leave Amelia. He wouldn't let her have friends; she only has me and Sarah in her life. I'm really worried about, please find her.'

'Well, as I said, we are taking this very seriously and we should be able to find out where the taxi took her.' The officers got up to leave.

‘You need to know,’ Kim stopped and wiped away the tears that had started to roll down her cheeks. ‘Kirsty is not safe with Charlie. You must keep her away from him. I think she left because she doesn’t feel safe around here with Charlie so near. You saw how violent he is. Please, I’m begging you, bring her home and reassure her that the police can protect her.’

Both officers smiled reassuringly at Kim but it was the shorter of the two that spoke. ‘We will be taking Charlie in for voluntary questioning and you can be assured we will be telling him, in no uncertain terms, to stay away from you and Kirsty. When we find Kirsty, you will need to convince her to press charges against him and then we can do the rest. We will be in touch as soon as we know something.’

Kim just about managed to keep her emotions together until both officers left but, as the door shut behind them, she broke down in a flood of tears. I rushed to her side and held her. ‘Hey they are going to find her and bring her back. The police are involved now and Charlie can’t get to her.’

John and I stayed late and only left when Kim decided to go to bed.

‘We will come back tomorrow morning,’ I told her as we hugged goodbye, ‘and remember, think positively, Kirsty will be back with us tomorrow.’

Kim smiled as best she could. ‘I really do hope so; I can’t take much more of this.’

John and I arrived home totally exhausted and decided to go straight to bed. I didn’t stir until the next morning when I was woken early by the sound of my phone ringing.

I looked up at the clock and it read seven twenty-two. I tried to focus on my phone screen and noticed it was Kim ringing.

'Hi Kim is everything okay?' I was still half asleep as I answered and the unfamiliar voice at the other end of the line threw me. 'Hi Sarah, this is Amy, I am a police officer. Kim has asked me to call you to find out if you could come round here as soon as possible?'

I quickly told her that we were on our way and ended the call so I could wake John.

'John, John.' I shook him and he turned over sleepily to face me. 'John, we need to go, the police are with Kim and she needs us.'

He was up within seconds and we were in the car within ten minutes. Thankfully, as it was a Sunday morning, there was hardly any traffic on the road. John didn't hang about and we arrived at Kim's in no time at all.

We were met at the door by Amy and I instantly sensed her sombre mood. We followed her into the front room to find Kim sitting on the sofa with her sister Suzanne. I could see they were both in a really distressed state so I looked back at Amy. 'What's happened? Has something happened to Kirsty?'

Amy took my arm and guided me to the kitchen. I could see John following closely behind. She asked us to sit at the table before pulling out the chair opposite. She looked me in the eye and cleared her throat to speak. 'I'm sorry to tell you that we found a body yesterday evening that matches the description of Kirsty.'

I felt light headed and the room seemed to spin so I closed my eyes and rested my head in my hands. It took a few minutes for the reality of what had just been said to sink in and John and I sat in total silence. As my head cleared I looked up at John and then over at Amy. 'What do you mean it matches Kirsty? Did Charlie kill her?'

Amy hesitated for a minute before replying. 'No. It looks like she took her own life. A dog walker found her body last night at the bottom of a cliff. It couldn't have been an accident as she would have had to climb a gate and small fence to get to the top. We know she ordered a taxi Friday morning and it has been confirmed, by the driver, that she was on her own and that was where she was dropped off.'

I could hear the words coming out of Amy's mouth but I didn't believe that she was talking about Kirsty. Still feeling a little shaky, I tried to get to my feet so I could go to Kim. John helped me make my way back to the front room where Kim was still sitting with her sister. She looked up at me and I immediately froze; all I could do was stare at her, not knowing what to say or do. She stood and came to me and as she grabbed hold of me I instantly burst into tears. I let her gently guide me to the sofa and I could feel Suzanne's hand squeeze mine as I sat down but all I could do was cling onto Kim.

John saw Amy to the door and politely thanked her for her help before returning to the front room.

We sat in stunned silence, not really knowing what to say or think. It was only broken by Amelia's sleepy voice calling for her Nan, from the stair gate at the top of the stairs. Kim immediately jumped to her feet and disappeared up the stairs. My heart broke as she returned with Amelia in her arms. A vision of how Kirsty used to greet me at the front door with Amelia in her arms immediately filled my mind. The thought that this little girl would never see her mummy again was too much for me. I couldn't accept that she was gone and I would never see her again.

I had honestly thought that the worst was behind her. I started to feel guilty that it was me that had persuaded her to leave Charlie and then I couldn't be there for her when she needed me the most. She wasn't strong enough to do it without me. My heart felt completely broken but I knew we had to put on a brave face for Amelia's sake.

We sat for a while and talked about Kirsty. Suzanne explained to me that the place Kirsty had taken her own life at was a popular beauty spot. She told me how she used to go there as a child with her mum and dad and how it was a place she had always loved.

I looked up at John. 'I want to go there, I need to understand and I need to see it for myself.'

Suzanne took my hand and nodded. 'Maybe we could all go there and lay some flowers but it can't be today. Kim and I need to go and identify Kirsty's body later this afternoon and afterwards Kim is going to come and stay with me and my husband for a while. How about Tuesday? We can all go and lay some flowers in her memory.'

'Yes I really would like that.' I half heartedly smiled and we arranged for them both to come to ours on Tuesday so we could go together.

I felt that Kim and Suzanne needed time alone as it was going to be tough for them having to identify Kirsty's body. I thought they would need some time to mentally prepare so John and I made our excuses and left.

When we got home it finally started to sink in that I would never see Kirsty again. I couldn't bear to think how Charlie must have been treating her in the last week of her life. He might not have physically pushed her over the cliff but he certainly pushed her mentally over the edge. I had lost everything: my dad, Tommy, my three unborn babies and now Kirsty. I also thought about Amelia and how she would have to live the rest of her life without her mum.

The next day I couldn't face anybody. John rang Kate and then my mum and told them both what had happened to Kirsty and that I needed time. I lay in bed for most of the day, thoughts of Kirsty's state of mind in the week leading up to her death went round and round in my head.

On Tuesday morning I had to force myself to get up. I realised John must have gone out whilst I had been in bed the day before as he had bought a beautiful bouquet of flowers for Kirsty. I smiled and thanked him; it meant so much to me that he had been thinking of me.

Suzanne and Kim were due at half ten and I sat anxiously staring out of the window waiting for them. It wasn't long before a car I didn't recognise pulled up outside and I shouted out to John.

'Are you ready?' he smiled reassuringly.

I gave a little nod and headed to the door to meet them. I gave Kim a hug and said hello to Suzanne who explained that they had left Amelia with Suzanne's husband as they thought it was for the best. John grabbed his car keys and

Suzanne and Kim clambered into the back as he started the engine.

'I'm not sure how to get there.' John said turning to Kim. 'Do you remember the way?'

Kim looked slightly unsure. 'I think I do. It's been a few years but I don't think it'll be that hard to find.'

It was a thirty minute drive from our house and the last ten minutes were off the beaten track but with Kim's help we managed to find it. It was a sobering thought realising that it was the place that Kirsty spent the last hours of her life.

We walked past a solitary wooden picnic bench and I couldn't help but wonder if Kirsty had sat there contemplating her very last actions. A thought came to me as we continued along the narrow path; by deliberately leaving her phone behind, she had no way of contacting the outside world, she must have already made her mind up that she wasn't coming back.

The cliff edge was fenced off and there was a large gate fixed shut with a rusty old padlock. The view was breathtaking. I could understand why Kim would have brought Kirsty here as a child.

Kim carefully squeezed her bouquet of flowers between the panels of the gate before taking a moment to reflect. I patiently waited to place mine and John's flowers beside Kim's. I sensed none of us were in a rush to leave so I suggested we go and sit on the wooden bench.

Kim told us of the times she sat on the same bench with Kirsty and her husband. The three of them would come once or twice a year and bring a packed lunch. 'Kirsty would love to play ball with her dad,' she said wistfully, 'then she would sit on his knee and watch the sunset in the distance.' As I imagined a young Kirsty enjoying the sunset it made me wonder if she had done the same thing before taking her life.

Kim hesitated for a second, deep in thought. 'Maybe that's what drew her here? She always said this place held some of the best memories of her dad.'

After a while we decided it was time to head back but before we left Kim turned to me. 'You two have been through so much. You and Kirsty were so close and I am so glad she had you in her life. You need time with John now but please don't be a stranger. I hope you two can find it in your heart's to spend time with me and Amelia, that little girl dotes on you.'

I grabbed hold of Kim. 'I want that more than anything, I was worried that with Kirsty gone you wouldn't want us in your life.'

'Oh goodness no. Please don't ever think that, we need you and want you in our lives more than ever now. I have always seen you and John as a part of my family.'

Over the following few days John and I spent most of our time alone together at home. We talked a lot about Kirsty and our miscarriages. My head was all over the place and I really didn't think I could cope with anymore heartache in my life. I didn't even want to think about trying for a baby again. All I could think about was Kim and Amelia; I was desperate to see them but thought it was best to give them time alone to grieve.

Then came the call from Kim confirming that Kirsty's funeral was booked for the coming Friday. I felt both sad and relieved that I could finally say goodbye to her. I had started to realise that all the decisions we make in life have an effect on someone else. Because I chose a different path and didn't meet Charlie, I had ended my best friend's life and left her little girl without a mum.

Chapter 29

The day of Kirsty's funeral arrived and I still couldn't believe it had come to this point. She was only twenty-four years old. She was my best friend and I would have to live with the guilt of her death for the rest of my life. I blamed myself; I knew what Charlie was capable of and I didn't do enough to help her. I let my best friend down when she needed me the most. If only I had made it to the club that night and relived my life with Charlie. Our paths wouldn't have crossed but at least she would still be alive. She would have been living a different life now. I could only guess at what sort of life she would have had but it could have been a beautiful life, with a decent man and maybe children. I had failed Kirsty when she depended on me and my best just wasn't good enough. That was something I would never, ever get over. I shouldn't have interfered with my past and because I did, I had lost two of the most beautiful people in my life, Tommy and Kirsty.

The funeral was at half eleven but John and I wanted to get there early, so we set off just after half ten. We hardly said a word in the car as I think John sensed I would prefer my private thoughts. We soon arrived at the crematorium but I really had no memory of the car journey what so ever. John parked up and opened my door for me. He took my hand and smiled at me sympathetically. We made our way to the crematorium entrance in silence.

There was a good size crowd standing outside but I didn't recognise many of them. I think they were mainly Kirsty's family as I didn't think any of Charlie's would turn up. I spotted Kim and Suzanne as they arrived in the lead funeral car and I headed straight over to them. As they got out I was the first to give Kim a hug. I tried to stay strong for her but I soon felt tears running down my face. I felt emotional and guilty. 'I'm so sorry. I haven't stopped thinking about how I could have done more to save her.'

Kim held me tightly and, with tears in her own eyes, she comforted me. 'Now you listen to me, you never, ever need to feel sorry. You were the best friend my daughter could have asked for and I'm really happy that she had you in her life. This is all that man's fault and don't you ever forget that.'

'I was really worried he was going to be here today.'

Kim gave me a knowing smile before looking around at the crowd of people who had come to pay their respects. 'I think there are enough people here today who would gladly escort him out, if he did have the nerve to show his face.'

I felt void of all emotions as we followed behind Kirsty's coffin. It was one of the hardest things I had ever had to do. Kim asked John and me if we would sit with her and Suzanne at the front. It brought back so many memories of Dad's funeral as it was the only other funeral I had been to.

I tried to comfort Kim the best I could but I felt so numb inside. Life was so unfair; Kirsty had her whole life in front of her but she had been living my old life and she had paid the ultimate price. It should have been me lying there, not Kirsty. It was too much for me and I couldn't help but cry. Both John and Kim comforted me but I felt I didn't deserve their love. I couldn't even begin to imagine how Kim must be feeling.

I would have done anything to swap places with Kirsty. I would have gladly given up my life to have brought her back to be with Amelia and Kim. How I wished, more than anything, that I could go back in time again and put things right. If the angels would send me back in time again, I would go to the club and relive my life with Charlie and correct this mistake.

The service was almost too much for me to bear. It didn't matter how many times I tried to convince myself it was all Charlie's fault that Kirsty took her own life, it always came back to me and it would always be my fault that their paths crossed in the first place.

After the service Kim invited us to the hotel for the wake. I wasn't sure if I could face Kirsty's family but I didn't want to let Kim down so I smiled and reluctantly agreed to go. I was nervous and Kim picked up on my nerves so one by one she introduced me to her family. They couldn't have been more welcoming; they knew that Kirsty and I had become really good friends and I could feel their love for her radiating around the room.

Over the next few hours, John and I mingled with all of her family and we all shared our own personal memories of Kirsty and the love she had for others. I heard that in her teenage years, although being quite shy, she was very focused and knew that she wanted to go into the caring profession, either nursing or working with disadvantaged children. That got me thinking all over again about where Kirsty would be now if she hadn't have met Charlie. She may have had a successful career and just thinking about it made me cry again. Everybody was so nice and tried their best to comfort me but I felt I didn't deserve any of their love. I blamed myself and if they had known what I had done then they would hate me as much as I hated myself. The guilt was eating me up and I really didn't think I could live with myself for much longer.

After a while Kirsty's family started to make their excuses and leave and it wasn't long before it was just me, John, Kim, Suzanne and a couple of others left. Kim looked at me and gestured me over to her. She patted the seat next to her and asked me to sit down. She looked deadly serious as she paused for a moment before speaking. 'Remember what I said the other day, I really do hope you will come round to see me and Amelia. I really want you to be a part of our lives. I have lost Kirsty and I don't want to lose you too. I have come to see you as a daughter.'

I tenderly cupped Kim's hands in mine and, moving slightly closer to her, I smiled. 'You and Amelia mean everything to me and I really couldn't imagine not being a part of both of your lives.' I looked up at John for support and he smiled as he spoke. 'Kirsty was my friend too and I have always been fond of Amelia. You have my word; we will always be here for you both.'

Kim got up and gave John a hug. 'You're a good man John. You and Sarah have been through so much but you should never give up hope. Amelia and I will always be here for you both and it will happen for you, I'm sure of that. I know you're going to make great parents one day.'

I smiled at Kim and John but inside the guilt had started to gnaw away at me. I was the reason my best friend was dead and her daughter had to live without her mum. How would I ever be able to look her in the eye again? I knew Amelia would grow and that at every milestone she would be missing her mum. Birthdays, school prom, her wedding day, these would be the days she would need her mum by her side the most and I had taken her away.

John and I made our excuses and I gave Kim one last hug before we left. I promised I would see her on Wednesday like I had seen Kirsty over the years.

On the journey back, reality hit home. Kirsty had gone for good and I couldn't bear the thought that I would never see her again. It felt so final. My whole world was crashing down around me. This really wasn't how I expected my new life with John to turn out.

We finally arrived home but John obviously didn't know what to say to me anymore and I really didn't want to make small talk. I was drowning in guilt and felt that everything had come to a head. For the rest of the afternoon John and I sat in awkward silence. I felt I was slowly losing my mind and I knew I had to get out. I knew where I had to be so I turned to John. 'Would you mind if I spent tonight with Mum?'

John came to sit by my side and as he did he took my hand. 'If that's where you feel you need to be tonight then I'm okay with it but please let me drive you there.'

'No!' I replied quickly. 'Don't be silly, I'll be okay to drive. Honestly. I just need to be with Mum tonight but I'll be back first thing in the morning, I promise.' I knew it was a promise I wasn't sure I could keep but I didn't want John to stop me. I stood to call Mum but I made sure John was still within hearing distance. The phone rang and I instantly hung up.

'Hi Mum.' I paused as if waiting for her to speak. 'Yes, I'm okay. I just wondered if I could stay over tonight?' I paused again playing over in my head what she might be saying. 'Thanks Mum, I'll see you in a bit. Bye.'

I ended the pretend call and headed upstairs to pack an overnight bag. When I came back down John was waiting for me in the hallway. He looked concerned as he pulled me close for a hug. 'I do get why you need to be with your mum tonight.' His arms tightened around me as though he didn't want to let me go. 'It's going to take time for you to get over this and when you are ready to talk I'm here for you.'

As he released me I smiled warmly at him. 'I know. We'll talk in the morning I promise.'

He leant down to kiss me and I knew it would probably be our final kiss goodbye. As he opened the front door for me I felt my heart breaking and I walked slowly towards my car without looking back. I instinctively knew John was still standing at the door and I really wanted to look round at him but a little voice inside me told me not to. I knew I had to be strong so I got in my car and pulled away.

After twenty minutes I drove through my local town and spotted the off licence so I pulled up outside. I don't know what possessed me to go in and buy a bottle of whisky as I hated it but I did.

I continued my journey along the dual carriageway before spotting a familiar looking turn off. I tried to remember the route that John and I had taken the previous week but it was all a bit hazy. The only bit that stuck clearly in my mind was the final dirt track.

About a mile further on I turned left off the main road and immediately recognised where I was. I followed the road for another mile before turning off onto the narrow dirt track I had remembered. I had to drive slowly to avoid the potholes as the bottle of whisky bounced wildly around on the passenger seat every time I misjudged one.

I soon reached the opening I was looking for and parked up. I grabbed the whisky and walked towards the large wooden gate. I stopped as I reached it. It had become a shrine to Kirsty and there must have been at least twenty bunches of flowers, some fresh and some wilting, tied to it. I spotted the bunch that John and I had brought last week and realised they had started to wilt which saddened me. I read the small cards attached to each bunch and the heartfelt tributes gave me comfort. I recognised the names as I had seen their faces earlier at Kirsty's funeral.

I climbed over the gate, totally ignoring the "do not enter, danger signs" and taking care not to disturb any of the flowers. I slowly edged forward but thought better of it and sat down to shuffle the last few feet on my bottom. I sat for a few minutes with my legs dangling precariously over the edge before curiosity got the better of me and I leaned forward to peer over. I quickly realised I wasn't good with heights and started to feel dizzy so I immediately leant back.

I forced myself to take another look down at the shear drop and tried to imagine the total despair Kirsty must have been feeling to do what she did. A shiver ran down my spine as I visualised her falling to her death. It was a bit unnerving to think that two weeks previously Kirsty would have been standing in this very spot contemplating ending her life.

I sat there thinking of all the good times I had enjoyed with Kirsty. I felt the warm evening sun on my face and I sat in total silence for a while, totally wrapped up in my thoughts of Kirsty. I watched the sun setting on the horizon totally mesmerised by the beautiful view and completely lost in the moment. I was so lost I had failed to notice the light fading fast and the temperature dropping. It was almost pitch black and I suddenly felt frightened and vulnerable.

I tried to focus on the reason I was there. I had gone to find answers and to pay a last personal tribute to my beautiful best friend who, like me, was badly let down by her angel. I hoped that if angels did exist that they were looking after her.

I searched through the songs on my phone, trying to find the one I wanted to play for Kirsty. I clicked on the word Angels and it started to play. It was the song I used to play when I was with Charlie. It gave me great comfort and got me through the really dark days. I set it to auto repeat and turned up the volume before placing the phone carefully down beside me.

I thought back over my so called perfect life; the life that I thought was going to be so much better after avoiding reliving my past with Charlie. What had my life become? Tommy would have been two and full of life but I had lost him and I believed my three miscarriages were punishment from Tommy's angel for turning my back on him.

I wasn't sure why my angel had stopped me from meeting Charlie and given my bad life to Kirsty. Surely Kirsty's angel could have protected her from him.

I took a few swigs from the whisky bottle. I wanted to blot out the pain for just one night. My angel had made a terrible mistake changing my past. So many other lives had been badly affected. I took a few more swigs even though I hated the taste. As the liquid settled in the bottle I heard a rustling noise in the bushes. I nervously turned and stared into the darkness but I couldn't make anything out. The beautiful surroundings I had enjoyed earlier as the sun set had become very uninviting.

After a few more swigs my nerves began to settle and I started to feel light headed. If only I had Kirsty's courage to lean forward and fall into the darkness, maybe then all my pain would go away. I listened to the words of the song playing over and over and I started to question my angel's motives.

I reached for the bottle again and noticed it was almost half empty. The taste had become more bearable but the burning sensation in my throat hadn't. I coughed before laying back to listen to the song.

I must have dozed off for a few minutes as I woke with a start. I sat up too quickly and the whisky hit me. My head spun as I stood up and stretched out my arms. I hummed the song to myself as I swayed erratically in the darkness. I started to fall forwards but steadied myself. It would have been so easy to just keep falling and to erase all of my pain in seconds. This is how Kirsty must have felt in the last few seconds of her life I thought to myself. I felt so close to her standing there. I closed my eyes and tried to imagine her jumping from that very spot.

My emotions started to take over and tears rolled down my cheeks as I stared up into the dark sky. 'Hey angel,' I shouted out bitterly. 'Can you hear me? Why did you have to introduce Charlie to my best friend? That wasn't a very kind thing to do and what about my poor little Tommy? He needed his mummy and you took him away from me and my three babies, my poor little babies, you knew how much I wanted them but one by one you had to keep taking them away from me didn't you.' I paused to wipe my tears with the back of my hand. 'I thought you cared about me. All my life I have put all my faith in you and for what, so you can bring me down.'

I stopped as thoughts of my Dad and the stories he told crowded into my mind. 'Sorry Dad,' I shouted at the top of my voice, 'you got it so wrong, angels don't exist. Mum was right all along, it's just a big fairytale. I have lost everything. We come into this world alone and we go out alone and that's just the way it is.'

I sunk to my knees and sobbed my heart out. Life had no meaning without Tommy and I was just kidding myself that I could live without him. I had lost Kirsty too and I needed her much more than she ever needed me. I couldn't do it anymore. Tommy's angel would never let me give John a baby of his own so I just hoped that, one day, he would find somebody who could.

I took another big swig trying desperately to silence the thoughts in my head. I felt really tired and I hoped I could sleep and never wake up. I took a few more swigs and lay back as the bottle fell to my side. I really wanted to believe that there was a heaven and I prayed I would soon be there with my dad, Tommy and Kirsty. I just wanted my pain to go away and for Dad to give me one of his hugs and tell me everything was going to be ok. I missed him so much. I begged, that if angels did exist, they would take my hand and show me the way to heaven tonight.

Chapter 30

I must have fallen into a drunken stupor with the song on my phone ringing in my ears. I must have laid there for quite a while as I had no sense of the time that had passed but, at some point, I became very aware of faint voices in my head. There was a sense of urgency in the voices. At first I could hardly hear them but soon they started to get louder and louder, just as if somebody was slowly turning up the volume on a television set. They seemed to be communicating with each other and there was a sense of controlled urgency. One seemed to be in charge; it was a male voice and he was telling the others what they needed to do.

Curiosity started to get the better of me and I tried to open my eyes to see what was going on. It took a few attempts and when I did manage to open them it took a few more seconds for my eyes to adjust.

I soon realised I was no longer lying on the cliff top. Instead I was in a hospital room and the voices I heard were the medical staff. I was standing at the back of the room and everything around me was chaotic. I could see a young woman lying in the bed and I had the feeling she was dying and the medical staff were trying to save her. I felt the urgency in the doctor's voice as he said they were losing her. I felt so sorry for her and shed a few tears. I wanted, more than anything, for the doctor to save this woman but I didn't know why I felt so strongly.

I looked around the room and could see that everybody knew what they had to do and were totally focused. Despite all their efforts, my gut feeling was that she wasn't going to make it which filled my heart with sadness. The sense of urgency increased but my eyes were drawn to a woman standing in the corner. She was different to the others; she was calm and smiling at me. She had the most beautiful eyes, long flowing auburn hair and she was wearing a long white dress. The moment our eyes met I started to hear her, I didn't know how but she filled me with a deep understanding of what was going on. It was a knowing, an influx of information that I knew I would need time to process.

I realised that she was my guardian angel and that she had taken a form that felt familiar and kind to me. She told me that she had never left my side but instead, she had given me free will to make my own way in life. I understood so much in that instant. I knew I was the young woman lying in the bed in front of me dying. I had been there for twelve days in a deep coma. The reality I thought I had been living was my conscious mind reinventing itself and taking me to another existence, another time and place where I felt safe.

The four years I had experienced were just a product of time running slower for me in my coma and the depressed, suicidal state that brought me back to this reality, was the cause of my body giving up.

I looked at my angel desperate for answers and help. I knew that Tommy was here, not in heaven, he was in this world with my mum, waiting for me and hoping I would pull through. I knew my body was dying and I pleaded with her. I had missed Tommy so much and I needed to be with him again. I couldn't die.

The expression on her face changed and became sombre as I heard her thoughts. 'What I am about to tell you is very important. I need you to close your eyes and only think strong, positive thoughts about Tommy and this life that you need to get back to.'

I closed my eyes and started to think about Tommy. It meant everything to me knowing that he was alive and well in this world and it gave me a renewed hope. I felt real excitement at the thought of seeing him again and holding him in my arms. Not making it back was not an option. I had to find a way no matter what it took. I felt I had been given something to fight for and I wasn't going to give up.

I felt an intense wave of unconditional love wash over me. In my minds eye I saw a strong image of me sitting up in a hospital bed with Tommy sitting on my knee. Thoughts of my miscarriages tried to creep in but I dismissed them and focused on Tommy. I felt really positive and opened my eyes to look back at myself in the bed. Within seconds I heard the doctor's voice again. 'She's stabilising, I think we've got her back.'

I looked back at my angel and she was smiling at me again. 'You did well but you are still not strong enough to wake up in this world just yet. You need a few more days to heal. I'm afraid you need to go back to your other existence for a little bit longer.'

I felt real disappointment as I really wanted to wake up. I was desperate to see Tommy but I knew I must stay positive because what happened to me in the other world affected whether I lived or died in my coma world.

'When the time is right I will come and find you.' She fell silent for a moment and I could sense she had picked up on my passing thoughts about my miscarriages. 'You must not try for a baby again while in your other existence. A soul is trying to be born to you but it can't happen and it will always fail there because the time and place are not right. You need to go back now.'

I felt an intense rush of love all around me, the type of love I had never experienced before and I felt sad at the thought of leaving her. I wanted to ask her about Kirsty but I suddenly felt two strong arms from behind, they gripped me around my chest and pulled me sharply backwards. The room was instantly plunged into darkness.

I soon felt myself coming round but it was still dark. As I started to get my bearings I realised I was back at the top of the cliff. I felt confused as John was with me and he was trying to sit me up.

'Are you okay?' I could hear the panic in his voice as he spoke. 'You know you could have died, you were laying less than a foot from the edge. If you had turned over you would have fallen. I had to pull you back to safety.'

I felt John tremble as he held onto me tightly. The song Angels was still playing on my phone and he leant over to switch it off. As he shone his torch around the light hit the half empty whisky bottle and a look of shear horror crossed his face. 'Please tell me you weren't planning on doing something stupid tonight.'

I smiled and tried to reassure him. 'No I wouldn't do that. I see my life more clearly now. Something happened tonight and I have clarity. How did you find me?'

'When I couldn't get through to your phone, I called your mum to make sure you got there okay. She said you weren't there and she knew nothing about you going over. After today, I thought this was the only other place you would have wanted to be.' John helped me up and we made our way to his car. 'You seem quite sober for someone who has just drunk half a bottle of whisky.'

I hadn't noticed before but I did feel okay, I think my angelic experience had somehow sobered me up. On the way home I felt a lot happier and optimistic than I had in a long time. Everything suddenly made sense.

That night, as I lay in bed and closed my eyes, I could see my angel in every detail. I was in no doubt that it had happened and the very fact that I should have been very drunk convinced me I had been touched by my angel. I recalled the things that I had been shown in those few seconds and they felt like memories from a long time ago not from a few hours ago.

Chapter 31

I woke up the next morning with a whole new outlook on life. The night before my angel had told me that I needed to stay in this existence a while longer as I needed a few more days to recover from my coma. I had been in this existence for four years and in my coma for only twelve days, so that meant for every year that passed here three days passed in my coma. I wondered if that meant I would have to stay in this existence until I caught up with my coma timeline. I had a feeling I couldn't exist here once I had caught up so I thought it would all come to a head in eleven months.

My angel had intervened the previous night to save my life and I realised if I wanted to get back to my real life then I had to stay positive. Memories of our meeting were still very fresh in my mind and I kept thinking about what she had told me. I remembered her saying that in this existence, the day Julie and I were going to the night club, she had to intervene to stop me so I didn't get back with Charlie. If I had relived my life with him he would have made it too negative and I would almost certainly have died in the first week in my coma. Seeing my other self so close to death focused my mind on staying positive for the next eleven months; I knew I had to put all of my trust in my angel.

I did wonder what would happen to John if I went back. Every part of the past four years had felt just as real as my other life and, as far as I was concerned, I'd been in a four year loving relationship with John but where did that leave us. The night before I slipped into my coma John had made it clear that he just wanted to stay friends. I wanted more than friendship from him but I wondered if I would have to make sacrifices when I got back.

I also wondered about Kirsty and if she existed there. If she did, she didn't meet Charlie and she would still be alive. I hoped she was living happily and maybe I could find her and we could become friends again. One thing I had learnt from Kirsty was that I couldn't let Charlie get away with hurting anyone else and I knew when I got back, I needed to press charges against him.

I had another eleven months in this existence and I felt I must embrace it and live it as if it were my last eleven months on earth but I had this terrible thought that I couldn't shake off. What if I came out of the coma but didn't make a good recovery and had a poor quality of life? I knew I needed to put this thought to the back of my mind and concentrate on the life I had in this existence, after all it was the only time I had left to be with John and I wanted to enjoy it.

Chapter 32

Later that morning, John and I made our way back to the cliff edge to pick my car up. We decided to stay for a while and as we stood together at the edge, John took my hand and asked if I was okay. I squeezed his hand and nodded. I did feel better about life but I was still upset about Kirsty. Over the past two and a half years I had built a really close friendship with her and my feelings were still very real. Whether this world was real or not, I still felt her loss just as much but knowing she may be alive and there was a chance I could see her again, made it all a bit more bearable. We stayed standing there in silence for a good hour, paying our own personal respects to Kirsty, before deciding to head home.

Over the next few days I thought about Amelia a great deal and I really wanted to be there for her. I had always been close and protective towards her, partly because I could relate to what the two of them were going through with Charlie.

John took Wednesday off and we decided to take Kim and Amelia to the local soft play area. Kim was really happy when I rang and suggested going. I felt much closer to John as the guilt had gone and I was really happy that he was supporting me seeing Amelia. I needed to be there for her and my only thought was to give her as much love as I possibly could and help Kim out whenever she needed me.

I had started to feel a lot happier about the future and the thought of having my old life back and more importantly having Tommy back, kept me feeling positive. However I also felt guilty about Amelia as one day I wouldn't be there for her.

I woke up on Wednesday in a really good mood and was really looking forward to spending the day with John, Amelia and Kim. I was really glad that Kim hadn't shut me out of her life as I felt we needed each other. Kim was like a second mum to me and since Amelia's birth I had loved being a part of all of their lives. Kirsty was there for me through my miscarriages and having Amelia around got me through all the bad times.

On the short drive to Kim's I felt that the day needed to be about Amelia. This was the first time we had spent quality time with her since losing Kirsty. Amelia was too young to know what was going on but she would be aware her mummy wasn't around anymore. I just wanted to be there for her and wrap her up in my love.

We soon pulled up outside Kim's and she must have been waiting for us as she opened the door just as we were about to knock. As we went in I noticed Amelia sitting in front of the television. She looked up at me and gave me the cutest smile ever and ran up to me. I lifted her up into my arms and felt such a rush of love for her. I looked at Kim and she gave me a knowing smile.

Amelia settled quietly on my lap, her eyes firmly fixed on the television screen. I inwardly smiled as I remembered Tommy loved watching the same programme and how it would keep him quiet for ages.

Kim made us all a cup of tea before joining us.

'How are you coping?' I asked as she sat down.

'Oh I'm okay. I have to stay strong for Amelia and she keeps me on my toes.'

'You do know you don't have to do this alone, don't you? We meant it when we said we are here for you both.'

Kim smiled. 'Sarah, I really do appreciate that.'

Later that morning, as we walked into the soft play area, memories of the times I had spent there with Kirsty came flooding back. It didn't feel right being there without her and it stirred so many emotions within me.

John went off to buy the drinks and I chose to sit at the table where Kirsty and I always sat; it was the table nearest the toddler play area. I remembered how we would take it in turns to play with Amelia as she wasn't quite at the age where she could be left alone and some of the over three's could be a bit rough. Watching Kim pushing Amelia on the soft dolphin swing brought back even more memories. Amelia had always liked that, ever since Kirsty first tried her out on it when she was just nine months old.

John soon returned with an overflowing tray, containing three mugs of tea, pre-packed sandwiches and an assortment of biscuits and crisps. I tried to contain my amusement. 'Did you leave anything for anyone else?' I laughed.

'Well' he laughed back, 'I thought I would cover all eventualities.'

I turned my attention back to Kim and Amelia, who were happily sitting in the ball pit and I decided I'd go and give Kim a break. I noticed Amelia had found a friend, a little girl who looked slightly younger than her. I politely smiled at the little girl's mum as I sat down beside her. Then I turned my attention to Amelia. 'Have you found a new friend?' I asked her.

She paid me no attention as they carried on passing the balls to each other and I looked up to see the little girl's mum smiling at me. 'How old is your little girl?' she asked.

I suddenly felt really awkward and glanced at Kim. 'Umm,' I hesitated and stuttered, 'she's just turned two.'

'Oh, only a few months older than Sophie then. By the way, I'm Emily. Is she your first?'

I felt really flustered and wished she would stop asking awkward questions. I looked back at Kim who gave me a reassuring smile so I turned back to Emily and answered. 'Er yes, she's my first. I'm Sarah and' I stopped not really knowing what to say. Emily was staring at me expectantly so I pointed at Kim. 'This is my friends mum Kim.' I didn't know where to look; I felt such an idiot. Why hadn't I just told her I wasn't Amelia's mum? Goodness only knows what Kim must have thought of me.

The girls carried on playing as I sat not knowing what to do. I was relieved when, after a few minutes, Emily finally lifted Sophie from the ball pit. She gave me another smile obviously unaware how uncomfortable I felt. 'What's your little girl's name?'

'Amelia' I said quietly, avoiding eye contact.

'Sophie, say goodbye to Amelia.' Sophie gave her one of those cute little waves, opening and closing her hand, before Emily took her back to their table.

After she left I turned to Kim. 'I'm so sorry.' I could feel my cheeks turning red as I spoke. 'I should have corrected her, it happened so quickly and I really didn't know what to say.'

'Look, don't be silly, of course she is naturally going to think Amelia is yours. Honestly, I don't expect you to explain yourself to everyone you meet.'

With a sense of relief I lifted Amelia into my arms and we made our way back to John. After a bite to eat I could see Amelia was itching to get back to the play area but before I could stand John was on his feet. 'I'll take her if you like?' he said quickly.

Amelia seemed to have taken to John and was quite happy to go off with him. We sat and watched them as they made there way to the top layer, Amelia leading. We tried not to laugh as John struggled to follow her through some pretty small areas to get to the tube slide.

'He's a natural with her,' Kim laughed. She turned and rested her hand on mine. 'I'm so glad you both decided to stay in touch. It's going to mean so much to Amelia to have you both around.'

'Kirsty was my best friend and I have known Amelia since she was born. She means everything to me and I really want to be a part of her life.'

Kim smiled sympathetically. 'Have you and John given any thought to trying again?'

'No' I replied. 'I don't really want to think about that now. I've told John I want to wait a while as my heads not in the right place at the moment.'

'I can understand that but when you and John are ready you need to know there is support out there for you. The hospital will help you as you've had three miscarriages. They can do tests. I really do feel for you both but whatever you decide, Amelia and I will always be here for you.'

Just at that moment John returned with Amelia in his arms, looking exhausted. 'I don't know where she gets all of her energy from,' he puffed.

We stayed for another half an hour before we decided it was time to make our way back to Kim's. Amelia was shattered and was fast asleep by the time we arrived back so John carried her up to her bed. We stayed a few hours but it felt a little tense between us. There were a few awkward silences and I wanted to talk about Kirsty but worried it would upset Kim.

Amelia woke just after five and John and I felt it was a good time to make a move as Kim needed to make her dinner.

As we reached the front door I gave Kim a hug. 'Can I come and spend next Wednesday with you and Amelia?' I asked.

'Oh that would be lovely. Amelia will love to see you and I will look forward to it too.'

We made plans for the following Wednesday before John and I headed home.

Chapter 33

I often thought back to my other life and the coma I was in. I had to keep reminding myself that this existence wasn't real but that started me thinking about Amelia. What would become of her as she wouldn't exist in my world because if Kirsty existed there she wouldn't have met Charlie? It would be exactly the same situation as Tommy in this existence; Amelia would become just a memory.

In the following weeks I felt I needed to see Amelia more than just a few hours a week.

It had been nearly three months since Kirsty took her own life and only eight months until I caught up with my present time and this existence would end. Time was running out for me and Amelia and I had grown to love this little girl as if she were my own. I couldn't get her out of my head and I wanted to spend more and more time with her. I wanted her to come and stay with John and me at the weekends but I didn't know how Kim or John would feel about it.

It slowly drove me crazy until one night I felt I couldn't keep it to myself any longer. That evening, after dinner, I decided to bring up the subject with John. As we sat together on the sofa I struggled to find the right words and it must have been a good hour before I built up enough courage to speak.

Thoughts of what I wanted to say kept swimming around in my head but I took a deep breath and decided to just go for it. 'John, I've been thinking about it for sometime now and wanted to know what you thought about me asking Kim if we could have Amelia stay over at ours at weekends?' I stopped but sensing a negative reaction I started to babble. 'I know she isn't ours and she has been thrust upon you and I am sorry about that. I know it must be hard for you, with the miscarriages and everything but you've got to understand I just want the best for her. I want for her to look at us as an aunt and uncle but I do understand if you say no as I am asking a lot of you.'

As I stopped for breath John smiled and laughed. 'I'm all for having Amelia stay with us' he said, 'but it's not me you need to convince. I think it may be a bit too soon to ask Kim that.'

After a lot of thought about what John had said I decided to ask Kim the following day.

The next morning I woke up shortly after John and made my way downstairs. As I walked into the kitchen he handed me a cup of tea. 'How are you this morning?' he asked.

'Yes I'm okay,' I smiled vaguely. 'I'm just worried how Kim might react. Are you sure you're okay with it?'

'Yes I'm one hundred percent committed to this. That little girl needs stability in her life. I'm sure Kim will see we only have Amelia's best interests at heart. It'll be fine you'll see.'

I knew John was right and I was probably worrying over nothing but I just didn't want Kim thinking I was trying to take Amelia away from her.

Running late as usual, John gave me the briefest of hugs before heading out of the door. 'I'll see you tonight,' he shouted back over his shoulder. 'Oh and good luck with Kim, try not to worry, remember the worst she can do is say no.'

After he left I sat rehearsing out loud what I was going to say. 'Kim I was wondering if you'd be okay.' I stopped as it didn't sound right. 'Kim I was wondering how you would feel about John and I having Amelia at the weekends?' I thought that sounded too full on so I started again. 'Kim I was wondering how you would feel about John and I having Amelia at the weekend now and again, to give you a break.' Everything I said sounded wrong and I was going out of my mind with worry. It was nearly nine so I decided to head off to Kim's early to get it over and done with.

Within seconds of arriving, Kim gave me a friendly hug and put me at ease; she always managed to do that. Amelia cheekily jumped onto my seat just before I had chance to sit down so I lifted her into my arms. 'Hey that's my seat you cheeky monkey.' She let out a little laugh before settling down on my lap and focusing back on the television. Holding her, I felt a little more confident and decided that I would be brave and pop the question into conversation at an appropriate point.

Kim started chatting away. 'So Sarah, have you had a good week?'

'Yes fine thanks, no different to usual, working and just a quiet weekend in, that's it really. How's your week been?'

'Not too bad, running around after Amelia bless her. She really loves her play dough at the moment and I'm always finding bits in the sofa.' She laughed out loud causing Amelia to turn and look at her.

'So she's been running you ragged then?'

'Yes, that and children's TV from seven in the morning to seven at night.' She rolled her eyes as we exchanged smiles.

'Yes but you wouldn't want it any other way would you.'

'No of course not but I must admit I do look forward to my Wednesday morning adult chats with you and I know Amelia looks forward to seeing you too.'

Feeling this was the perfect opportunity, I tried to find the words but my mouth instantly went dry and I clammed up. Kim could obviously tell something was wrong. 'Are you alright Sarah?'

'Erm,' I hesitated, 'yes. I was going to ask you something but I don't want to upset you or for you to think I was in some way trying to take over.'

Draping her arm over my shoulder Kim smiled. 'Sarah, you know you can tell me anything and honestly I won't be offended.'

I paused for a moment and then looked nervously back up at her. 'John and I have been talking and, only if you agree, we would love it if Amelia could stay with us some weekends, you know, just to give you a break.'

Kim let out a little laugh. 'Have you really been worrying about this? Oh Sarah, I've been hinting to you for months that you and John are most welcome to take Amelia at weekends but because you never took the hint I didn't think you were interested.'

'So I have been worrying over nothing then,' I sighed. 'I thought you might think we were trying to take Amelia away from you.'

'Come here and give me a hug you daft thing. Amelia needs more in her life than just me. All she has ever known is me, Kirsty, you and John. I have always wanted you both to spend time alone with her. We are a team and she needs us all.'

'Thank you, John's going to be made up. Please don't think we are doing it because I can't have a baby though. I'm doing this for Amelia as she deserves to be happy.'

'I know and one day it will happen for you. Kirsty would have been so proud of you.'

I felt the excitement in me building as I thought about Amelia staying over. 'How about a week on Friday? That would give us time to get a little bed for the spare room and maybe we could have her until Sunday?'

'Yes that'll be fine.'

I looked down at Amelia who was still sat on my lap. 'Would you like to come and stay with me and John for a few days soon?'

'Okay,' she said without moving her eyes from the programme she was watching.

Kim smiled. 'That's her new word at the moment, she say's okay to everything. I'll make sure she understands by next Friday.'

When I got home I couldn't wait for John to get in from work so I could tell him the news. He was over the moon and soon started talking excitedly about redecorating the spare room.

'We'll go and get a little bed for her on Saturday. How about that princess one we saw the other week with the matching curtains?'

'Yes' I laughed, 'I was thinking about that one earlier.'

John really took to the idea of having Amelia stay and he spent all Saturday afternoon getting the spare room just right.

The whole of the next week I worried that Amelia wouldn't adjust to spending time with us and was so nervous when Friday finally arrived. It was a big day for both of us and John even took the day off work. I could see how much he was looking forward to it but I just hoped he was doing it for all the right reasons and not because I couldn't give him a baby.

We arrived at Kim's just after ten in the morning and planned to stay the day. It had been four months since we lost Kirsty and I was very aware that it would be the first time Amelia would be away from Kim. All through the day I worried and imagined Amelia crying her eyes out when it was time to go but I needn't have worried. At five o'clock, after a little persuasion from Kim, Amelia was standing by the door and raring to go. I really felt for Kim though as she waved us off. This would be the first time that she had been on her own since Kirsty died.

Back home, John and I made such a fuss of Amelia. The following morning we took her shopping and for a meal. She reminded me so much of Tommy and just like Tommy she had the same facial expressions as Charlie. Pushing Amelia through town in her pushchair a horrible thought suddenly came to me and it put me on edge. What if we bumped into Charlie? Kim hadn't heard from him since Kirsty died and we all wanted it to stay that way.

The weekend went so quickly and before we knew it, it was time to take her back home.

'Did you have a good time?' Kim asked when we arrived.

'Yes we had a great time thanks,' I smiled broadly. 'We went into town and took Amelia out for a meal. I think she really enjoyed herself. Did you have a nice rest? I hope you managed to put your feet up?'

'Yes I did, I forgot what it was like not to have to worry about anybody but myself for a few days but I did miss this little one.' She ruffled Amelia's hair as she spoke.

'Well hopefully you'll let us look after her another weekend.'

Kim sensed the hesitation in my voice and took my hand to reassure me. 'I meant what I said, Amelia only really has us three and we are a team. She needs you two in her life.'

I glanced over at John for support. 'We are happy to have her most weekends unless you have plans for her of course. We only want the best for Amelia. I'm just glad we can do our bit too.'

'If it's okay we could have her next weekend.' John butted in with a smile.

'Yes of course.' Kim looked down at Amelia. 'You'd like to stay with John and Sarah again wouldn't you Amelia?'

Amelia briefly looked at me, nodded and then went off to sit at her little desk to do some colouring.

Over the next few months Amelia stayed over at ours most weekends. We couldn't help but spoil her: John bought her a little slide and plastic wendy house for the garden, even though it would soon be winter and she wouldn't get outside much.

Chapter 34

Christmas was fast approaching and Kim invited us to hers for the festive season. John started shopping mid November which was unusual for him as he normally did a last minute dash in the final week. We tried not to go overboard as Amelia already had plenty of toys, both around Kim's and at ours and it was her third birthday a few months after Christmas.

I was really excited in the build up to Christmas and Kim came with us to the Town's Christmas lights switch on. It was the first one I had been to in a long time. I had always regretted not taking Tommy but Charlie didn't like crowds.

We spent all three days over Christmas with Kim and Christmas Eve was magical. I couldn't believe how many toys Amelia got on Christmas Day itself and it must have taken her over half an hour to open them. There was an air of sadness without Kirsty and I knew Kim felt it too; it's why I couldn't bear the thought of her spending her first Christmas alone with Amelia since Kirsty's death.

Once Christmas had gone I struggled to face the New Year. It brought me back down to earth with a sobering bump as I had less than five months to go before I caught up with present time. Over the previous few months I had made the best of this existence and had totally wrapped myself up in John, Amelia and Kim but the New Year meant I had to face up to the fact that, come the 25th of May, I would be in unfamiliar territory.

The longer I lived in this existence the more I doubted myself. How could this world not be real? If I cut myself I bled, I felt physical and emotional pain and if I was to jump in front of a car I would most probably die. This existence had been my life for the past five years; I had John and a beautiful little girl that I adored but it wasn't my life.

Everyday I had to remind myself, that in reality, I was lying in a coma in a hospital bed and I could be waking up on the 25th of May. I didn't think I could exist in this reality after that date and I had to get back to the life that I left behind five years ago. It was still hard to get my head around the fact that my real life had only moved forward by two weeks.

Amelia's wellbeing was really important to me and I needed to know that John would take good care of her when I was gone. I would never know for sure if this reality was just in my head or if it would carry on without me but I knew John well enough to know that he would always be there for Amelia.

I started to get an uneasy feeling with each day that passed and I feared the future. The unknown scared me and I constantly worried how or if I would get back and what the future had in store for me. Would I just wake up in the hospital bed? Would this existence just become a memory? I was well aware that the only reason I was here was because Charlie beat me to within an inch of my life causing horrific head injuries. Then, out of the blue the answer came to me and I knew what I had to do. I knew what my angel had been asking me to do and it made total sense.

On the 24th of May, at 6 p.m. precisely, I had to go back to Charlie's house and recreate that violent scene again. I would have to provoke him enough so he would beat me to within an inch of my life and then I could fall unconscious in this existence and wake up from the coma. It made perfect sense; it was the gateway back and I had to create it.

My angel said she would come for me when the time was right and I felt she had just presented me with the answer. The thought of reliving that night sent a shiver down my spine but I knew it was the sign I had been waiting for. With my angel by my side I felt strong and I knew she would get me through it.

I still had a few months before I needed to face Charlie so I pushed the thoughts to the back of my mind and concentrated on giving all of my time and love to John and Amelia. Amelia spent almost every weekend with us over those months and I grew really close to her. I couldn't imagine life without her but that was exactly what was going to happen.

Chapter 35

Time seemed to be speeding up and it was soon mid May and in just over a week my two existences would reach the same point in time.

I had one week to prepare for next Thursday, the twenty-fourth. The confrontation with Charlie needed to go exactly as it had done before and somehow I knew I needed to get John to come and save me. He would need to come in ten minutes after I entered the house but I wasn't sure how I could make that happen.

I had one week left and I wanted to make that final week with John and Amelia special. I had suggested to Kim that I would like to take Amelia to the beach for a few days and she was more than happy to let us have her for the week.

'I think this will be the first time Amelia's ever been to the beach,' she said sadly. 'It's going to be a really good experience for her. Charlie never took them anywhere; he's such a selfish man.' I could see how annoyed the thought made her so I lifted Amelia up in my arms. 'Well' I said spinning her around, 'you needn't worry about this little one. She is going to have a wonderful time as John and I are going to spoil her rotten.'

Amelia let out a little laugh much to Kim's delight. 'I have no doubt of that. You have a good time and I will see you both on Wednesday.'

As it was May, we had no problem booking four nights in a child friendly bed and breakfast on the Norfolk coast. John had managed to take the whole week off work at very short notice and we were really looking forward to our break with Amelia.

We set off early on the Friday morning and it looked like the weather was going to be kind to us. It was unusually warm for the time of year and looking at the forecast it seemed like it would stay that way for the whole break.

We arrived at the bed and breakfast just after twelve and the owner greeted us with a smile. 'Did you have a pleasant journey? She asked as we placed our cases down. 'I'm Sally but please call me Sal and who's this pretty little girl.'

'This is Amelia.' I replied as she hid behind me. 'She's a bit shy at first but she'll liven up when she gets used to you.'

'Oh bless her; I can see a lot of her dad in her.'

John smiled at me awkwardly.

'She looks even more like him when she's got one of her pouts on.' I said jokingly before laughing.

John laughed and instantly his mood lifted.

Sal showed us to our room. It was only basic with a double bed, child's bed in the corner and a small flat screen television attached to the wall but it was clean and comfortable. Much to Amelia's delight on the chest of drawers, next to the kettle, was a selection of biscuits on a plate.

Sal smiled as she turned to leave. 'Just fill in the form to let us know what you would like for your breakfast and leave it in reception before eight tonight.' With that she pulled the door to behind her.

I couldn't wait to take Amelia to the beach as it was just a five minute walk away. Amelia was a bit unsure at first as she walked on the sand. John and I walked her to the sea and I could see another couple with a little boy further out and the sea was only up to their knees so we paddled out a little further. Amelia loved walking with the water beneath her feet and it instantly brought back happy memories of the last time Kirsty and I took Amelia to the local swimming pool. That gave me an idea.

'John, why don't we take Amelia to the swimming pool one day in the week? She would really love that.'

'Yeah that's a great idea. We'll have to buy her a little swimming costume.'

Amelia sat happily making sandcastles with John and much to my amusement she kept jumping on them before he could finish.

On the Saturday, we took Amelia to play in the amusements. John tried to win her a princess doll in the crane grab machine but to no avail. He looked very defeated as he suggested we go and buy one in the shop instead.

In the afternoon we played a game of crazy golf. John let Amelia take his shots, with a lot of help from him but they still managed to beat me. As we neared the end of the course Amelia kept saying she wanted to go to the beach and John couldn't resist. He smiled and lifted her into his arms as we headed back.

The weather had been really good to us; it felt like the perfect summer's day and watching John and Amelia splashing away in the sea warmed my heart. John doted on her and seeing them together like that made me realise, for the first time, that whatever happened to me I would be leaving her in safe hands.

The following morning, we frantically looked for a shop that sold swimming costumes suitable for a three year old. We eventually found one and just after twelve we headed for the pool. John looked very much the proud Dad as he carried Amelia into the water. She made a beeline for a little slide with running water and climbed the small set of steps and quickly slid down. John looked worried when she hit the water at the bottom but it was only about a foot deep and she was standing back up within seconds. We took her into the deeper end but she looked unsure and wrapped her arms tighter around John's neck so we took her back to the shallower water.

The weekend was over so quickly and as I woke on Monday morning I felt down. I really didn't want our time away to end but I was happy that at least we still had Amelia until Wednesday. Over the last eleven months we had become a proper little family and I couldn't bear the thought of never seeing her again.

On the Tuesday, I wanted to spend one last special day with Amelia so we took her to the soft play area. Later on in the evening I was very aware that it would probably be the last time I was ever going to put her to bed. She was worn out and as I sat beside her, reading her favourite book, she quickly fell fast asleep. I lay with her for at least an hour, not wanting to leave her side, trying desperately to freeze frame this image of her in my mind forever.

Early on the Wednesday morning, Amelia walked into our bedroom at just after seven and cuddled up to me. Later that morning after breakfast, I reluctantly packed her little suitcase and we made our way back to Kim's.

Kim met us at the door but quickly turned her attention to Amelia. Scooping her up into her arms she kissed her cheek. 'I've really missed you. Come and tell Nana all about your holiday,'

John and I followed them in before heading to the kitchen to make a cup of tea. I knew that this would probably be the last time I would see Kim and Amelia and I wanted to enjoy every minute I could. At just after three, John suggested that we should make a move but I really didn’t want to leave. I knew this day would come but it didn’t make it any easier. I managed to put John off for another hour as I continued to play with Amelia but I had to face facts. I lifted her into my arms and held her tightly. I had lived this life for five years and saying goodbye didn’t feel right anymore.

‘You be good for your Nana and John and don’t ever forget I love you.’ I whispered in her ear before giving her a kiss on the forehead and placing her gently back on the floor. I really didn’t want this moment to end and I couldn’t help but shed a few tears.

Kim picked Amelia up before turning and handing me a tissue. ‘Hey what’s all this? Anybody would think you were saying your final goodbyes.’

I smiled through my tears. ‘Sorry don’t mind me; I’m just a bit over emotional at the moment.’

‘Well we’ll see you on Saturday then.’

‘Yes, err, Saturday, okay then.’ I replied before leaning over to Amelia and giving her one final kiss on the cheek.

As we pulled away in the car I looked back at Kim standing in the doorway with Amelia in her arms and with a smile, I gave them a little wave.

John didn’t mention what had happened and back home we decided to order a takeaway and watch television. We didn’t really talk and at just gone nine I decided I’d have an early night as I knew tomorrow was going to be a big day.

Chapter 36

On the morning of Thursday May 24th I woke up bright and early. I was filled with both excitement and fear about the day ahead. I was dreading having to relive the beating from Charlie but I believed it was the only way I could wake up from my coma. I had been going through this day in my head, over and over again, for months. I just knew this is what my angel was asking me to do and I knew I had to make sure the evening happened exactly as it had last time.

I wasn't sure how everything would work out initially but over the months I had prepared a plan. I would give Charlie some home truths about Kirsty. I knew only too well which buttons to press to set him off and I would provoke him into beating me to within an inch of my life. I knew I would have to time it just right so that John could come in on time and save me but I trusted that my angel would make it work. Then tonight I would fall into a coma in this existence allowing me to wake from the coma in the real world.

I knew this would probably be the last day John and I would spend as a couple in this existence as I didn't know what tomorrow would bring. I wanted to make our last day together special so I booked us a table at The Mill restaurant for lunch at one o'clock. I also felt I really needed to see Mum to say goodbye in this existence and John was more than happy to come with me.

On the way we stopped for lunch at The Mill. It was one final thing I could do for John as I really didn't know what was going to become of my life or his. We left at two fifteen and made the twenty minute drive to Mum's.

As we arrived I thought back to the last time I had lived this day. The beating Charlie had given me had been imprinted in my mind for the last five years and I felt I needed Mum to give me the courage to deal with what was going to happen. I also wanted a couple of hours of normality before I had to face my destiny.

Mum noticed how quiet I was and instantly sensed my nerves. ‘Sarah are you okay? You look really tense.’

John hadn’t picked up on how I was feeling and looked over at me inquisitively as I tried to bluff Mum. ‘I’m fine Mum. There’s nothing to worry about. I was just thinking about Kirsty. It’s been nearly a year now since she died.’

Mum smiled at me sympathetically. ‘The anniversaries will always bring it home to you, especially the way she died. Her boyfriend should have been locked up for the way he treated her.’

‘I know and there’s nothing stopping him from doing it again to some other poor woman. People like that don’t change.’

‘You really have to let it go and try and put him out of your mind or it will eat you up and make you bitter. You need to put all of your efforts into looking out for Amelia. She’s the one that matters now. That little girl is going to need you both and I am so proud of you for what you are doing for her.’

Her words made me feel guilty as I knew I wouldn’t be around for Amelia. I also felt so confused about what would happen. For months it had all been going round and round in my head. Was this existence only playing out in my mind? If I did wake from the coma would this life no longer exist? Or, on the other hand was this a parallel universe? If that was the case then I wouldn’t be here for her but at least I knew John would take care of her when I was gone. The hardest thing to accept was the fact that I would never know for sure what would happen to this existence.

I looked at the time and it had just gone four o'clock so I turned to John. 'I think we'd better get going.'

I gave mum a big hug as it felt like it was the last time I would see her and in a way it was. The Mum I was returning too would have shared different experiences with me. As we pulled away I glanced back to wave at her; saying goodbye to this reality was going to be a lot harder than I thought it would be.

All the way home I focused on Charlie and what I would say to him. My past fear of him was slowly coming back and I was petrified at the thought of having to go through that beating again. My only comfort was the thought of my angel standing by me and guiding me back to my other existence.

We arrived home just after five and I had an hour to prepare myself. I made John a sandwich and handed him the plate. He noticed my hand shaking and looked concerned. 'Are you okay?'

'Yes I'm fine.' I smiled vaguely and he didn't push it any further but he knew something was wrong. I sat with him for twenty minutes trying to compose myself.

When I next looked at the clock it was nearly six. My mouth became dry and my body tingled with nerves.

'I need to pop to the shop.' I lied and I was half expecting him to question me but he didn't. To my relief I noticed John's mobile was next to him, I just hoped he would answer my text as soon as I sent it as I knew my life may depend on it.

'I won't be long.' I called out as I headed for the door.

John looked up from the television and smiled. ‘Okay, I’ll have the kettle on by the time you get back.’

I drove the mile or so to the lay-by and it suddenly felt like déjà vu, the only difference this time around was John, he wasn’t in the car with me. I pulled in at six twenty and sat nervously waiting. I hadn’t seen Charlie in almost a year and I couldn’t believe I was about to walk back into his house and put myself back in the firing line. This day had been burnt into my memory ever since I entered this existence five years ago. The beating Charlie gave me that evening was the reason I was here and now it was time for me to put things right.

My hands started to tremble as I typed out a text to John.

“John I have gone to Charlie’s house, I have to do this for Kirsty. I am going to tell him exactly what I think of him. I am going to stand up to him for Kirsty. She couldn’t stand up to him so I owe it to her to give him some home truths. I love you. Sarah xx”

I looked at the time. It was half past six, time to go. I got out of the car and slowly walked towards the house. I started to feel all of the same bad feelings I felt last time. A shiver ran down my spine as I pictured the whole violent scene and how it played out. Charlie’s car was parked outside and my heart was in my mouth as I walked the last few yards. I stopped a few feet from the front door and looked at my phone and at the text I had just written. I knew it would take John at least ten minutes to get to Charlie’s after I sent it. I was putting all of my faith in him getting there in that time. I paused for a moment, my thumb hovering over the send button before taking a deep breath and pressing send.

The message disappeared as it sent and I knew there was no going back. I took another deep breath, slowly opened the door and took a few steps inside. Nervously I called out Charlie's name. I so wanted to be the strong one and to stand up to him as an equal but I started to shake uncontrollably. My head was telling me to turn and run but I was frozen to the spot, my heart pounding uncontrollably.

Charlie walked into the hall from the living room. At first he looked surprised to see me but he soon hardened and his face contorted into a sarcastic smile as he spoke. 'Oh just let yourself in why don't you.'

My mouth was really dry and I started to stutter. 'Yyyou don't scare me, I know exactly what you are.'

Charlie walked right up to me and slowly moved his face close to mine. 'Okay then, so what am I?'

I knew he was trying to intimidate me and he may have been able to in the past but I wasn't going to let him anymore. I was determined to show him my strong side and tell him what I thought. 'You are just a bully that beats women up. Kirsty died because of you.'

His mood changed and he moved even closer until I could feel his warm breath on my face. 'I would be very careful what you say if I were you. That is a very serious accusation you are making.'

I took a few steps back. I knew I would have to push him harder so I summoned every bit of strength I had. 'Kirsty told me everything about you. She didn't love you, she didn't even like you and she only stayed with you because she was scared of you.' I forced a laugh. 'How does that make you feel? You can only get a woman to stay with you through fear and intimidation.'

Charlie grabbed a fist full of my hair and pulled me sharply back towards his face. He stared deep into my eyes and I could see that I had really rattled him. 'You really need to watch your mouth. That boyfriend of yours obviously doesn't keep you in line. Somebody needs to teach you some respect.'

He tightened his grip on my hair and yanked my head back sharply causing a searing pain in my scalp. The pain made me even more determined not to show him any fear. 'Is that how you taught Kirsty respect,' I replied through gritted teeth, 'with your fists? No woman will ever love you. You are a pathetic excuse for a man.'

That really hit a nerve and he flew into a rage. I felt another sharp agonising pain in my scalp as he twisted my head. I stumbled to the floor and he pulled me across the room by my hair before yanking my head back towards his face so he could yell at me. 'You really don't want to get on the wrong side of me. If you want the truth, Kirsty took her life because of your meddling; her blood is on your hands.'

I tried to prise his fingers from my hair but his grip was too strong. The pain was excruciating but I wasn't going to let him win. 'What are you going to do then? Smack my head against the wall a few times and knock me unconscious, then maybe kick me in the head a few more times as I lay on the floor defenceless just like you did last time.' I stopped and looked him straight in the eye. 'I hate you,' I said calmly, 'and the four and a half years I spent with you were a living hell. I'm just glad I got away from you. Tommy and Amelia are better off without you.'

'What the hell are you going on about you mad cow?' He loosened his grip on my hair and threw me to the floor. 'Get out of my house and think yourself lucky I didn't really hurt you.'

I got straight back up and lunged towards him. 'I'm not scared of you and I'm not going anywhere, not until you admit you are a cowardly bully that beats women.' I gave him the smuggest grin I could muster. 'How does it feel when a woman stands up to you then?'

It was obviously the final straw and he let out a loud growl. He grabbed me by the neck and almost lifted me off of my feet before marching me to the door and throwing me down the steps. I fell into a clumsy heap at the bottom.

I heard a car pull up sharply, brakes screeching and then I saw John running past me towards Charlie. He threw a flying punch at him and hit him square on the jaw. Charlie fell back into the house and flat onto his back. I could see John crouching down beside him as I got to my feet. 'That one's for Kirsty' he shouted in his face.

Charlie picked himself up and shoved John back out of the door. 'You are both mad,' he yelled 'don't think you have heard the last of this. I'm going to have you done for assault?' He slammed the door shut behind him and I heard the lock click. That's when I realised he was a coward and not the powerful man I used to fear.

As we walked back towards the lay-by John turned to me in total bewilderment. 'Whatever possessed you to do that? He could have seriously hurt you. Mind you, I must admit it did feel good giving him a taste of his own medicine.'

When we got home John made me a cup of tea to settle my nerves. I was buzzing from what had happened and it felt good to have finally stood up to Charlie.

As I contemplated my actions, it soon dawned on me just how stupid I had been. I realised I had got it so wrong, if Charlie had beaten me up like he had last time then it could have killed me in both realities.

I couldn't help but wonder what was to become of me over the next few hours and days. I was so sure that my angel had wanted me to follow the same path as last time and I really thought by going into a coma in this existence, it would bring me out of the coma in the real world.

I was lost and confused; I remembered her saying she would come and find me when the time was right so I resigned myself to waiting and leaving my future to her. One thing I thought I knew for sure was that I couldn't exist in both places at once.

As it reached ten o'clock I felt myself nodding off. John was engrossed in a programme he was watching on the television so I leant over to give him a kiss goodnight before heading upstairs. I felt overwhelmed with sadness as I realised this could be the last time I would see him in this existence.

As I lay in bed I thought about the future and I prayed to my angel to keep me safe. 'Whatever happens, I trust you and will never doubt you again. Just knowing you are by my side will keep me strong. I know you only have my best interests at heart.'

I also prayed to my Dad. 'Dad,' I said fighting back my tears, 'I need you more than ever. I am so scared right now. Please keep me safe, and Dad, if things go wrong and I can't make it back to my life or my quality of life is so bad back there, then please come and find me and keep me safe until I can be with you again. I love you Dad.'

I set my alarm for 5.24 a.m. as that was the time that I woke up in this existence. I hoped that this would be the time I would wake up in the real world back with Tommy.

As I started to drift off to sleep I realised I was placing my life completely in the hands of my angel. 'I need you,' I thought hoping she would hear me. ‘Please look out for me tonight.’

It wasn’t long before I fell into a deep sleep.

Chapter 37

At 5.24 a.m. I woke with a jolt as my alarm clock went off and I quickly looked around the room. Within seconds I realised nothing had changed and I sat in stunned silence, not really sure what to think.

The alarm clock carried on ringing unable to pull me from my thoughts.

'Why did you have to set the alarm so early?' John mumbled as he leant over to switch it off.

'Sorry I didn't realise I had, I must have set it by mistake.'

He rolled over and went back to sleep as I pulled on my dressing gown and headed downstairs. I tried desperately to make sense of everything as crazy thoughts swam around in my head. Nothing had changed. Did that mean if I went to the hospital I would find my other self there in a coma? Did I dream of meeting my angel? Maybe this was the real world after all and I wasn't in a coma and life would carry on like this until I died. What about Tommy? I was confused as I was so sure that I had met my angel on the cliff top. I really didn't think I could live in this existence after I had caught up with time.

Out of the corner of my eye I saw John come in. He made himself a cup of tea before kissing me on the cheek. 'Is everything okay?' he asked as he sat down.

I nodded but I must have seemed really distant to him and all morning my mind was elsewhere. I couldn't get the night I met my angel and saw myself lying in a hospital bed out of my head; I just knew I hadn't imagined it. The thought niggled at me all morning and I had to be sure.

'John, I need to go out for an hour.'

'Do I need to be on standby for round two with Charlie?' He gave out a little laugh.

'No, you don't need to worry; I won't be repeating that again.'

I drove the short distance to the hospital and parked up. My nerves were building as I walked through the main entrance. There was a queue of about six people at the main desk which gave me time to get my nerves under control and plan what I was going to say. I hadn't thought it through at all and as I got nearer to the front, I started to feel tense. I wasn't sure if that was because I felt silly for what I was about to ask or worried that I would find out that I was actually there in a coma. As the minutes passed I found myself standing at the front of the queue anxiously waiting for one of the two receptionists to become free. Every minute started to feel like an hour.

Finally the young couple talking to the dark haired receptionist moved away and she looked at me and smiled. 'Can I help?' she asked as she beckoned me over.

My legs felt like jelly as I walked to the desk. I gave her a nervous smile as my brain whirred. 'Hi, my sister was brought in a few hours ago as an emergency case.'

'Okay, what's her name?'

'Oh, err, her name's Sarah Connell.'

She started tapping away on her keyboard for what seemed an age and I could feel my whole body trembling. After a few minutes she looked up. 'I'm sorry but nobody by that name has been admitted today.' She smiled at me sympathetically. 'Are you sure they didn't take her to Cambridge?'

I felt confused and silly as I nodded. 'Oh maybe, I'll check.' I thanked her for her help and turned to make a quick exit.

I knew it was a stupid thought and deep down I knew it was impossible for me to exist in two places at the same time. I just felt I needed to know for sure.

I headed back home and found John cooking lunch. The smell made me feel ill but I made the effort to eat as I didn't want to upset him. As the afternoon progressed, I started to feel worse and thought I was coming down with something as my head was banging and I had really bad stomach pains. All I wanted to do was lie down and sleep.

I poured myself a glass of water and went upstairs to bed. I wanted some paracetamol for the pain and knew that John kept some in his sock drawer. As I pulled a few pairs out hunting for them I spotted a small red box tucked away at the very back. Curiosity got the better of me and I opened it and realised it was an engagement ring. Just at that moment I heard John coming up the stairs so I quickly put the ring back in the drawer, pushed some socks over the top of it and lay on the bed. John knocked quietly on the door before coming in and sitting beside me.

'I'll get you some paracetamol' he said, 'and then you should try and rest.'

I didn't argue as he passed the pills to me and for the next few hours I drifted in and out of sleep. I couldn't get the engagement ring out of my mind and I felt I had spoilt his surprise. He had been acting a bit secretively over the past weeks and now I understood why. One thing I knew for sure was that when he proposed the answer would most definitely be a yes.

John must have come up again at about ten. I could hear the door slowly open and felt him gently place his hand on my forehead. 'How are you feeling?' he asked.

I looked at him through bleary eyes. 'I'm still not feeling at all well and my stomach really hurts. Could you get me some more paracetamol please? My head is really throbbing.'

I knew John was really concerned about me and he came to bed early. I cuddled up to him and lay there waiting for the paracetamol to kick in. Eventually I must have drifted off.

Chapter 38

As I slept I had a wonderful dream. I was in the park that Dad used to take me to as a little girl and he was pushing Tommy on the swings. John was standing next to him holding a new born baby wrapped in a pink shawl. I stood there watching Dad playing with Tommy and I was overwhelmed with emotion. I just wanted to tell Dad how much I had missed him. I started to feel really upset because they couldn't see or hear me. I called out to them but I was invisible. I walked up to Dad and kept repeating over and over again "Dad can you hear me". I was upset and frustrated as I stood beside Dad and watched him pushing Tommy on the swing but then, all of a sudden he turned to me and smiled. He opened his arms and I went to him. I held on to him tightly and instantly felt like I was twelve years old again and daddies little girl.

After a few minutes wrapped in his arms he looked at me and smiled. 'You will always be my little girl' he said, 'and I am so proud of the way you have coped with everything that's happened to you. You need to wake up now; it's time for you to go home.'

I woke almost immediately and looked over at John who was fast asleep. I felt so uplifted by my dream and I felt an urgency to write it all down before I forgot it. Still half asleep, I picked up my diary and jotted it all down, trying to remember every last detail. As I finished and rested the pen back on the side I looked over at the clock. It was exactly five twenty-four. As the significance of the time sunk in I felt an overpowering urge to turn and look towards the door. I noticed it was wide open and there was the most beautiful pure white light radiating from the hallway. It took a moment for my eyes to adjust and as they did, they quickly became transfixed by two beautiful figures. I recognised one as my angel and she was holding the baby in the pink shawl from my dream, unlike the last time when I saw her at the hospital, she had beautiful white wings. She was standing with another angel and I sat mesmerised by their beauty.

Once again our eyes met and I was able to hear her, although she didn't speak. 'You need to follow me into the light.' She smiled and held out her hand.

I looked over at John as he slept before leaning over to give him a tender kiss on the cheek. It felt like I was saying goodbye to him and I just couldn't bring myself to leave. I was torn between John and this existence and following my angel to my other life. I thought about all the love and support John had given me over the past five years and I really didn't want to lose his love but I knew I needed to go.

I gently picked up Johns hand, careful not to wake him. 'Whatever happens to me, I will always love you and I need you to know you mean the world to me. I wish you had got the chance to ask me to marry you.' I kissed him tenderly on the forehead. 'The answer would have been yes.'

I reluctantly let go of his hand and slowly got out of bed. I walked towards the open door and as I reached both angels they smiled at me. My angel handed the baby to the other angel and they both turned and walked into the light.

I took one final look at John as he slept. 'I love you' I whispered before walking through the door and into the unknown.

I felt myself being drawn into the light and it embraced me. I felt no fear just an overwhelming feeling of love, warmth and comfort. My eyes couldn't adjust to the light but I sensed my angel close by. I felt the same intense, unconditional love as I did on the night when we last met. The light was pure and inviting and it almost felt alive.

I heard my angel. 'Close your eyes.'

As I did I felt myself falling forward and I instinctively put out my hands but I soon realised I wasn't in danger. I felt the floor disappear from beneath me and I gently floated for what felt like eternity. All my worries instantly disappeared and nothing seemed to matter anymore. I felt like I wanted to stay wrapped in the light forever. I was free, safe and surrounded by a love I'd never experienced before. I sensed my angel was very close to me, guiding me. I didn't know how long I had been drifting as time didn't exist in the light but as I moved on vivid images filled my mind. Long forgotten memories crowded in all at once.

I saw Mum and Dad and I was instantly transported back to my childhood and the joy I felt being with them both. All the wonderful times we spent together seemed to merge into one but before I could enjoy them, feelings of despair took over as images of Dad dying filtered in. These images gave way and Charlie came through, I saw all of the bad times but I had the power to rush past them and I no longer felt fear. I felt an inner strength emerge and an overpowering rush of love embraced me as I felt Tommy arrive. The three beautiful years I had with him in my life completely filled my being.

As I was transported through my life's journey I began to feel enlightened. I saw everything from a different perspective and for the first time, I realised all the things that had happened to me, both good and bad, were all part of a bigger plan.

I started to gently drift further down into the bright abyss and I felt my angels arms wrap around me to stop me falling. 'You need to sleep now,' she whispered. Before she had even finished speaking I fell into a deep, dreamless sleep. I don't know if I slept for seconds, hours or days as I had no sense of time but at some point I found myself wanting to wake up.

I struggled to open my eyes, I kept trying but they wouldn't open. I felt that my body wasn't working and I didn't understand why. I tried to cry out but I could only make a grunting noise. A deep panic began to rise up within me until I heard the sound of a familiar voice.

'Sarah, Sarah, listen to me. You are going to be okay please stay calm, everything will be okay I promise.'

I felt two soft hands on my face and the panic subsided. As I started to relax I tried to open my eyes again, this time slowly. As they adjusted to the light I started to see the outline of a face and I blinked a few times in confusion.

'Hello Sarah, I'm Kirsty, you are in hospital. I'm one of the nurses who have been looking after you. You have been unconscious for fifteen days and we have all been really worried about you.'

I was so happy to see her and she gave me such a warm smile. I tried to speak but my mouth was really dry. I knew what I wanted to say but it wouldn't come out and I started to get really upset.

Kirsty gently reassured me. 'Its okay, it will take time.'

I slowly mouthed the word Tommy to her and she smiled. 'Oh yes, little Tommy. He's been keeping us nurses entertained over the last few weeks, he is such a cutie.'

I mouthed the word where.

'Don't worry, its okay, we have just phoned your mum and she is on her way in.'

I felt weak and must have fallen back to sleep but I was soon woken. Sitting on the bed right next to me was Tommy. I instantly burst into tears as he jumped on top of me and wrapped his little arms around my neck.

'No Tommy,' I heard Mum shout out. 'Mummy's not well.' She tried to pull him away from me but I quickly wrapped my arms around him. I had waited five years for that moment and I wasn't going to wait a second longer. It felt so good to finally feel the warmth of my little boy's body next to mine; I couldn't believe I had him back. I looked over at Mum and John and through my tears I smiled at them. Mum tried to speak but started to cry instead and John put his arm around her. I moved my hand on top of hers and squeezed it tightly.

The rest of the day was a bit of a blur as I drifted in and out of consciousness but the next morning I woke feeling much stronger.

Chapter 39

Kirsty was in the room and I could see her checking the monitors by my bed. She seemed so much more confident in this life and I was so happy for her. My speech was improving and I had so many questions for her but I couldn't help just smiling at her as she worked.

She spotted me smiling and came and sat beside me. 'Somebody looks pleased with themselves.' She laughed.

'Are you happy?' I asked looking deep into her eyes.

'Yes I'm fine.'

'No, I mean are you happy with your life? Is your life going as you planned? Have you got a husband and family?'

She looked at me a little oddly before smiling. 'I love my life, its perfect. I have a wonderful boyfriend and a beautiful little girl called Amelia who is eighteen months old. I am lucky really because my mum, Kim, looks after Amelia so I can carry on doing the job I love.' Kirsty took my hand and started to look a bit more serious. 'I hope I am not speaking out of turn,' she paused, 'I know you have had a few really rough years. Your mum told me all about Charlie. I couldn't even start to imagine what you must have gone through for all those years and if that had been me I don't think I could have coped.'

I gave her a smile. 'I wouldn't wish him on anyone. I just thank my lucky stars that I am still alive and I am free of him.'

'Yes I think you definitely have an angel looking out for you. Oh, that reminds me, I have something for you. I'll just go and get it, I won't be long.'

About five minutes later she came back clutching a small envelope which really intrigued me. She sat back by my bed to explain. 'Eleven days ago a lady came in claiming to be a medium and saying she wanted to help you. Your mum got really upset, called her a parasite trying to profit on her grief and told her to leave. Well, she came back the next day and asked me to give you this letter if you regained consciousness.' Kirsty looked a bit unsure as she handed the letter over. 'I was in two minds whether or not to give it to your mum but I thought you had the right to choose. I hope I'm doing the right thing by giving it to you.'

I took the letter from her and carefully opened it. I recognised the address straight away; it was from Claire, the medium that I went to see in my other existence. I started to read it with excited anticipation.

Dear Sarah,

If you are reading this letter then you must be well on the road to recovery.

Please forgive me for contacting you like this as the last thing I want to do is to put you under any more stress than you have already suffered. Please also let me assure you that I am not writing to you for any financial gain.

I am a medium and last night I had a vivid dream about you. You were very distressed and you told me that you had gone back in time. You said that an angel had changed your life plan and your son, Tommy couldn't be born. In my dream state I wasn't much help to you but the next morning when I woke I realised this was much more than just a dream. At first I thought you were a lost soul that couldn't pass on but when I remembered your full name, I searched for you on social media. I soon found your page, read about your coma and saw all the messages wishing you well.

I remembered you telling me that you had been back in time for seven months, so time must have been running a lot faster for you there.

I'm not sure if it's possible but I have been trying to get back to you through meditation. I've been trying to enter your coma world so that I can ease your mind and explain to you where you are and what's happened to you. I will pray to your angel every day and ask her to bring you back safely.

I really do hope me writing to you hasn't upset you as that is the last thing I want to do.

If you do have any memory about our meeting then I will always be here for you but if you have no memory of this then please throw this letter away.

Please realise that this letter was sent to you with genuine love.

Always in my thoughts and prayers.

Claire.

I had begun to think that my other existence was more than just in my own head as Claire had become linked to me. Maybe there was a place between life and death or a parallel universe, I wasn't sure what it was but there was something. It meant so much to me that Claire was trying to help me so I vowed to go and see her when I got out of hospital.

As I put the letter down Kirsty noticed the tears in the corners of my eyes. 'Do you mind if I read it?' she asked.

I told her to go ahead but after she finished she looked slightly annoyed. 'How do these people sleep at night?' She shook her head in disgust before smiling at me sympathetically. 'Try not to let it get to you; the best place for this is the bin.'

'No!' I said, 'its okay, I will keep it for now.'

She handed the letter back to me and I hid it away in the locker next to my bed.

Kirsty returned to work and I sat thinking about the future. I knew it wouldn't be for a few days but I was really looking forward to getting home and spending time with Tommy and Mum. My joy was tempered with sadness as I thought about the five year relationship I had enjoyed with John, in my other existence and how back here in the real world, we were no longer a couple.

After lunch Kirsty came back over to re-examine the monitors and she soon noticed my change in mood. 'Cheer up. Your mum and Tommy will be here soon.'

I gave her a half hearted smile as she sat down.

'Are you okay? Do you want to talk?'

'Yes I'm fine, it's just all the time I was with Charlie I always regretted finishing with John. I always dreamed of being with him again one day but now he's back in my life he only wants to be friends.'

'Well I wouldn't give up on him too quickly.' Kirsty gave me a knowing smile. 'Us nurses see and hear a lot as we go about our business and I don't want to speak out of turn but John has spent every night here over the past few weeks. I think he feels more for you than you realise.' She took my hand and gave it a reassuring squeeze. 'This didn't come from me but every night he sat with you for hours, holding your hand. Let's just say he did quite a bit of reminiscing about your past and he said he would protect you from Charlie and would always look after you and Tommy. I'm no expert but even I can see he still thinks a lot of you.'

It was just what I wanted to hear and as a tear started running down my cheek Kirsty gave me a hug, pulled a fresh tissue from her pocket and proceeded to gently wipe it away.

'Hey, things will work out for the best you'll see.'

I knew in that instance why Kirsty and I had become such good friends and I really didn't want to lose her friendship again.

Just then Mum and Tommy walked in. Kirsty must have sensed that Mum wanted a few minutes alone with me as she stood and made a big fuss of Tommy before lifting him up into her arms. 'Hello Tommy, how's my little soldier? Do you want some of those biscuits you like?'

I smiled as she carried him back out of the room.

Mum sat down beside my bed and took my hand. I could see she was trying to keep her emotions in check.

'It's okay Mum, I'm going to be alright.'

She started crying. 'I thought I had lost you.' She said between sobs. 'On that morning two weeks ago, about five twenty, I was woken by Tommy crying. I knew something was wrong and I tried to wake you but I couldn't.' Her sobs deepened as she thought back to what had happened. 'I called for an ambulance and you were rushed to hospital. We didn't know if you were going to make it. Then, four days ago, you took a turn for the worse and nearly died. Tommy could have lost his mum.'

I thought back to when I first met my angel and I saw myself dying. I squeezed Mum's hand tightly as she carried on talking. 'The police are coming to see you in the next day or so but only if you are up to it.'

I squeezed her hand again. 'Mum I'm ready to tell them everything; I won't let him do this to anybody else. I've seen how he ruins lives.'

Just then Tommy ran back in closely followed by Kirsty. 'He's eaten all of our biscuits,' she laughed. 'I don't know what my colleague's are going to have with their cup of tea later.'

It was Mum's turn to laugh. 'You can't leave biscuits lying around when Tommy's in the room.'

'He's a little love, I'm sure they will forgive him.' Kirsty laughed before leaving again.

After a few wonderful hours with Tommy and Mum, visiting time ended and they headed off. It upset me to see Tommy go and I had to remind myself that I had the rest of my life with him and I would be going home soon. Although home would no longer be a place I shared with John.

John was due to visit me that evening and it would be the first time that we would have together to talk since I slipped into the coma. I felt exhausted after spending time with Tommy so I let myself drift off to sleep as I wanted to be bright and awake when I saw him. As I closed my eyes Kirsty came over and gently whispered in my ear. 'Sarah, my shift is about to finish, so I thought I would come and wish you good luck with John tonight. Remember think positive, I have a good feeling about this.'

As she turned to leave I grabbed her hand. 'Thanks for the chat earlier. You are a really good friend.' I stopped and hesitated for a moment. 'I lost all my friends when I got with Charlie; he only ever let me out to see Mum. Maybe, when I'm better and if you fancy it, we could take Tommy and Amelia out somewhere and make a day of it?'

'Yes I'd love that,' Kirsty replied enthusiastically, 'I think Amelia and Tommy will get on really well. I'll speak to you tomorrow, you get some rest.'

As I lay there I started to think about my other life. If it was all just in my head then it no longer existed but what if it did exist. It pained me that I would never know for sure. One thing I did know was that Amelia in this world wouldn't be the same soul as in the other existence, as they had a different dad and this Amelia was eighteen months younger. With those thoughts running around in my head I soon fell into a deep sleep.

I woke several hours later at about half past six. I started to feel nervous at the thought of seeing John again. It felt strange that he wouldn't have any memory of our five years together and I found that very hard to deal with.

After a very anxious wait I heard the door open and my heart raced as John walked in. I felt it beating even faster as he pulled up a chair and sat down beside me. I gave him a nervous smile and he smiled back and took my hand before gently leaning in to kiss my cheek.

'You gave us all a real scare' he said warmly. 'You don't realise how worried I have been about you and four days ago was the worst day of my life. I don't know what I would have done if I had lost you that night.'

I squeezed his hand as tightly as my strength would let me and took a deep breath. 'John, I need you to know,' I said throwing caution to the wind, 'I have always regretted finishing with you all those years ago. You just never know what's around the corner and I know life is just too short and fragile for regrets so you need to know I never stopped loving you. Charlie was the biggest mistake of my life and I would do anything to turn the clock back and be with you again.' I smiled sadly. 'But I suppose I wouldn't have Tommy in my life would I?'

John moved even closer and gave me a thoughtful smile. 'I've had a lot of time to think over the past two weeks. I never stopped praying for you and I know how much you believe in your angel, so every night I asked her to look after you and for her to bring you back to us. Now I just want to take care of you and Tommy and give you both a better life.' He hesitated for a moment before looking deep into my eyes. 'I know this is going to sound really strange to you but I woke up yesterday morning and I just knew that yesterday was going to be the day that you were going to wake up. I had this really vivid dream where I was in a park, standing next to your dad while he was pushing Tommy on the swing. I was holding a new born baby girl and then suddenly you appeared, out of thin air and gave your dad a big hug. He told you how proud he was of you and how well you had coped with everything. Then he said you needed to wake up now and that it was time for you to go home. At that point you vanished into thin air. My dream got a bit weird after that.'

I couldn't believe what John was telling me. I was hanging onto his every word and I sat up and pleaded with him to tell me the rest. 'Oh no, you can't leave me hanging, I need you to tell me every last detail of your dream, no matter how weird it sounds to you.'

He shrugged his shoulders. 'Okay if you're really that interested. Your dad then turned to me and said that he was really glad that you had found me and he could see I was a decent man and he knew I would take good care of his little girl and two grandchildren. He gently lifted Tommy off of the swing and passed him over to me before taking the baby girl from my arms. He then winked at me and said that he needed to give her back to the angels for now as she needed to be looked after for just a little while longer. Then he smiled and looked me in the eye before asking me to tell his little girl that she must not be afraid to try again.

Weirdly he said it would be fourth time lucky for us. Then I woke up in a really positive mood and I don't know why but I just knew you were going to be okay and would wake up.'

By the time John had finished I was in floods of tears. I grabbed hold of him and hugged him tightly. Dad had come through for me. I would never doubt Dad or my angel again. John was my good life decision and I smiled at him through my tears.

'You and Tommy are the best things that have ever happened to me and you'll see, one day I am going to marry you.'

Authors thought

When hope has been replaced by hopelessness and life's troubles are stacking up at your door, it's nice to think that, when you need help and all you have left is your total faith in your Guardian Angel, angelic help could be just a heartbeat away.

Printed in Great Britain
by Amazon